OTHER BOOKS BY
ANNABELLA MICHAELS

Souls of Chicago Series
Feeding the Soul, Book 1
Music of the Soul, Book 2
Protecting the Soul, Book 3
Renewing the Soul, Book 4

PROTECTING *The Soul*

SOULS OF CHICAGO #3

ANNABELLA MICHAELS

DEDICATION

This book is dedicated to Lee Rey. Thank you for cheering me on, making me laugh and giving me the push I needed to reach my goals. I appreciate your friendship and look forward to our talks more than you'll ever know.

CHAPTER
One

Landon

"THANKS FOR COMING, GUYS. THIS WON'T TAKE LONG, BUT I needed to speak with you about an important matter."

I let my brother Carter and his fiancé, Ryan, into my spacious hotel room and motioned for them to have a seat on the couch. "Would either of you like a drink?"

"I'm good, thanks," Ryan said, looking at me suspiciously.

"What's going on, Landon? You're acting weird. Well, weirder than usual," Carter teased. I plopped down in one of the chairs and looked at them with a serious expression. I hated to be the one to cause them worry, but there was no getting around the situation we were in. They needed to know what was going on so they could take necessary precautions.

"Look, there's no easy way to say this. We've received some

strange letters lately and you need to be aware of what's going on."

Carter's brow furrowed in confusion. "What kind of strange letters?"

I pulled a plastic bag out of my briefcase and laid it on the coffee table so they could see it. Carter leaned forward to get a closer look at the letter which had been typed neatly on a thick piece of blue stationary. There was no signature other than a stamped picture of some sort of flowers and the words on it were shocking to say the least.

You are mine, Mr. Greene. You belong to me and no one else.

Carter's eyes were wide as he looked at me. Ryan grasped his hand tightly and he sounded angrier than I had ever heard as he stared me down. "What are you going to do about this? Is this the only one? We have to keep him safe, Landon." He fired off his words until I raised my hand to stop him.

"I know how you feel. He's my brother and I'll always do everything I can to keep him safe. This is the third letter we've received, all on the same stationary, all typed and they seem to be escalating. The first two we thought were fairly mild, just your usual fan adoration, but this one has a more sinister undertone. The person sending these letters is obviously obsessed with you and they seem to be getting more agitated." I ran my fingers through my hair tiredly.

I had recently helped Carter's band, which I was the manager of, obtain a full contract with Golden Entertainment Studios and he was finally living his dream of travelling the world, performing in front of sold-out crowds. I wished so badly that this could have been handled without Carter ever knowing about the danger. He deserved to be happy, but with each new letter it had become apparent that whoever was fixated on my brother wasn't going to just go away.

"So, what do we do now?" Carter asked me. Sensing my nervousness, he reached over to lay a comforting hand on my knee. My heart swelled with love for my little brother that he would be more concerned with me than himself at such a time.

"Now, we increase your security. I've already contacted the studio and Lachlan Edwards is sending a personal friend of his to head up the security team. Since this threat involves you too, Ryan, you each will be assigned a security team that will be with you whenever you go anywhere until we determine that there's no more threat."

Ryan and Carter exchanged a look and I opened my mouth to try to reassure them, but was interrupted by a heavy knock at the door. My heart beat wildly in my chest. I knew who was waiting on the other side of the door. I had been thinking of little else ever since Lachlan had called to let me know who was being assigned to deal with the situation.

Schooling my features so I wouldn't give away my thoughts, I straightened my back and clenched my fists at my sides. My jaw ticked nervously as I made my way to the door and opened it. It had been months since I had seen the man on the other side and I wasn't sure if the swirling in the pit of my stomach was excitement or dread.

"Landon, it's good to see you again." Micah's gruff voice tickled over my skin, leaving goose bumps behind and I opened my mouth to say something, but my mind suddenly went completely blank. I let my eyes travel over his dark hair which he kept neatly cut in a military fashion, down his perfectly straight nose, finally landing on his plump lips. I remembered all too well the way they felt against my own. Without any conscious thought on my part, I leaned towards him as if I was being pulled by an imaginary rope.

The sound of his deep chuckle snapped me out of my daze and I pulled back in horror as I realized my mouth had been gaping open the whole time. My eyes flew to his and I saw the humor shining in their gray depths. *Smooth, Landon, very smooth.* I wanted to smack the smug smile off his face, but instead I narrowed my eyes at him, turned on my heel, and quickly stalked back over to Carter and Ryan.

"Guys, this is our new head of security, he's going to get to the bottom of our problems," I said by way of introduction. My eyes flickered to his and my breath caught as I found him staring at me. His face gave away nothing, but he winked at me before turning to face the other men in the room. My face flushed with heat and I swallowed thickly.

Carter stretched his hand out to shake. His voice held a hint of surprise as he spoke. "Micah, it's good to see you again. Thank you for coming."

"It's my pleasure," Micah responded.

"How do you know each other?" Ryan asked as he shook Micah's hand.

"Micah is Giovanni's best friend," Carter explained. Giovanni was married to my other younger brother, and Carter's twin, Caleb.

"I think I remember Giovanni mentioning you. Weren't you with him the night he mistook Carter for Caleb and nearly punched a guy that was dancing with him at a club?" Ryan asked.

"Yes, I was. That was classic." Micah laughed and I found myself mesmerized by the way his face lit up when he smiled. I felt an odd sense of jealousy that I wasn't the one to have put the smile on his face. *Oh my God, get a grip!*

I cleared my throat and all three heads turned to look at me. "I think we need to discuss the situation and how you plan on dealing with it," I said abruptly. Carter narrowed his eyes at me suspiciously, so I turned away from him and sat down in the chair. Micah took the seat opposite mine while Carter and Ryan returned to the couch. I refused to look at him, but I could feel his eyes on me as he spoke.

"I was sorry to hear about the letters, Carter. I take it this is one of them?" Micah asked. He scowled as he read over the note on the table.

"Yes, that's the most recent. There were two others before that," I stated. Ryan placed his hand over Carter's and I smiled at him. I was thankful that my brother had found such a loving man to help him through this, to share his burdens with as well as his joys.

"I'll need to see those as well," Micah said to me and I gave him a single nod. "Lachlan briefed me on what's been happening so far and we agreed that I would need to do a total overhaul on your security setup."

He leaned forward, his eyes serious as they scanned over each of us. "Lachlan asked me here as a favor for a friend, but I want to be very clear before I commit to anything. I know you each have jobs to do and I'll do my best to stay out of your way as you do them, but I have a job to do as well. If I agree to this, then I'm in charge." My skin suddenly felt too tight and my blood thrummed in my veins as I heard those words.

"I will have carte blanche when it comes to all decisions regarding security and I don't want to hear any complaints about the extra men I bring in to watch over you. Carter's safety is my top priority and I'm going to make damn sure nothing happens to him on my watch. Is that clear?" He arched a brow at us as we each spoke our agreement. He nodded once, seemingly satisfied. "Alright, we'll get started first thing in the morning. Carter, you should let the rest of the band members know what's going on as well. They need to be aware of the changes that are being made and they can also help keep an eye out for any suspicious behavior they may see."

"I'll talk to them right away," Carter agreed.

I hugged Carter as he and Ryan got ready to head back to their room. "I'll take care of everything, Carter, you just keep doing what you do best."

His mouth quirked up in a sly smile. "Guess I better hurry and get Ryan back to our room if I'm going to do what I do best," he teased.

"Good night, brat," I laughed, relieved to see he hadn't lost his sense of humor. I watched the two men holding hands as they walked down the hallway to their room. I tensed as I heard Micah walk up behind me and I schooled my features as I turned to face him.

There was a stiffness in the way he held himself that conveyed his military background and his eyes held both intelligence and a wariness only seen in people who had lived a hard life. Micah was the same height as me, but there was something about the man that seemed larger than life. His expression was unreadable as he looked me over and I had to make a conscious effort not to squirm under his scrutiny. "I'll meet with you tomorrow to see the other letters and I'm going to talk to your security team so I can see what I have to work with."

"That's fine. Just let me know what time works for you." I opened the door for him, but he made no move to leave.

"Are you okay with this?" he asked.

"With what exactly?" I hedged carefully.

He took a step closer and I could feel the heat radiating off of his body. He smelled like fresh rain and mint and I fought the urge to breathe his scent in deeper. "With me telling you what to do," he responded huskily.

I swallowed hard at his implication, but stood straighter and puffed my chest out a little, refusing to let him see how his words affected me. "I'll do whatever you say." I watched his eyes darken and damn if that didn't make my pulse kick up a notch. "When it comes to security only," I tacked on quickly.

I thought I heard him say, "We'll see about that," but I was too distracted by the sight of his lips as they tipped up at the edges, the bottom one a bit fuller than the top. I wanted to lick them, but then I felt a surge of anger as his words caught up with me. How dare he toy with me. Especially after the last time.

"Goodnight, Micah," I said with more force than I had intended.

"Goodnight, Landon." My cock twitched at the sound of my name on his lips and my skin burned where his arm brushed mine as he moved past me. I watched him walk down the hallway but quickly shut the door when he glanced over his shoulder, wearing a knowing smile as he caught me staring.

I leaned my head against the door and let out a loud sigh. What kind of game was Micah playing? It didn't matter anyway because I refused to play along. I had enough going on in my life right then and I didn't need any further complications. Besides, he had made it clear the last time I saw him that he wanted nothing to do with me.

With a frustrated groan, I pushed away from the door and made my way to the bedroom. I quickly brushed my teeth and changed into a comfortable pair of pajama pants before climbing into bed. I shivered as I burrowed down into the blankets, willing the sheets to warm with my body heat.

Even after several months of being on the road with my brother's band, I still found it difficult to fall asleep. Spending night after night in an unfamiliar hotel bed had started to take its toll on me and I could feel the effects of my restless nights in my daily routines. I wondered idly what it would be like to have someone to curl up with at night, to have strong arms to hold me, and to be able to hear a heart beating its rhythm under my cheek as I slept.

I wasn't surprised when my thoughts brought up an image of Micah Hamilton. The man had sparked something in me from the first time I laid eyes on him. Memories of that night flowed through my mind.

I had been caught up with something at work and had to rush to get to Caleb and Giovanni's bachelor party. By the time I got to the strip club, the party was in full gear and several of the attendees were well on their way to being drunk. I spotted Caleb talking to someone at a table, so I made my way over just as Carter and Giovanni arrived with a tray full of drinks. I walked around the table, hugging each of my brothers then pulled up short, my eyes widening as I got my first real look at the man Caleb had been talking to.

Fierce, raw, and sexy were just a few of the words that came to mind as my eyes raked over the stranger's sculpted body. He was wearing a plain gray t-shirt that stretched tightly across his broad chest and his right arm was covered in tattoos. I could make out muscular thighs beneath the material of his jeans and my eyes widened as I took in the prominent bulge between his legs, barely contained by the denim.

I looked up quickly to find him taking inventory of my body as well and I stood still, letting him look his fill. My eyes locked with his as a sexy smirk formed at the corner of his lips and I had to fight the urge to groan out loud.

Caleb cleared his throat, pulling our attention back to him as he made introductions. "Micah, this is my brother Landon. Landon, this is Gio's best friend, Micah." My hand slid into his and I cursed my treacherous body as goose bumps broke out across my skin at the feel of his calloused fingers. We held on longer than was necessary, neither of us seemed to be in a hurry to let go.

Reluctantly, I pulled my hand from his grasp and felt my face heat when I noticed everyone watching our exchange. I met Caleb's gaze which consisted of a mixture between surprise and delight. I rolled my eyes at him and pulled a chair up to the table.

Ever since my little brother had found his soulmate, he seemed determined to help the rest of us find ours. I didn't have the heart to tell him, but I wasn't sure I believed that I had a soulmate out there anymore. At that point, I was just hoping for someone to share my life with that would treat me halfway decent and laugh at my jokes. So far, I hadn't found either.

I quickly downed a shot, not caring what it was. I just wanted to catch up with everyone else at the party. I set the glass down on the table and looked up, surprised to find Micah staring at me. Feeling a boldness that was totally out of character for me, I let my tongue slide across my lower lip, catching the drop of alcohol that lingered there. I gave myself a mental fist bump when I saw his eyes widen and he shifted in his seat, crossing his ankle up onto his leg to hide his sudden discomfort. I couldn't help but chuckle as he glared at me, the look in his eyes promising retaliation.

Our attention was soon pulled to the stage where my other brother, Carter, was announcing a lap dance for the two grooms. We all laughed at the horrified expressions on Caleb and Giovanni's faces, then stood, cheering as two scantily clad dancers made their way over to the men and began grinding their bodies against them. I don't think I had ever seen Caleb's face so red in his life.

Giovanni stood and took the place of one of the strippers, putting on his own show for his fiancé. I was about to let out a loud whistle to lend my support when I felt a chest press against my back. The warmth emanating from the rock-hard body caused my breath to catch in my throat and the smell of newly fallen rain filled my senses.

My heart beat wildly in my chest as Micah spoke, his warm breath in my ear causing a tremor throughout my body. "I had no idea Caleb had such an alluring older brother."

I glanced over my shoulder at him, arching my brow. "And I had no idea Giovanni had such an enticing friend."

I was shocked at my own brazenness. I couldn't remember the last time I had flirted with another man; well I could, I just didn't want to. Most of the men I slept with didn't require flirting. They were usually guys I met at a club and after a few drinks or dances we would just sort of agree to take things back to one of our houses. A few had asked if they could see me again, but I hadn't met anyone who really sparked my interest so I gently turned them down.

I turned back to watch the action taking place with the grooms and was thankful for the noise level in the room which hid the moan that escaped my lips as Micah's hands found their way to my hips and he pulled me back against him roughly. I bit down on my lower lip as he pressed even closer to me, the evidence of his arousal rubbing up against the crack of my ass in a delicious way. I felt sweat trickle down my back as my body threatened to burst into flames. Never in my life had I been so affected by someone I'd just met. Holy fuck, the man was dangerous!

Micah stepped away quickly as the dance ended and my brothers made their way back to the table. My dad and two brothers-in-law came over to join us and I sat so no one would see the obvious bulge in my jeans. I ignored the surprised look Dad gave me as I quickly downed two more shots. I noticed Micah kicking back a few more also and was *relieved that he seemed a bit shaken by what had happened also. He caught my eye and raised his glass in a silent toast.*

We spent a long time talking and laughing as we all drank more than we should. By the time the two love birds began opening their gag gifts, I was a little wobbly on my feet and more than a little grateful that I had been smart enough to take a cab to the club. Given the shape I was in, I had no business getting behind the wheel of a car.

Caleb and Giovanni opened matching bright yellow smiley face shirts to the raucous laughter of Carter. I didn't understand the joke, but given my drunken state, I found it hilarious all the same. I turned to see Micah staring at me through hooded eyes. My laughter died in my throat as he stood and made his way over to me. I glanced around at my family, but they were all busy watching the grooms open their presents.

I held my breath as Micah placed his hands on the arms of my chair, caging me in, and leaned down so that his eyes were level with mine. He was so close that his breath ghosted across my lips and I licked them eagerly, wanting a taste of him. "Do you want to get out of here?"

I nodded so quickly that he had to back up or risk getting head butted. He chuckled as he scanned the room to be sure no one was look- ing and then held his hand out to me. His large hand nearly engulfed mine as he helped me stand, grabbing onto my elbow as I swayed.

He eyed me cautiously for a moment. "How drunk are you, Landon?"

"Drunk enough to feel no pain, but not so drunk that this is a bad idea," I said with what I hoped was a naughty smile. He shook his head and chuckled so I took that as consent and tugged him towards the door.

We were each laughing at nothing in particular as he flagged down a cab and we stumbled into the back seat while I gave my address to the driver. As soon as the door shut we were all over each other. His hands held the back of my neck as he pulled me in for a toe-curling kiss. He groaned loudly as I slid my tongue into his mouth and I moved my hands up to feel the short hairs that graced the top of his head. I loved the way they tickled against my palm.

His hand lowered to my erection and I whimpered as he gently squeezed my cock through the rough denim of my jeans. My hips punched up of their own accord, seeking more from him, and his lips latched onto my neck as I threw my head back in pleasure. My head swirled as Micah continued his assault on my body. I was lost in his intoxicating kisses and the feel of his palm pressing against my hardness. I gripped his shirt as he backed up, not wanting him to retreat, but he just laughed as he pulled me from the back of the car. I hadn't even noticed its arrival at my home.

Micah paid the driver and slid his hand to my lower back, guiding me to my front door as I fumbled with my keys, trying to find the right one. Once the door shut behind us, I heard the lock click into place and then I was shoved up against the door as Micah's body closed in on mine.

Given the height similarity, our bodies aligned almost perfectly and we both sighed as we felt our straining cocks connect. I ground my hips into his and he grabbed my wrists, placing them over my head and holding them in his firm grip as he reached with his other to unsnap my jeans. My eyes rolled back as his thumb reached in to rub over the head of my dick. If I hadn't had so much to drink, I probably would have been embarrassed by the sound that escaped my throat as he pulled his thumb up and swiped his tongue over it, tasting me. His answering groan nearly brought me to my knees.

He continued to hold me against my front door and I thrilled at the feeling of being held captive by the man. I had never been with someone who consumed me so completely. My legs gave out from under me as his rough fingers slid around the width of my erection and I dropped my head to his shoulder as he slowly moved his grip up and down my length. He moved one leg in between mine to help steady me as he applied more friction.

The only noise in the room was the sound of my ragged breathing and the heady sound of his slick hand slipping over my skin. "Micah, I'm close," I gasped and then regretted it immediately when he withdrew his hand.

"Show me your bedroom, Landon," he said gruffly and I hurried to comply, stumbling a bit as I made my way through my darkened hallway.

When we reached the large master bedroom, I switched on the low lamp beside my bed and turned to him. Good Lord, the man was a wet dream as he sauntered over to me and slowly began lifting the hem of my shirt. The backs of his hands rubbed against me as he raised the material over my head and his eyes held mine steadily as he lowered my pants down over my hips. I helped to kick them off the rest of the way and then waited. I don't know why, but I wanted Micah to tell me what to do next.

"Get on the bed," he said as if he'd heard my thoughts. I didn't have time to question whether I had spoken out loud before I scrambled onto the bed and lay down against the soft comforter. I watched, mesmerized as he lifted his shirt, displaying miles of tanned skin stretched over corded muscles and more tattoos that I wanted to explore further. Very nice!

"Very nice!" My eyes darted to his, surprised by his mirroring words and my skin caught fire at the hungry look in his eyes as they skimmed over the length of my naked body. I felt his gaze like a caress over every exposed inch of me and I was suddenly desperate for the feel of his skin against my own. "Where are your supplies?" he asked, his words sounding hoarse. I pointed to the table on the opposite side of the bed and he smiled before moving around the bed and opening the drawer. I watched the way his ass moved tantalizingly as he walked.

I blinked my eyes several times then let out a pained moan as the sun streamed in through my window, piercing my aching head. My stomach churned violently and I lay as still as possible, willing it to settle and sifting through my memory of the night before.

I remembered flashes of the bachelor party and the disturbing *image of Giovanni grinding against my little brother as he gave him a lap dance. I remembered my dad making friends with several of the strippers and there was something else that kept tickling at the back of my brain but refused to come to the forefront.*

I sat up slowly, hoping my stomach wouldn't revolt at the movement and was surprised to see a glass of water and a bottle of aspirin on the table beside my bed. I tilted my head in confusion and glanced over my shoulder at the other side of the bed. I lived alone and it didn't appear that I had brought anyone home with me. Regardless of how it got there, I was grateful for the medicine and I quickly took two, washing them down with the water. I went to put the glass back down and that's when I noticed the piece of paper that had been tucked under it.

I unfolded it and let out an audible gasp as I saw what was written: I figured you might need these in the morning. It was a pleasure meeting you, but it was probably best that it ended this way. —M.

All of the events of the evening came flooding back, including the feel of Micah's hands on me and the taste of his mouth.

I let out a loud curse and regretted it immediately as my head felt like it would split in two. I leaned forward, cradling my head in my hands as I realized that I had lost the opportunity to be with the first man to make me feel alive in years. How could I be so stupid as to pass out?

After several minutes, I eased myself from the bed and made my way to the shower. It wasn't until I lathered shampoo onto my head that my mood began to brighten because I suddenly remembered that I would see Micah again at the wedding. I promised myself that I wouldn't let another opportunity pass me by.

I shook my head at the memories and sighed loudly, breaking the silence of the hotel room. What happened between Micah and myself that night didn't matter anymore and neither did what occurred at the wedding. The only thing that mattered was finding out who was sending the letters to Carter and putting a stop to it. I leaned up in bed and fluffed the pillow under me, hoping to get comfortable enough that sleep would finally come.

I would need as much rest as possible if I was going to have to constantly fight the myriad of emotions that man brought out in me. It would do me good to remember, he was there to do a job. Once Carter was safe, Micah would leave and I could go back to trying to forget all about him.

CHAPTER
Two

Micah

I LOCKED THE DOOR BEHIND ME AND TOSSED MY KEY CARD ON the table before heading over to the little refrigerator in the corner of the room. I didn't normally allow myself to drink when I was on a job, but seeing Landon again had left me feeling jittery and I needed something to take the edge off. Besides, I wasn't technically on the job until the next morning.

I grabbed a tiny bottle of scotch out of the fridge and poured it into a glass before taking a sip. The alcohol was smooth and it didn't take long before I was filled with a warm, pleasant feeling.

I looked around the large room. Apparently, Landon's little brother was doing well for himself if the lush accommodations of the hotel were any indication. Of course, I wouldn't have expected any less from one of Lachlan Edwards' clients. Lachlan always insisted on treating his clients like royalty. It was just one of the many reasons musicians were volleying for a chance to sign on with him. Most important though was the fact that Lachlan had an uncanny eye for recognizing raw talent. If he liked you then not only were you the real deal, you were also guaranteed to make it big.

I wasn't tired yet so I pulled the sliding door open and stepped out on the balcony. The night was warm and clear. I sank down on a lounge chair and leaned my head back to look up at the stars. I sipped at my scotch, letting it soothe the frayed edges of my nerves that being near Landon had caused. I hated feeling unsettled. It had taken a long time for me to feel as if I finally had control of myself. Yet one meeting with that man had me off balance again.

I had thought about him a lot over the last several months. I wasn't even sure what it was about him that kept pulling me in. I mean, sure, the guy was gorgeous; with his broad shoulders, thick dark brown hair, and warm golden-hazel eyes. It was more than that though. I had met plenty of men over the years that were good looking; slept with a lot of them too, but there was something about Landon Greene that called to me like a siren. I closed my eyes as my mind drifted off to the night we met.

From the moment I met Landon, I hadn't been able to take my eyes off of him. I had spent the better part of Giovanni's bachelor party observing the way Landon interacted with his family, the way he moved, and the deep timber of his voice.

I tried to be discreet, but he had caught me staring several times and I was thrilled to find that he didn't seem to be completely unaffected by me either. When our hands touched for the first time as we were introduced, I had felt a buzzing in my veins like I had never experienced before and as I looked into his eyes, I was almost positive that he felt it too.

The combination of copious amounts of alcohol along with the explosive chemistry between the two of us soon had us in a cab making out like randy teenagers. I knew I should stay away from him. After all, G was like my brother, the only family I had left and I was sure it wouldn't go over well to have a one-night stand with my best friend's new brother-in-law, but one taste of Landon's mouth and I was lost. I wanted nothing more than to strip him bare, experience the feel of his warm, smooth skin under my fingertips as I buried myself in his tight depths.

Unfortunately, the universe had other plans and Landon passed out right before the fun began. A surprising wave of tenderness had swept through me as I'd stared down at his sleeping form and I realized what a colossal mistake it would have been to sleep with him. Landon was a good man, he deserved better than to have someone as messed up as me intruding on his life, even if it was just for one night. With a new sense of clarity, I made the decision to stay away from him no matter what.

It had taken more strength than I knew I possessed to keep my distance when I ran into him once again at the wedding. I could feel his eyes drilling into me as we stood alongside the grooms and the palms of my hands bore the crescent shapes left behind by my nails digging into them as I fought the urge to look back into those beautiful hazel orbs.

Several times throughout the night, I saw him approaching me and each time, I would turn quickly, getting lost in the crowd. I knew it was cowardly of me and that he had to have questions about the way I had left things, but the truth of the matter was, I just couldn't be trusted to be alone with the man. All it would take was the smell of his skin and I would abandon my good intentions and not stop until I'd had my fill of him.

I had succeeded in staying far away from him throughout most of the reception, but he eventually caught up with me, pulling me into an alcove.

"Why are you avoiding me?" he asked. His expression was apprehensive, guarded.

"I'm not avoiding you. I'm just focused on the happy couple," I responded flippantly.

His eyes darted around us, making sure no one was close enough to overhear. "Can we talk about the other night?"

"There's nothing to talk about. Nothing happened, right?" I regretted my words immediately as his cheeks colored with embarrassment.

"I'm sorry about that. I guess I had more to drink than I'd realized," he said quietly, looking at the ground as he spoke.

I could feel myself beginning to cave. My hands itched to pull him to me and wrap my arms around him, but my phone chose that moment to vibrate in my pocket. I pulled it out, thankful for the distraction then glanced at the message quickly before turning back to face Landon.

"I'm sorry, I have to go." I started to walk past him, but he reached out and grabbed my arm, the heat of his hand searing me through the thin material of my dress shirt.

"Will I see you again?" He studied me with a mixture of wariness and hope.

I refused to look directly at him as I shook my head. "Like I said in my note, it's probably best that nothing happened between us."

"We may not have had sex, but how can you say nothing happened? I know I'm not the only one who felt the chemistry between us," he insisted.

"I'm sorry, I have no idea what you're talking about. The other night was nothing but a hazy blur from indulging in way too many drinks. Now if you'll excuse me, I really have to go." I walked away before he could see the lie in my eyes and made my apologies to the grooms for having to leave early.

Against my better judgement, I glanced in his direction one more time. Even from across the room it was easy to make out the defeated look in Landon's eyes. Before I could change my mind, I slipped out the back door, wincing when it slammed shut behind me. I hated that look on Landon's face and I would have given anything to see him smile again, but I knew I was doing the right thing. Someone as inherently good as Landon would never be able to understand someone like me.

I took another sip of my scotch, draining the glass and let out a loud sigh. Despite my reasons, the look of hurt and confusion on Landon's face as I walked away was still etched in my memory. I had debated not taking the job when Lachlan called me, but I couldn't bring myself to say no to the man. Not to mention the fact that it was a member of Giovanni's family that was in possible danger.

I knew it would be a test of strength to be in such close proximity to Landon, but I had promised myself that I would behave professionally around the man. *How well did that turn out, jackass? Not one hour with the guy and you were flirting with him.* I hadn't missed how angry Landon had seemed at my last comment. That was a good thing as far as I was concerned. With any luck, Landon would be pissed enough to keep his distance from me then I wouldn't have to worry about being tempted by him.

With a resigned sigh, I headed back inside to get some sleep. The next day was going to be a long day and I would need to keep my wits about me. I had a job to do and it didn't include seducing Landon. He was a good guy who came from a loving family, he was also smart and successful. He was everything I wasn't. The things I needed, the things that I *required,* had no place around a man like Landon Greene.

—· ⟫•⟪ ·—

I was up before the sun, a result of my years spent in the navy. I made my way out of the swanky hotel and began my morning ritual of a five-mile run. As I ran, I made a mental list of what I needed to do for the day. While the letters Carter had received up to that point were relatively tame, they also held a hint of something more sinister that didn't sit well with me. I had learned long ago to listen to my instincts and everything in me was telling me to proceed with caution.

I was soaked with sweat when I arrived back at the hotel, so I called for room service then jumped in the shower while I waited for my breakfast to be delivered. I pulled on a pair of cargo pants and a t-shirt then picked up my phone to check in with my office in Chicago.

For years, I had planned on opening my own security firm when I retired from the navy. I had always imagined working beside some of my closest friends, SEALs like me. Together, we would help to protect the citizens of Chicago while enjoying the twilight years of our lives. I would live close enough to Giovanni that I could watch his children grow up and be the fun uncle that they came to when their dad was being too parental. Maybe I would meet someone special that I could share my life with and we would live happily ever after.

I snorted derisively at how naïve I had been. Sure, I would get to see Giovanni become a dad and yes, I was able to open my own security firm, but my navy buddies wouldn't be joining me and I most certainly wasn't going to find someone to share my life with. I knew from watching G and Caleb that some people do in fact get their happily ever after, but I also knew that I wasn't one of them. I had been exposed to too much, been damaged too badly by some of the vilest creatures on the planet. No one would ever be able to love the person I had been forced to become, a former shell of myself.

I shook off the depressing direction my thoughts had taken when I heard a knock at the door. I answered and stepped to the side, allowing the server to enter the room. The young man, who barely looked legal, slid his eyes over me appreciatively and gave me a hopeful grin. I pulled my wallet from my pocket and tipped him before ushering him back out. I smothered a laugh at the disappointed look on his face as I shut the door.

I sat on the couch, placing my breakfast of fresh fruit, granola, and milk on the coffee table in front of me and as I ate, I checked my phone for emails. When I was finished eating, I leaned back against the couch and dialed my office in Chicago, waiting for my office manager to answer the phone.

Mary had shown up one day as I was moving office furniture

into the building. Boxes were piled up in every available corner, files tossed around haphazardly, and the phone had been ringing off the hook. I was both happy and overwhelmed with the way my business had taken off before the doors were even officially opened.

I had just set a heavy filing cabinet down on the floor when I heard a small gasp behind me. I spun around and was surprised to see a tiny woman standing in the doorway, her eyes wide and her mouth hanging open. Her gray hair lay in soft curls around her caramel-colored face and her black wool coat hung down below her knees. She quickly recovered and straightened her shoulders as she slowly scrutinized the state of the office.

"It looks like I got here just in time. Don't worry, I'll have this all put together before you know it," she stated, her voice hinting at a Southern accent.

"I'm sorry, but we haven't opened yet. Is there something I can help you with?" I asked her.

"No offense, but it looks like you need my help more than I need yours, honey." Her eyes levelled on me in a way that brooked no argument and I felt myself wanting to squirm under her steady gaze.

"Excuse me?" My confusion was evident in my voice.

She rolled her eyes and let out a sigh of exasperation. "I saw your Help Wanted sign out front. My name's Mary. I can work Monday through Friday until seven and I can do Saturday mornings until noon. I won't work Sundays because that's the day I spend with the Lord. I'll let you determine the salary; I don't need much. Although it wouldn't hurt you to be generous considering the current condition of this place." Her voice trailed off as her eyes swept over the room once again.

My jaw was on the floor at that point and my brows had climbed to the top of my hairline. I wondered for a brief moment if the guys I had hired had sent this woman in as a joke, but one look at her serious expression told me otherwise. Before I could formulate a response, she had shrugged off her coat, revealing a floral print dress, and set her purse down in a nearby chair.

"Well, don't just stand there, we have a lot of work to do. Hand me that stack of files and I'll start organizing this place while you finish unloading the truck." She turned her back on me, leaving me with no choice but to do as she said.

Since that day, we had been operating for several months and Mary had more than delivered on her promise, quickly organizing both the office and the ever-growing client list until the place ran like a finely tuned machine. Mary was a tough woman, but she was fiercely loyal and protective of those she cared about and that included me as well as the men who worked for me. Her husband was a business tycoon who had passed away a year earlier and she found herself suddenly alone with too much time on her hands. Although they had tried for years, she and her husband had never been able to have children of their own, but she had quickly become a mother figure to all of us and we adored her.

After several rings, I heard Mary's familiar Tennessee drawl as she picked up the phone. "Hamilton Security, how may I help you?"

"Hi, Mary, it's Micah."

"Micah! You were supposed to call me last night to let me know that you arrived safely," she scolded. Rather than being offended, I warmed under her concern. Other than G's mother, I had never had a mom to worry about me.

"I'm sorry, Mary. I had a meeting as soon as I arrived which didn't end until it was late. I didn't want to wake you."

I heard her harrumph through the phone. "Next time, wake me. It's not like I sleep that well when one of my boys are gone anyway."

"I will, Mary. I really am sorry," I said sincerely, feeling badly for causing her stress.

"Ah, you know I can't stay upset with you, Micah. Now, what can I do for you?" I smiled as she switched to business mode.

"It looks like I'm going to need extra help for this one. Who's available?" I had been fortunate enough to hire six incredibly skilled men. Each of them had served in the various branches of the military and were some of the highest trained and specially-skilled men in the country. I knew that whoever came to help, Carter and Ryan would be in the best possible hands.

After getting everything set up with Mary, I hung up and decided to take a look around before my meeting with Landon. I saw Carter and Ryan as they were leaving the hotel gym and they introduced me to the security guards that had been hired by the record label. While they were nice guys, they clearly were in over their heads when it came to protecting someone in the public eye. I listened as they described their system to me, clenching my jaw at the obvious flaws. I made a mental note to address each of the issues with Landon.

—· ———⟫•⟨——— ·—

I stood outside the door to Landon's hotel room, trying to calm my racing heart before I had to face him again. I had been trained as a Navy SEAL to deal with intense situations, sometimes even life or death scenarios, but none of my training had prepared me for the way I felt every time I looked into Landon's golden-hazel eyes. *How is it that a man I barely know has gotten under my skin so completely?*

I looked up in surprise when the door swung open before I could knock. Landon seemed just as surprised to see me standing there, but he hid it behind a nervous cough.

"Excited to see me?" I said, deciding to use humor to break the ice.

His eyes widened as if he'd been caught, but then flickered quickly to the floor. "I thought I heard someone," he explained quietly.

"And you just opened the door without checking to see who it was?" His eyes grew in alarm at the anger in my voice, so I took a deep breath to calm myself before speaking again. "I'm sorry, it's just that we have someone out there who's obsessed with your brother. This person could very easily decide to use you to get to him. You

23

need to be more careful."

"I promise to be more careful next time. I appreciate your concern." His lips lifted in a gentle smile, transforming his face. *He should smile more often*, I thought and then gave myself a mental shake for not being stronger around the man. I was supposed to be there in a professional capacity only.

"It's my job," I said gruffly as I brushed passed him.

"Your job, of course," he responded frostily, shutting the door behind him. "So, why don't you tell me what your plan is to keep my brother safe since that's what your *job* is." Without looking at me, he sat at the table and gestured for me to have a seat.

He still didn't look at me as I pulled a chair out and sat down. I told myself it was easier that way, if he was angry with me then we could focus on the job at hand instead of the lust that seemed to flare between us whenever we were in the same room.

"To start, I'd like to see the first two letters please." I followed his movements as he stood and walked across the room. He was dressed professionally in a blue-button down shirt and black slacks that hugged his delectable ass in a way that made my mouth water. I remembered all too well how that ass had felt in the grip of my hands and I felt my cock stirring within the tight confines of my cargo pants. *Down, boy!*

He retrieved a briefcase from the coffee table and sauntered back over to the table, unaware of the turn my thoughts had taken. His eyes flickered to me as he set the case down on the table and the sunlight streaming through the large windows lit upon him, turning his beautiful hazel eyes into the color of rich, warm honey and revealing the natural golden highlights that streaked throughout his hair.

"This is the first one we received." He set the letter and envelope on the table in front of me and I turned my attention to them.

I was pleased to see that someone had had the sense to bag each piece separately, so as not to ruin any evidence should we need to get the police involved. Considering the amount of fan mail the band and

Carter, in particular, received on a daily basis and the fact that none of the letters contained a direct threat, I knew there wasn't enough evidence of criminal intent to call the police at that point.

However, I had learned from years of avoiding my father's bouts of drunken rage and then later through my SEAL training how to hone in on my instincts and listen to my gut and my gut was telling me that whoever was sending the letters meant business. I was taking this case very seriously.

"Where were the letters found?" I asked.

"Each one was found somewhere different. The first was left with the front desk of the hotel, but none of the staff saw who had left it. The second was found by one of the guards, near the tour bus that the band uses when they're travelling in the States. The last one was waiting for him in his dressing room after a concert." I saw Landon shiver and I had to agree. The hairs on the back of my neck were standing at attention with the thought of how close this person had gotten to Carter.

My eyes scanned the contents of the clear zippered bags. Just like the letter that Landon had shown me the previous night, it was made of the same thick, blue stationery and *Mr. Greene* was typed evenly on the front of the envelope. The letter itself contained only a few words: *You are more beautiful every single day.* I recognized the small stamp on the bottom right corner of the page that was the same bouquet of flowers that were present on the other letter.

Silently, Landon laid the second letter out on the table. It was an exact replica of the other letters; the only difference was its message. That one read: *When I close my eyes, I can only see your face. You are my forever.*

While the notes themselves were fairly tame, they weren't what I would consider normal fan mail. I had looked over some of the other letters sent to Carter from adoring fans and they all seemed to hold a general theme: *I love your music, You're so talented, I would love to meet you someday.* Those letters conveyed someone who was looking at Carter from the outside in. The matching letters, however, spoke of something more intimate, as if the person already knew Carter personally. The third letter: *You are mine, Mr. Greene. You belong to me and no one else* displayed a new level of possessiveness that had me concerned. The intensity of the letters was increasing with each one.

"These are the only letters of this kind as far as you know?" I asked, finally glancing across the table at Landon. I was surprised at what I saw. Landon's eyes were wide, fixed on the papers spread out on the table, and his hands were noticeably shaking as he smoothed them down his silk tie over and over as if he needed something to do with them.

Obviously he was worried about his brother and the sight of the letters was disturbing to him, but this seemed like something more. He looked as if he were struggling to hold himself together. My protective nature was screaming at me to take him in my arms and shield him from anything that might cause him distress, but I had to keep my distance; for his sake, as much as my own.

"Look at me," I said calmly. He continued to stare at the letters so I spoke more firmly the second time. "I said look at me, Landon." His eyes darted to mine and I held his gaze steadily, making sure he heard what I was about to say.

"I know you're worried about your brother, but you're not doing this on your own. It is not your responsibility to keep him safe. This is what I'm trained for, Landon. I'm here now and I'll make sure no one hurts Carter, okay?" He gave me a slight nod of his head and I breathed a sigh of relief as I saw him visibly relaxing with my words.

"So, what do we do now?" he asked softly.

"I've already called in a few of my guys. They'll meet up with us on our next stop. They'll be in charge of watching over Carter and Ryan, as well as helping me to upgrade the everyday security on the tour. I've already taken a look around to familiarize myself with how things are done and I noticed several areas that need improvement as far as security goes."

I held my hand up as I saw the panic returning to his eyes. "I already have a plan in place to address each of these issues and I've spoken to Lachlan and he's in full agreement of me doing whatever it takes to ensure Carter's safety."

Landon's body sank back in relief, but his fingers continued to tap out a nervous rhythm against the wooden arms of the chair. I was surprised when he met my eyes, tilting his head to the side curiously. "Can I ask you a question?"

"Of course," I responded, ready to tell him anything I needed in order to assure him that I wouldn't let anything bad happen to his brother.

"How is it that you know Lachlan? I mean, he's the most sought after record executive in the world, he grew up in England and currently resides in California. How did he become friends with a Navy SEAL from Chicago?"

He must have noticed the rigid set to my jaw because he hurried to explain. "I didn't mean that in a bad way, I just can't figure out what connection the two of you might have."

My mind was flooded with memories, like snapshots of the worst time in my life and I squeezed my eyes shut as I willed the painful memories away.

I opened my eyes to see Landon looking at me with concern. "Lachlan and I are close friends; we have been for a while." I hoped Landon didn't ask any more questions because that's all I was willing to say on the matter.

"Right, it's none of my business. I'm sorry for asking," he said, his cheeks turning pink with embarrassment as he avoided my gaze and began to chew on his nails.

I hated the look in his eyes and I knew he was probably jumping to conclusions about my relationship with Lachlan, but that was better than having him find out how Lachlan and I had really met. That was a story that I hoped I never had to tell.

"Well, if that's all, I have a lot of work to do." I stood awkwardly, needing to make my escape before I said too much.

"Sure, I'll see you later." He walked me to the door and began closing it before I had even made it out all the way. I stopped it with my hand and he looked at me in surprise.

"I know you barely know me, but I promise you, I will do whatever it takes to keep your brother safe. Do you trust me?"

I think we were both surprised when he gave me an immediate, "Yes!"

I let out the breath I didn't realize I had been holding and nodded at him. "Then you have nothing to worry about."

Without another word, I turned and strode down the hallway, thankful that somehow I had made it through that meeting.

CHAPTER
Three

Landon

"Just a second, Akio. I know I had it here somewhere." I sifted through the stack of files on the table and rolled my eyes as I heard him chuckle through the phone. "Go ahead, laugh it up. I doubt you could do much better if you were trying to run a business out of a suitcase, living in a different city every night."

That caused him to laugh louder. "Aww, poor little traveler, having to see parts of the world most of us will only ever dream about. Besides, you weren't any more organized when you were here in Chicago. That's why you needed me so badly, remember?"

"Yeah, I remember," I agreed grudgingly. I'd met Akio Forrest four years before when he was working as an office temp at the same agency where I was employed as a talent scout. I had been miserable in that job. Instead of finding talented bands and handing them off to someone else, I wanted to stick with those bands and manage their careers, helping them reach their fullest potential.

Finally, I had decided to take a chance and start my own agency. Akio and I worked well together and when I mentioned my idea to him, he'd offered to join my team. I had agreed immediately, knowing that he would run the place better than someone with twenty years of experience managing an office. Despite his small size, Akio was a spitfire who didn't take crap from anyone, including me. He was a dedicated employee, an incredible person and besides my brothers, the best friend I'd ever had.

"Here it is!" I held the file up triumphantly as if he could see it through the phone.

"Good. Now get it signed and fax it back to me right away so I can get the venues scheduled for Wizard's Wrath."

After successfully getting Carter's Creed signed on with Golden Entertainment Studios and launching their first world tour, a second band that was managed by my agency was getting ready to headline their own U.S. tour and I couldn't be happier. The guys of Wizard's Wrath had worked very hard to get where they were and it was also an affirmation that I had made the right decision in starting my own business. It almost made the sleepless nights and the ulcer that I was sure I was developing, worth it. Almost.

I heard a knock on the door and stood to answer it. "I'll get it taken care of today. I have to go, someone's at the door."

"Oooohhhh! I hope it's Military Micah! If it is, you'd better send me some pictures this time."

"Why do I tell you things?" I groaned as my friend cackled wildly in my ear. "Goodbye, Akio."

"What? I'm a visual person," I heard him yell as I hung up. I shook my head, but couldn't help the smile that pulled at my lips. My smile faded quickly though when I saw who was on the other side of the door. I had been dreading this meeting all morning.

"Rocko, I appreciate you coming. Please, come in." I moved aside so he could step into the room and I was immediately concerned by his appearance.

Rocko was the drummer for Carter's Creed and a close friend of my brother's. He had always been an extremely good looking guy with well-defined muscles in his arms from years of playing the drums, bright blue eyes, and silky black hair that hung down to his waist. As I followed him to the couch, I noticed that he had lost weight and his usually tanned skin looked pale. His hair had lost its usual glossy sheen and was pulled into a messy ponytail.

I sat down at the opposite end of the couch and tried to hold back a gasp as I saw the dark smudges under his eyes which refused to meet my own. It hurt to see the man that was usually the life of the party looking so lost, but that was the reason I had called the meeting to begin with. Rocko was lost and he needed to find his way back before everything he had worked so hard for was taken away from him.

"Rocko, I wanted to talk to you because I'm worried about you. Everyone's worried about you."

"Why?" he asked, sounding confused.

I paused as I wondered if he was trying to act as if nothing was wrong or if he was genuinely surprised that someone would be worried about what happened to him. I knew from things that Carter had told me about the wildest member of his band that Rocko must have had something terrible hidden in his past, but so far, he had refused to open up to anyone about it.

"Because we care about you, Rocko. You're our friend as well as an important part of the band." I saw his forehead crease, but it was difficult to get a read on his thoughts because his attention was focused on his hands, which he was tapping nervously against his legs. "We've all noticed that you seem to be having trouble focusing lately. Do you want to talk about what's going on?"

His eyes shot to mine and I was glad to see a spark of temper hidden in their depths. If he still had some fire in him then maybe there was a chance that we could reach him. "Why is everyone on my case lately?" he asked as he stood and began pacing back and forth.

"Nobody's on your case, Rocko, but you have to admit you haven't been acting quite right lately. You've been showing up late for rehearsals, you take off as soon as your shows end instead of joining the rest of the band to meet with fans, and you look like shit."

"Fuck y..." His words cut off as I faced him head-on with a glare.

"Look, I've given you more chances than most because I know how important you are to my brother and the rest of the band, but I won't be disrespected. I don't know exactly what's going on with you, but you better fix it and I mean immediately. I am contractually obligated to report any problems to Golden Entertainment." I held my hand up when he looked like he was going to argue.

"They've been keeping a close eye on you and I'll tell you, they're not happy with what they've seen. You're an incredible drummer, but right now you're a liability. If you don't get your head on straight, the higher-ups won't hesitate to replace you with someone else and there won't be a damn thing I can do about it."

Rocko's shoulders sagged and for the first time I saw true fear in his eyes. I knew that the members of Carter's Creed were like family to him and it killed me to have to say those things to him, but perhaps a wakeup call was exactly what he needed.

I put my hand on his shoulder as my tone became gentler. "I'm willing to help you with whatever you're going through, Rocko, but I'm not a mind reader. You have to tell me what's wrong. If it's the stress of the job, maybe we can find a healthier way for you to deal with it."

He looked at me for several long seconds, considering my words. Just when I thought he might finally open up to me, his eyes filled with what looked like regret mixed with hopelessness. "Thanks, Landon. I appreciate that, I really do, but this is something I've got to deal with on my own."

Without another word, he walked out of the room and shut the door behind him. I sank down onto the couch and put my head in my hands, massaging my temples to help relieve my pounding head. *If it's the stress of the job, maybe we can find a healthier way for you to deal with it.* My words to Rocko played back on a continuous loop and I knew I should learn to take my own advice.

Even though I wanted nothing more than to crawl back into bed and hide under my covers, I knew that would be the worst thing I could do. I needed to find a way to cope with my growing anxiety and closing myself off from the rest of the world wasn't going to help. With a renewed determination, I changed into my workout gear and headed down to the hotel gym.

Most of the hotels we stayed in while on the road offered gyms for their guests to use, but this was by far the nicest one I'd seen. Every imaginable piece of equipment was lined up neatly throughout the large room and each wall was made up entirely of mirrors.

I noticed a few people out of the corner of my eye but ignored them as I made my way over to the treadmills. I put my headphones in and pulled up my favorite playlist then set the controls on the equipment, starting out at an easy jog and eventually picking up speed.

I loved exercising. By pushing my body to its limits and then forcing myself to go even further than that, I was able to sweep aside everything except the steady rise and fall of my breathing. My mind didn't have time to wander over meetings, budgets, or crazy stalkers.

As I ran faster, I could feel my muscles becoming limber and my head began to clear. The anxiety that knotted my stomach on a daily basis flowed out of me as my feet pounded the surface of the machine. I took a deep breath, filling my lungs like I was surfacing from a long dive beneath murky waters.

I focused on the rhythm of my movements and the music playing in my ears, allowing myself to lose track of time as I ran full-stop.

After a while, my lungs began to burn and my legs felt rubbery from exhaustion and I was forced to slow my pace. As invigorating as it was to finally feel like myself again, I knew it wouldn't do me any good to end up injured.

I grabbed my towel from the side of the treadmill and wiped at the sweat that dripped down my face as I began my cool down. I took a long drink from my water bottle and for the first time since I had started my workout, I became aware of my surroundings.

The group of men and women who had been in the gym when I arrived were gone and there was only one other person in the room with me. He was facing the opposite direction and was bent over, preparing to pick up a large set of weights. With the endorphins still flooding my body, I took a moment to enjoy the view as I jogged.

The man wore black basketball shorts that showcased a perfectly sculpted ass and I felt my cock twitch within my own shorts. As he straightened, I could see the muscles in his back, rippling under the material of his gray t-shirt as he lifted the weights and I let myself imagine just what he would look like without the shirt on.

I was so caught up in my naughty fantasies that I hadn't noticed that the man had put the weight back down and was now staring at me through the reflection of the mirror. My eyes widened in shock as I realized I'd been caught ogling none other than Micah Hamilton and that was when it happened.

I tripped over my own feet and began slapping wildly at the power button on my machine, but before I could get it to stop, I felt myself being launched off of the treadmill, landing on the floor with a loud thud. I lay there, sprawled out awkwardly on my stomach, my face burning with embarrassment as I assessed what, if any, damage I had done to myself.

Fortunately, nothing seemed to be hurt except my pride, but I stayed where I was, my forehead pressed to the floor as I wondered if there was any chance at all that he hadn't just seen that. I prayed that he had been wiping the sweat from his eyes and had missed the entire thing, but my hopes were soon dashed when I saw a pair of shoes out of the corner of my eye.

"Are you alright, Landon?" I heard Micah's deep voice rumble.

I chanced a quick glance up at him and was surprised to find that instead of laughing, he looked concerned as his hand stretched out in a silent offer. Picking up the tattered remnants of my dignity, I slid my hand into his, allowing him to help me off the floor.

"Thanks," I managed to mumble. I could feel his eyes on me as I grabbed my towel and threw it around my neck and then began searching for my phone which must have gotten thrown at the same time I had.

"I think it landed over by the door," he said quietly. If possible my face flushed even hotter as he walked over and bent down to retrieve my phone which appeared to have weathered through the embarrassing episode better than I had.

His fingers brushed over mine as he handed my phone to me and my senses were suddenly assaulted with the intoxicating smell of clean sweat and man. I watched as a drop of sweat ran down his neck and pooled in the hollow of his throat. I licked my lips, wishing I could lap it from his heated skin.

My treacherous cock thickened beneath the smooth material of my shorts which did nothing to hide my condition. *You have got to be kidding me!* How the hell I was able to have any response other than the overwhelming urge to hide my head in the sand was beyond me, but somehow my dick had plans of its own.

I needed to get out of there before I made things worse, although I wasn't really sure how that would be possible. I turned to walk away, but stopped when I felt his hand on my arm. His eyes raked over my body, lingering on the prominent bulge on display before finally coming up to meet my gaze. My breath caught in my throat at the hunger behind his beautiful gray orbs.

"Is there a problem?" he asked pointedly.

I felt my anger rising to the surface as it usually did when he was around. Micah had done nothing but reel me in and push me away since the day we met and I was tired of it. I had enough of my own problems and I didn't need him toying with me for his own amusement.

"You made it abundantly clear at the wedding that you weren't interested in my *problems*," I responded coldly.

I could feel the heat radiating from his body as he leaned in close and ran a finger slowly down my throat, making me shiver. His breath ghosted over my ear as he whispered, "I said it wouldn't be a good idea. I *never* said I wasn't interested."

I swallowed thickly as he straightened back up and with a cocky smirk, sauntered out of the room. I sank back against the wall, too weak to stand on my own. *One of these days, the man is going to make me spontaneously combust.*

CHAPTER
Four

Micah

THE LOUD ROAR OF THE CROWD WAS A BIT SHOCKING AT FIRST for someone like myself who wasn't used to it. I had attended my fair share of concerts, but I had never been on the performance side of the stage, hearing the collective screams of over fifty thousand fans coming right at me. I could only imagine what it was like for the band who were preforming center stage.

My eyes ran over the many people scurrying around behind stage. It was mind boggling to me how many people were required to help pull off a show of that magnitude. I was in awe of how much time and effort Landon had put in just to ensure that everything ran as smoothly as possible so that the band could focus on their music.

It had been several weeks since I had taken over security for Carter's Creed and so far, things were running very smoothly. Tony,

Greg, and Carlos, three men who worked for me at my security firm, had arrived shortly after I had and they had taken over the various functions of implementing a better security system, not only for Carter and Ryan, but for the entire band.

Each person was assigned their own security guard who escorted them from the venues to the hotel rooms or tour bus. I also had a guard watching over the bus at all times to keep anyone from getting on that wasn't supposed to be there. I made sure that there was adequate security watching each entrance onto the floor of the hotel where the band stayed and someone was in charge of vetting which fans were allowed access to the band behind the stage.

While the guards that were hired on by Golden Entertainment Studios were capable of watching over the band members, I only allowed my guys to watch over Carter and Ryan. The men who worked for me were the best in the business and I trusted them completely. I had promised Landon that I would keep his brother safe and I was determined not to go back on my word.

Although there hadn't been any new letters in the weeks since I had arrived, I wasn't convinced that the threat was over. I had researched the stationery used, but so far, I hadn't found any significance to it. Whoever sent them seemed to have chosen their words carefully and had somehow managed to deliver all three letters without being seen.

As usual, my thoughts wandered back to Landon. He had been avoiding me ever since the incident at the gym, but once in a while we would catch each other's eye as we passed in the hallway and he would turn that perfect shade of crimson just like he had when he fell in front of me. I felt horrible that he had been so embarrassed, but mostly I was flattered that I could make him so flustered.

While I had sworn to myself that I would leave Landon alone, when we were near each other, I wanted more. More of his smell, his taste, his touch. Every time I saw him, the pull between us became stronger and I was unable to resist him. That alone should have sent me running, because I refused to ever let someone have power over me again.

I turned back to the stage and watched as the band started the first song in their set. I had to admit, they were incredible. Carter was extremely talented and he worked the stage like a true professional. I watched as he leaned down to sing directly to a group of women at the base of the stage, reaching out to touch their raised hands. I chuckled as some of the women giggled, a few screamed, and one poor girl burst into tears.

"He's amazing, isn't he?"

I turned to see the man who stood beside me. Ryan Marshall was a gorgeous man with blond hair and smoky gray-blue eyes; eyes that only ever noticed one man, Carter Greene. Ryan stared at his fiancé in awe, as if it were the first time he had laid eyes on him and I turned away, feeling as if I were intruding. *What would it be like to have someone look at me with that much adoration?*

"Yes, he's very talented," I agreed.

Ryan shook his head with a gentle smile. "It's more than just his talent. Carter is the kindest, most generous person I know. He's also incredibly smart, sexy as fuck, and has a wicked sense of humor."

Ryan tilted his head toward the crowd of fans. "He could have had anyone he wanted and somehow he picked me. He's my whole world." Ryan turned to look at me for the first time and I was surprised at the intensity I saw in his eyes. "Please, keep him safe. I can't lose him."

The weight of my responsibility threatened to pull me down. The lives that would be ruined if I failed again…No! I couldn't afford to think like that. This time would be different.

"I'll find out who's sending the letters and I'll stop them. I won't let them hurt him, okay?" I knew better than to make promises I couldn't keep, but I wanted to ease the worry from his eyes. Luckily, it seemed to work because Ryan's shoulders relaxed as he nodded his head.

He stuck his hand out to me and I shook it. "Thank you, Micah. I feel better knowing you're here. Everyone does." I knew of at least one person who would disagree, but I decided to change the subject to a lighter topic.

"So, I hear congratulations are in order. When's the big day?"

Ryan smiled wide, showing off a set of perfectly white teeth. "We haven't decided yet. The tour schedule is so crazy we haven't even had time to talk about it much. Carter wanted to take me to some exotic beach where we could get married on the sand. I don't really care where we do it, I just want him to be my husband. I want the whole world to know without a shadow of a doubt that he's mine and I'm his."

"Oh, I think the world already knows that, Cryan," I teased.

Ryan threw his head back with a laugh. "Isn't that name horrible? Hollywood sure likes to blend couples' names, but I think ours might just be the worst."

I laughed with him. "Yeah, it's pretty bad."

We spoke for a few minutes before I got the strange feeling that I was being watched. I looked around discreetly, not seeing anything out of the ordinary. Finally, I looked across the stage to the other side of the curtains and saw Landon standing there looking at me.

He held my gaze, surprising me because he was usually the first to look away. His lips lifted in a small grin and my cock stirred inside my jeans. I had missed that smile, since I tended to piss Landon off when we were together. His tongue darted out to wet his lips and I hardened even more as I pictured Landon on his knees, those perfect lips wrapped around my dick. I suddenly resented the fact that there was a whole stage between us.

A woman walked up with a clipboard in hand and began speaking to him. He smiled, but I noticed the reluctance in his eyes as he turned his attention away from me and on to her. Since Landon was busy and everything looked secure on stage, I said goodbye to Ryan and headed outside to check on the limos that would be taking the band back to the hotel for the night. I took a deep breath of the crisp night air as I stepped out, willing my cock to settle down before anyone noticed the effect Landon had on me.

I hung up the phone and grabbed a water from the mini fridge before collapsing into one of the plush chairs in my hotel suite. I had been worried that calling three of my guys to come help would leave Mary short staffed at the agency, but as usual she had everything under control.

Hearing Mary's voice had made me feel homesick for Chicago. Despite my horrible childhood, I had a lot of great memories of living there; particularly with Giovanni and his parents. They loved to take us on day trips, exploring all that the city had to offer, including catching a Cubs game at Wrigley Field and seeing the breathtaking view from the Observation Deck. The Romeros had shown me what unconditional love was like, treating me like another member of their family. They had given me a home when I might have otherwise ended up in a jail cell.

After spending years in the navy, I had been tired of constantly moving around. I was looking forward to starting my own business and finding a place to live near Giovanni. I hadn't expected to get called away on a job that would take me clear around the world, but there was no way I could say no to Lachlan. It wasn't all bad though; everyone on the tour had been very nice and of course, Landon was there.

I drank the last of my water and decided to indulge myself by crawling into bed and watching some mindless TV. I had just pulled my shirt over my head when my phone rang in my pocket. I glanced at the screen, surprised to see Landon's name.

"Hello?"

"Micah, thank God." I stiffened as I heard the strain in his voice.

"What's wrong, Landon?" I asked, already pulling my shirt back on and shoving my key card in my pocket.

"Can you come to my room please? There's been another letter."

"I'm on my way," I said as I shut the door behind me and hurried down the hall. A few seconds later, I knocked on his door.

"That was quick," he said as he let me in.

"It's not like I'm far away," I teased, but he barely smiled as he turned and walked back into the room.

I followed him to where he had the new letter spread out on the table. "Where was the letter found?" I asked as I read the neatly typed words.

No matter how hard you try, you can't break the bond between us. I won't let you.

"It was at the front desk with the other mail. I asked, but no one saw anyone drop it off." I made a mental note to question the hotel staff myself, later.

"Have Carter and Ryan seen the letter yet?"

"No, the concert just ended. Carter should be getting cleaned up and then he has a meet and greet with the fans after. Ryan always stays with him until they're ready to go back to their room," Landon explained.

I pulled my phone out and sent a text to Carlos, Greg, and Tony to let them know about the newest letter so they would be extra careful about who came into contact with Carter. When I was finished, I put my phone away and looked up to find Landon staring down at the letter, but his eyes were unfocused. His lips had turned a pale white and were pressed into a thin line. He was visibly shaking and his nostrils flared as his breathing increased.

With the rigorous training and challenges that they put us through to become Navy SEALs, I had seen my fair share of panic attacks and I knew how to recognize the signs. I rushed over to Landon and put my hands on his shoulders, trying to get him to make eye contact.

"Landon, look at me. I'm right here."

His eyes darted around the room, not really seeing anything. I wasn't even sure he knew I was there as he began hyperventilating and grabbing at his throat. A sob tore from his chest and I knew I had to get him under control before he lost consciousness.

I used one hand to pull his fingers away from his throat before he could hurt himself and locked them in place between us. I grasped his chin firmly in my other hand and forced him to look in my eyes. I leaned in close and spoke to him in a voice that left no argument about which one of us was in control.

"Landon, look at me damnit! I'm in charge and you're going to do exactly what I say. You. Need. To. Breathe." Slowly, I saw him take notice and focus on my eyes and the sound of my voice. "That's it. Take a deep breath and hold it. Now, slowly let it out." I released a sigh of relief as he followed my instruction. "Again." We stood that way for several minutes until his breathing evened out and most of the shaking had subsided.

The fear in his eyes had been replaced with embarrassment and something else. *Was that arousal?* He glanced down at my mouth and I wet my lips unwittingly. He leaned forward slowly and pressed his lips to mine and I realized I still had his hands locked between us, but I didn't let go.

He opened his mouth, inviting me in and I swallowed his gasp as my tongue swept in to taste him, reacquainting myself with the sweet flavor I had been craving since that very first night. A surge of lust flooded my veins, making my knees weak. The cold metal of my zipper pressing against my hard cock brought me back to my senses. I wouldn't take advantage of Landon in a vulnerable state, no matter how intoxicating his kisses were.

Reluctantly, I pulled back and slid my hands from around his wrists. It killed me to see the disappointment and confusion in his eyes and it took every ounce of willpower I had to step away from him. I picked up the letter from the table.

"Don't worry, I'm going to take care of this. It's actually a good thing that we got another letter because each one gives us another clue and brings us that much closer to finding this asshole," I rambled as I made my way to the door. I turned back to look at him.

Landon shoved his hands into his pockets and stared silently at the floor. I wanted to take him back in my arms and pick up where we had left off, but I let myself out instead, knowing I would just fuck things up more if I stayed. I leaned against the closed door and let my head drop back as one question ran through my mind, begging to be answered. *Was it possible that Landon had been as turned on as I was when I took control?*

CHAPTER
Five

Landon

I STOOD IN THE SHOWER WITH MY HEAD BENT, LETTING THE SPRAY of the water clear the fogginess from my mind. I hadn't slept much, tossing and turning all night long as I replayed what had happened. I knew my anxiety was getting worse, but I had never experienced anything quite like that before and I was more than a little embarrassed that Micah had been there to witness my breakdown.

As the oldest boy in our family, I always looked out for my two sisters and younger brothers. I became even more protective as my sisters began dating and the twins announced that they were gay. I loved my siblings and I wasn't going to let anyone hurt them. That's why I went on tour with Carter. Even though I knew he was an adult and a professional, I felt like if I were there then maybe I could stop anyone from taking advantage of him.

Things were going well for a while. I had been given the opportunity to organize the entire tour and the shows were going off without a hitch. Carter's Creed was gaining popularity and my brother was happier than I'd ever seen him. His fiancé, Ryan, was travelling with him and he was writing new songs every day.

Then the first two letters arrived and I felt like the rug had been pulled out from under me. How could I keep my brother safe if I didn't know where the danger was coming from? The hardest part for me was not being able to talk about it with anyone. I had kept the letters secret from Carter and Ryan because I didn't want them to worry unless they had to and I knew it wouldn't be fair to tell anyone else in my family about them since there was nothing they could do from so far away.

Instead, I kept my worries to myself and as a result, my anxiety began to grow. I was no longer able to sleep at night, I had no appetite, and I had trouble keeping still. Sometimes it felt like the weight of my responsibilities would crush me.

With the arrival of the third letter, I knew I had a responsibility to tell Lachlan Edwards what was going on. As CEO of Golden Entertainment Studios, he wanted to know everything that was happening with the people he held contracts with. Unfortunately, my relief at having finally shared the burden with someone else was short lived when Lachlan informed me that Micah would be coming to take over security.

I had tried my best to hide my growing anxiety from everyone around me, but when I saw the words written to my brother in the fourth letter, something inside me snapped. Four letters had come, each one becoming more aggressive and personal, and we still were no closer to figuring out who was behind all of it. For all we knew, the person who wrote the letters could work for us and be in close proximity to Carter.

Before I knew it, I had broken out in a cold sweat and began shaking all over. My heart was racing and no matter how much air I'd tried to pull in, I couldn't fill my lungs. I had begun to feel lightheaded and my vision was swirling when I heard Micah speaking to me in a firm voice.

I focused on the sound of his voice, grabbing onto it like it was a life raft and before long my breathing began to even out. As my brain was once again fed the oxygen it desperately needed, my head began to clear and I was able to see Micah more clearly. I hadn't even noticed that he was standing so close to me or that he had my hands locked firmly in his grip.

Instead of making me feel trapped, his hands wrapped tightly around my wrists made me feel free; free of my worries and the burden of having to make every decision on my own. In that moment, all that was required of me was to follow his directions and do what I was told. It was the safest I had felt in my entire life and an unknown part of myself that must have been craving that security all along, came clawing to the surface.

I leaned forward and kissed him. I wasn't sure how he would respond and a part of me had braced for his rejection, but instead he kissed me back. The first swipe of his tongue against mine had me aching for more and I could feel my cock straining to be let free.

All too soon, he stepped back and I'd shivered at the loss of his body heat. I understood why he would want to stay away from me, after all, I was a complete mess. Carter was the one in trouble, yet here Micah was having to calm *me* down. He was here to take care of my brother, not to babysit me.

I turned the water off and reached outside the shower for the towel I had left hanging on the rack. I dried myself and then continued getting ready for the day as I wondered how I could possibly avoid having contact with Micah ever again.

Since I had met him, I had passed out right before we had a chance to sleep together, followed him around like a lost puppy at the wedding, made a complete ass of myself as I fell off of a treadmill, and now had a total meltdown in front of him. I had done nothing but look like an utter fool in front of the man so there was no other reasonable explanation for why he had kissed me back except that he must pity me.

That thought had me wanting to crawl beneath the covers of my bed and hide until Micah had returned to Chicago and was once again hundreds of miles away from me. Of course, that meant that I would need to move to a new place to avoid any possible run-ins with him. *Perhaps Australia would be far enough away.* Then I remembered my family and I knew that I could never leave them, not to mention my agency and everyone who worked for me.

As I buttoned up my shirt, Micah's words came back to me, "I said it wouldn't be a good idea, I never said I wasn't interested." Perhaps it wasn't pity that had made him return my kiss after all, but then what had he meant when he said that? We were both adults and the chemistry between us was off the charts, so what exactly was holding him back?

I finished working my tie into a knot and smoothed it down as I checked my reflection in the mirror. The skin around my hazel eyes creased as I smiled. If there was any chance that Micah was still interested in me then it was time I found out once and for all.

* * *

I walked up the stairs that led to the stage and carefully stepped over the maze of electrical cords that were taped to the floor. I stopped at the side of the curtain and watched as the band warmed up for their show. The usual easy-going banter between the friends was nowhere to be found and had been replaced by a tension that could be felt by even a casual observer.

"Something is off with them. What is it?" I turned in surprise when I heard the familiar British accent.

"Lachlan, what are you doing here?" The handsome man was

dressed in a preppy light blue sweater and tan dress pants, making him look more like an ivy league college student than the CEO of one of the most profitable record labels in the world.

"I like to pop in here and there to check on my bands." He gave me a knowing smile. "People tend to behave differently when they know I'm going to be around. If I catch them by surprise, I can get a better feel for how things are truly going."

"Well, everyone wants to put on a good show when the boss is around." He chuckled and then grew serious as his attention was drawn back to the stage.

"What's wrong with them, Landon?" he asked with concern.

"They're trying to keep it all together like the professionals they are, but they've been through a lot of stress lately," I said, stepping in to defend them.

Lachlan held his hand up. "Don't get me wrong, they're still amazingly talented and if I were someone watching from the crowd, I probably wouldn't be able to tell that anything was amiss, but knowing them like I do, I can tell that something just isn't right. Is it the letters Carter's been receiving?"

I let out a low sigh. "Partly. We received another letter the other day. Micah's hopeful that it will provide a new clue that will lead us to whoever is sending them."

Lachlan nodded thoughtfully and his eyes softened. "Micah's a good man; the best. He'll do whatever it takes to keep your brother safe."

I was surprised at the sudden rush of jealousy I felt as I wondered once again how well Lachlan and Micah knew each other. "I know," I murmured. I was afraid to say more for fear of giving myself away.

"I'm sure I could guess the other source of their tension." Lachlan's gaze slid back to the stage. His jaw twitched as his eyes landed on Rocko.

I nodded even though he wasn't looking at me. "Yes, you already know about the problems with Rocko."

"Anything new?" We both watched as the drummer kept a steady beat on the instrument in front of him. Rocko was one of the best drummers I had ever heard and even distracted, he never missed a beat. His performance wasn't the problem; the problem was that liveliness between the friends, the energy they produced when they took the stage, was missing.

"Nothing specific. He hasn't gone on any binges that I know of, but there's definitely something not right with him. Everyone can feel it and we're all walking on eggshells just waiting for the other shoe to drop. I had a talk with him, but I'm not sure I really got anywhere. Whatever ghosts are chasing him, aren't giving up and he's not letting anybody in."

Lachlan glanced at me out of the corner of his eye. "You have good instincts, Landon. I've been in this business a long time. I've seen people with the whole world at their feet who have lost it all because they wouldn't let others in. Some things are just too big to deal with on our own."

His words made me think of Micah and I remembered how safe he had made me feel in those few moments while he held me; like I wasn't alone and I had someone to help me shoulder my responsibilities. I wanted to feel that way again and I was more determined than ever to talk to Micah and find out why he thought something between us would be a bad idea. I tried to focus when I realized Lachlan was still speaking.

"He's tried to deal with his problems all on his own and in very unhealthy ways and he's become a ticking time bomb. The questions that remain are when will he explode and who will be caught in the blast." I shuddered at the thought. Rocko was a client of mine, but he had also become a friend and I didn't want to see anything happen to him.

"Well, look who it is." Lachlan and I each turned at the sound of Micah's voice and I watched as a warm smile spread across Lachlan's face. I stood to the side as the two men embraced, holding on to each other longer than I thought was necessary. Alarms went off in my head as Lachlan leaned back and cupped Micah's face gently, intimately.

"Micah, it's been so long. Too long." I wanted to tear them away from each other, but I cleared my throat loudly instead. They each turned to look at me as if they were surprised to see me there and I had to resist the urge to roll my eyes.

"Gentlemen, perhaps we should take this reunion somewhere else so we don't disturb the band while they practice."

Micah's lips tugged up at the corners in amusement. "You mean the band who currently has my ears ringing because they're so loud? That band?"

I realized how ridiculous my words sounded, but I narrowed my eyes at him. "If you mean the band who will be playing to a sold-out stadium and needs to concentrate, then yes." Micah's eyes flared at my haughty tone and I wondered if it was turning him on.

"You're right. We should continue this somewhere more private, like your room," Micah conceded. I swallowed hard at the double meaning in his words and my eyes flickered to Lachlan to see if he had heard it too. Luckily, Lachlan had redirected his attention back to the band and was staring with a thoughtful expression on his face.

"Lachlan, are you coming?" Micah touched the man's arm to get his attention.

"Yes, sorry. My thoughts got away from me," he smiled sheepishly then glanced over his shoulder once more before following us out of the venue. Not much was said as we rode back to the hotel in Lachlan's limo and I led them to my room.

"So, Micah, Landon told me there was a fourth letter delivered," Lachlan said as he and Micah settled onto the couch. With no other option, I took the chair across from them.

"Yes." Micah nodded his head seriously. "Whoever's sending them obviously hasn't given up, not that I thought they would, but as

I told Landon, each letter brings more clues that will help us track the person down."

"Do you have any idea who it could be? A jilted lover perhaps?" Lachlan asked.

"Carter never dated anyone before Ryan. His previous encounters with men were never what anyone would consider serious," I explained carefully. I didn't want to give the impression that Carter had been a slut, but he had definitely had a lot of fun exploring before finally meeting the love of his life.

"Ahh, I see. Then perhaps it's someone who wanted more from him. There's been a lot of media coverage about his engagement to Ryan. Maybe this person wants Carter all to himself." Lachlan's speculations brought a voice to my own fears and I felt my heart rate increase.

"There's something about the letters that has been bugging me. Something tickling at the back of my mind, like when you're trying to remember someone's name and it's right on the tip of your tongue, but you just can't get a clear grasp on it." Micah leveled his stare at me. "But I'll figure it out. I won't give up until I do."

I felt my heart rate slow with his words and I gave him a small smile, knowing that he had picked up on my distress and was trying to calm me down. I felt the same level of comfort I had felt when he had held me close to him. That was until Lachlan spoke.

"That's why I called you to take care of this." Micah's head swiveled to the other man when he laid his hand on Micah's knee. "There's no one in the world I trust more to handle this situation than you, Micah." My hands turned into fists as I fought the urge to reach over and smack Lachlan's hand away.

"I'll do my best," Micah said quietly.

"I know you will." Their eyes held for a few moments as they seemed to hold a silent conversation and I had to clench my jaw as I battled the green-eyed monster within me. I didn't know how the two men had met or what they meant to each other, but I didn't like it. Not one bit.

Luckily, Lachlan stood and said goodbye before I could make a jackass out of myself. Drawing on the manners I had been raised with, I politely showed him to the door and gave myself a mental pat on the back when I didn't slam it behind him.

I turned to see Micah leaning against the back of the couch with his arms crossed, his mouth quirked in a sexy smirk. "If there's something you want to ask me, now would be the time."

I hated that the man could read me so easily. I brushed past him and went to the table that I had been using as my makeshift desk and stood with my back to him, rifling through a stack of mail. "I have no idea what you're talking about, but I do have a lot of work to do, so if you could just show yourself out, that would be great."

I gasped as I suddenly felt him right behind me. He spun me around and leaned forward until I was forced to sit on the edge of the table or risk falling. Blood rushed to my dick as the now familiar scent of fresh rain and musk that was all Micah, surrounded me.

He held me captive in his stare as he spoke. "Lachlan and I are friends. Very good friends..." I tried to turn away, not wanting to hear any more, but he grasped my chin in his hand, forcing me to concentrate on what he was saying.

"We've been through some things that have made us very close, but that's all we are. There's never been anything between us except friendship and there never will be."

Relief washed over me, but I refused to let him see it. "I don't know why you're telling me this, I wasn't even wondering about that."

A devilish grin spread across Micah's face. "Have you forgotten that I'm trained to read a person's body language?"

"And what is my body language telling you?" I whispered.

Micah looked me up and down slowly, his eyes lingering on certain parts of my anatomy and making me feel exposed, as if I were standing in front of him without any clothes on. "It's telling me that you're curious, jealous...and turned the fuck on."

CHAPTER
Six

Micah

L ANDON LEANED TOWARDS ME, HIS EYES LOCKED ONTO MY
mouth, but I pulled back instinctively. Everything in me was
screaming to let go and have him the way I had wanted him
since the night we met, but a part of me that must have been stronger
than the rest hesitated. He pulled back and cocked his head, studying
me curiously.

"You admitted before that you were interested and I could tell
when you kissed me the other night that it was true. So why did you
say it would be a bad idea for anything to happen between us?"

I stepped back and slid my hands into the pockets of my jeans
so I wouldn't be able to grab him and spread him out across the table
the way I wanted to. "G is my best friend. He's like a brother to me;
the only family I have. I don't think he'd like me hooking up with his

brother-in-law."

"Bullshit!" Landon stated firmly and I looked at him in surprise. "That's just an excuse and you know it. Giovanni knows you're a good man or he wouldn't be friends with you and I'm pretty sure he trusts me. He wouldn't care who either of us were with as long as the person treated us right."

I stared at the floor until Landon stepped closer and lifted my chin so he could look directly at me. "What's the *real* reason you're fighting this, Micah?"

I moved out of his reach as I took a deep breath, deciding it was time to finally level with him. I just hoped he didn't look at me with disgust once I explained. "You're an incredible man, Landon. The way you've turned your whole world upside down to take care of your brother, making sure that he has whatever he needs to be a success; putting your own needs aside to keep him safe and happy. You own a successful business and you're incredibly smart, but I see the toll it's taken on you and you deserve to have someone beside you to help carry the load. Someone who hasn't made a complete mess of their own life. Someone who isn't…me."

Landon looked at me incredulously. "What are you talking about? You're an amazing man…"

"You don't get it. I'm messed up. There are things I need; things I require from a lover that have no business in your world."

He looked at me warily for the first time and I didn't know if I should feel relief that I was finally getting through to him or disappointment that my assumption had been correct. Landon deserved someone who would be gentle with him and lavish him with romance.

"What kind of things?" His voice sounded husky and I was surprised to see the spark in his eyes. *Good Lord, he's actually turned on by this.*

Hope flared through me as I responded. "Do you really want to know?" I fought back a smile as he nodded emphatically.

"I need to be in control. I need a lover that will submit to me." I watched his reaction closely for any sign of trepidation, but instead he cocked his head curiously.

"So, you're looking for a sub/Dom relationship?"

"I never said I was looking for a relationship." I said more harshly than I had intended. I made sure my tone was gentler as I continued. "And I don't want to dominate someone all of the time. I'm not interested in collaring a man or hard-core BDSM. I just want someone that will give control over to me during sex. Someone who is willing to put their own ideas aside and let me decide what happens, when it will happen, and where it will happen. That person would have to be willing to hand everything over to me when it comes to intimacy."

Landon shivered and his lids were heavy over his hazel eyes as he stared at my lips as if in a trance. "Are you ready to run now?"

When his eyes met mine, they were filled with a steely determination. "I'm not running anywhere. I want you to show me."

"You deserve better than that. You deserve someone who will be tender and gentle with you."

Landon stepped closer until his chest brushed up against mine, leaving no space between us. "*Show me!*" he stated forcefully.

Without thought, I gave in to the demands, both his verbal one and my internal. I had been craving the man in front of me for too long and he had just given me his blessing. If he wanted to know what he was in for with a man like me then who was I to stop him?

With a desire that I had never felt before, I grabbed the sides of his face and pulled him towards me, devouring his mouth in a fierce kiss. My fingers ran through his silky hair and my head spun as he kissed me back just as passionately. My tongue delved in, exploring the deep recesses of his mouth. My hands located his belt and I quickly undid the buckle then slid it from the loops of his dress pants.

He gasped as I pulled his hands behind his back and wrapped the belt around his wrists. I arched my brow at him in question and he gave me a single nod, telling me without words that he was still with me. I finished tying him up and then stepped back to look at my handiwork.

Landon was the most beautiful man I had ever seen. We were just getting started, but already he looked completely trussed up. His hair was a sexy mess from where my fingers had run through it, his arms were tied tightly behind him, and I could see his impressive cock was straining inside his dress slacks. The man was pure decadence and I couldn't wait to indulge in him.

I slowly unsnapped my pants and released my swollen shaft from the confining material of my jeans. Pre-cum beaded at the tip of my cock and I watched as Landon stared at it and licked his lips boldly, making his wishes clear.

"Next time," I growled as I reached for his zipper. My movements faltered when he smiled at me and I realized what I had just said. I had never meant to imply that there would be a next time, but now that it was out there, I wasn't sorry. I already knew that one time with Landon was not going to be enough to slake my need.

I leaned down to kiss him and swallowed his sigh as I reached in and traced my hand over the head of his dick. Wetness coated my fingers and I brought them to my mouth for a taste. He tasted salty, slightly sweet, and absolutely delicious. I groaned my appreciation and then pulled his pants and briefs further down until they cupped his ass. I ran my hands down the full length of him, learning the weight of him in my hand. He was long and had a good width that I couldn't wait to stretch my lips around.

"Are you sure about this?" I asked, giving him one last chance to walk away.

"Yes!" he answered breathlessly. He looked hot as fuck with his cock standing at attention while his shirt and tie were still in place. His eyes never wavered from mine as he waited to see what I would do next. The fact that he was giving control to me, allowing me to decide what would happen next, had me on the brink of coming and I had to take a deep breath to steady myself.

I watched him carefully as I placed a hand over his throat and applied a bit of pressure. Then I pressed harder, not enough to cut off his air, but enough to excite us both and the fire burning in his eyes was my reward. My other hand snaked down between us and grabbed both of our cocks, making them slide against each other. At the first contact of our skin, Landon let out a cry of relief and I leaned forward.

"Those sounds are all mine. They belong to me and no one else is allowed to hear them unless I say so. Do you understand?" Landon nodded and whimpered quietly.

Pre-cum dribbled from his cock making it easier to glide my hand up and down. I circled my hand around our paired shafts, forming a tight sleeve for us to fuck. I could tell Landon was close, but I wasn't going to let him come just yet.

"You will wait for me. Even though your balls are drawing up tight and you can feel the burning at the base of your spine. You will not come until I say you can."

Sweat beaded on his upper lip with the strain of holding back and I licked it from him, wanting every part of him for myself. I had never felt so wildly possessive about another person and it almost scared me with its ferocity.

I worked our cocks at a steady pace, feeling my own control reaching its breaking point. Landon shook all over as he struggled to do as I commanded, wanting to please me. After a few more strokes, I couldn't hold back any more. "Now!" I growled as cum shot out the tip of my cock. I could barely hear the sounds of Landon coming over the roaring in my ears.

When my breathing had evened out, I helped steady him so he could stand and put himself back together. Instead he leaned forward and rested his head against my shoulder. My arms hung loosely at my sides as surprise swept through me. I had never been the cuddling type, nor had I been with a man who was, but I found myself liking the few extra moments of intimacy.

Tentatively, I reached up and placed my hand on his head. I watched his shoulders relax and I realized he had been waiting to see how I would respond. I ran my fingers through his silky hair and I felt his warm breath as he sighed, awakening something inside me that I thought had died long ago.

Startled by my reaction to him, I stepped back and quickly released the belt from his wrists. I could feel his eyes on me as I grabbed a couple of tissues from the table, cleaned up, and then tucked myself back into my pants. I needed to get out of there and we both needed time to think this through before it went any further.

I reached for him, cupping his face with my hands, and brushed my lips across his. "That was amazing. *You* were amazing and there's definitely something strong between us that I would like to continue exploring, but I think it would be best for both of us if we took some time to think about this. You need to be sure that the kind of things I need are really what's best for you." I held up my hand as he started to protest. "Like I said earlier, you are a great guy who deserves someone who will romance you. That guy is *not* me. I'm not looking for a long-term commitment, but I like spending time with you and I wouldn't mind seeing where this could go. So, I want you to think about it long and hard before you give me an answer."

I pressed my mouth to his, kissing him thoroughly then forced myself to pull away before I could drag him to bed like my body was begging me to.

I went to the door and swung it open, surprised to find Carter with his hand up. Apparently, I had caught him just as he was about to knock. "Hey!" he said as he leaned back to check the room number.

"Hi, Carter! You've got the right room. I came to talk to Landon, but I was just leaving," I explained awkwardly.

He smiled at me and then his brows raised as he looked at something behind me. I glanced over my shoulder and saw Landon with his hair all a mess. His lips were red and kiss swollen and I thought to myself that he looked absolutely delicious. Unfortunately, that probably was not how he wanted his brother to find him.

"I just got out of the shower," he said lamely, his eyes darting back and forth between the two of us as he hurried to fix his hair.

"Yeah, Ryan and I like to hold our meetings in the shower too. You know, kill two birds with one stone and all," he said with a playful smirk and walked past me, letting himself into the room.

Landon shot me a murderous look when I laughed, but I couldn't help myself. If Carter hadn't figured out what had been going on by his brother's appearance, the scent of sex lingering in the air surely would have clued him in.

"Did you need something or did you just come here to be an ass?" Landon asked with a scowl.

"Can't I do both?" Carter asked, fluttering his lashes innocently. Landon tilted his head at the younger man and narrowed his eyes at him. Carter held his hands up in surrender. "Okay, okay I'll stop. I really did come here for a reason and it's a good thing you're here, Micah, because this involves you too."

"What's wrong? Did you receive another letter?" I asked him, switching over to protective mode. "And why the hell isn't Tony with you?"

"Easy there, G.I Joe. Nothing's wrong, there's no new letter and Tony's right outside the door."

"So what's this about then?" Landon questioned.

A smile spread across Carter's face and he held his phone up in the air, shaking it back and forth. Landon's answering grin was just as wide. "Is it finally happening?"

"Yep!" Carter managed to get out as Landon swooped him up in a big hug.

"Can someone please let me know what the hell is going on?" I looked at them both in confusion.

Landon spoke first. "You're going to need to gather your security guys, we're going home."

"Hurry!" Carter smiled at me exuberantly. "Caleb and Giovanni are adopting Sarah tomorrow. We have to hurry if we don't want to miss the ceremony."

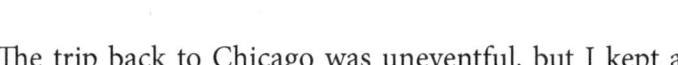

The trip back to Chicago was uneventful, but I kept a close eye on Carter just in case his stalker decided to make a move. I positioned myself in a seat between Tony and Greg, stating that we needed to formulate a plan for while Carter was at home, but really it was an excuse to avoid Landon.

The time I had spent with him was mind blowing, but I meant what I said when I told him he needed to really think things through before agreeing to anything further between us. I had almost convinced myself that I would never find anyone who wouldn't think I was a complete deviant for the things I needed in a man, but then I met Landon.

I had my reasons for needing to feel like I was in control, but the few men I had tried to explain it to had looked at me like I was crazy. Landon hadn't made me feel that way at all, in fact he seemed almost relieved when I explained that I wanted to make all of the decisions when it came to sex.

If he agreed and then changed his mind it would hurt. Not to mention the problems it could cause among our friends and family. As much as I wanted to press him for an answer so we could get back to the fun stuff, I also knew that nothing about the man was simple and that no matter what ended up happening between us, Landon had already left a lasting impression on me.

Carter and Ryan were gracious enough to agree to stay at their parents' house while we were there. That made our jobs much easier since there was only one location to secure. After checking over the property, I left them to get settled in and headed over to my office to check on things there.

The building I rented was brown brick, squeezed between a

bookstore and a Chinese restaurant located just a couple of blocks over from the heart of Chicago. It was long and narrow and cost a fortune in rent, but it was perfect for what I needed and most importantly, it was all mine. I couldn't help the proud smile I got every time I saw the words *Hamilton Security* etched on the large picture window at the front of the building.

Growing up, I had been told repeatedly that I would never amount to anything. I probably would have started to believe it too if someone hadn't stepped in to show me otherwise. The woman who gave birth to me decided when I was only six years old that I was too much of a hassle and took off with another man on the back of a motorcycle.

That left me with one parent, who blamed the simple fact that I existed as the reason for everything that ever went wrong in his life. The fact that he couldn't keep a job because he was too passed out to show up for his shift or the way he lost the trailer we had been living in to a bookie he owed money to, held no bearing whatsoever. According to John Hamilton, I was the source of everything bad that had happened to him and he took every opportunity he could get to remind me of it.

When I was fifteen, he stumbled home early from the bar one night and caught me making out with a boy on the couch. That was the first time he realized I was gay and subsequently, the first time he beat me. After that, it became a regular occurrence.

I started hanging with some bad kids from my neighborhood to avoid spending time at home and before I knew it, I was in the back of a cop car for breaking into a convenience store. When the police asked me who I wanted them to call, there was no choice as far as I was concerned. I wanted the only father I had ever known so I told them to call Giovanni's dad.

That moment was a turning point for me. After a long talk with the authorities, where I explained where the bruises on my body had come from, I was released into the Romero's care where I remained until I graduated and enlisted in the navy. It was G and his family who taught me what love really was and that I was worthy of receiving it. They were the ones who made me feel like I could be anything and do anything that I wanted with my life.

Other than that brief period of happiness where I had lived with the Romero's, I had spent my entire life with people telling me what to do and breaking me down until I bent to their will; first with my dad and then with what happened in the navy. I finally had my business to be proud of and I refused to let anyone have control over me ever again.

I let myself in the front door and breathed in the familiar smells of herbal tea and the floral perfume that was Mary's favorite. Voices led me to one of the back offices where I found Brandon, an ex-Marine who worked for me, laughing at something Mary had said.

"Who's in charge around here?" I barked.

They both looked at me in surprise before Mary answered in an authoritative tone. "Everyone knows *I* am in charge." Breaking out in a broad grin, she came forward and threw her arms around my waist. "How are you, Micah? It seems like you've been gone forever."

Brandon shook my hand. "It sure has been quiet without you around here. And with you and the others gone, Mary's focused all of her mothering on me, Nolan, and Jeremy." He rolled his eyes in mock irritation even though I knew he was joking. All of the guys that worked at the agency, myself included, adored Mary, and while she tended to hover sometimes, we wouldn't have it any other way.

"Oh, hush, you." She playfully swatted at his arm.

"You know I love you, Mary," he said as he bent to kiss the top of her head. "I have to get going. Got a call about some suspicious phone calls the governor's been receiving at his home. It's great to see you, Micah."

"You too," I said as he clapped me on the shoulder and walked out.

I was still smiling when I turned back to face Mary who was

studying me closely. "What?" I asked.

"There's something different about you and I'm trying to figure out what it is."

"What do you mean? I'm the same old Micah."

She cocked her head at me and narrowed her eyes, making me feel like a bug under a microscope. I struggled not to squirm under her watchful stare, but I was finding it more and more difficult as the minutes ticked by.

Mary had always had an uncanny ability to read people. I had asked her once if she ever considered opening her own shop as a fortune teller. She laughed and explained that after all of her years on this earth, she had simply learned to watch and listen. "It's amazing what you can find out about a person if you just keep silent and observe," she had told me.

"You've met someone," she finally said.

I scowled at her trying to hide my shock. "I've been working. When would I have had time to meet anyone?"

A small grin spread across her weathered face and her warm chocolate colored eyes sparkled. "Very good point. So whoever it was, you met him on the job. Interesting."

"Why is that interesting?" Her eyes widened. "Not that I met someone," I quickly tacked on when I saw her victorious smile.

"It's interesting because I've never known you to focus on anything other than the job at hand. Whoever the man is, he must be really special to have captured your attention while you were working. Also, you seem more relaxed, lighter."

I cursed under my breath, knowing that there was no use arguing with her. Mary grabbed my hands and her soft skin felt soothing against my own work-roughened hands. "Micah, listen to me. You are an amazing man with a kind heart. You deserve to find someone who can shower you with all the love you deserve and never got before." My eyes widened in surprise. I had never told Mary about my childhood.

"Don't look so surprised, boy." Her eyes were full of awareness and compassion as she continued. "I can tell that you've had a lot of people in your life that have failed you. I'm guessing your parents were a part of that and probably the ones who hurt you the most. I know you try to put up a brave front and you've shut most people out because you assume they're going to let you down, but, Micah, not everyone will let you down. Whether it's the man you recently met or someone you will meet in the future, perhaps it's time to let someone in. It's time to open your heart up and start trusting again. Think about it."

She patted my cheek lovingly and then walked out of the office, giving me a moment to myself. I swallowed around the lump in my throat and was surprised to feel tears roll down my cheeks. Mary saw more than even I had given her credit for. Although she was wrong about one thing. Other than my parents, the only person who had let me down, the only person I wasn't sure I could trust, was myself.

CHAPTER
Seven

Landon

I SHUT THE DOOR BEHIND ME AND LET OUT A FRUSTRATED breath. I needed a few moments to myself before I faced my family. Tiredly, I flopped down on the bed and looked around the room. It looked exactly the same as the day I moved out, from my old basketball trophies on the shelves to the easel in the corner from when I had decided to try my hand at painting. That was until I realized that I couldn't even draw a stick figure properly.

My mind wandered to Micah and what had happened between us. He'd worked my body until there was no room for any thought in my head outside of the two of us and it had been the single most erotic moment of my life. But once again, when the moment had passed he withdrew, avoiding me on the entire flight home. He claimed it was because he wanted to give me time to decide if I really wanted what he was offering, but I couldn't help but feel that he was doing it to protect himself as much as me. The question was why? Micah was strong, intelligent and brave. What could he possibly be afraid of?

A knock at the door interrupted my thoughts. "Landon? Are you in there?" The door slid open and Dad peeked his head in. Out of all of his children, I resembled him the most. All of my siblings took after our mom, but Dad and I had the same thick dark brown hair and hazel eyes, although his hair had become streaked with gray along the temples and his eyes crinkled at the edges from years of laughing. He worried he looked old, but Mom assured him that she thought he looked more distinguished with each new year and if the adoring way she gazed at him was any indication, she was telling the truth.

"Hey, Dad!" I said climbing off the bed with a smile.

"It's so good to have you home. It's been way too quiet around here without you boys stopping in."

I gave him a disbelieving look. "Caleb's still around and Emma and Michelle are both pregnant. How can things possibly be quiet around here?"

He chuckled. "Well, you've got a point, it has been a bit crazy here. Between the pregnancies and adoption, we're adding to our family quickly. This place will be busting at the seams when you and Carter each start your own families."

An image of Micah popped into my head unbidden and I pushed it away as quickly as I could. "Well, I'm sure Mom's over the moon about all of the new grandbabies."

"You have no idea. It's all she can talk about any more," he said lovingly. "Now why don't you get changed. We have to be at the courthouse in an hour for the ceremony."

"Okay, Dad, I'll be down as soon as I can." Carter and I had agreed on the plane not to mention the threatening letters to our family. They would only worry, plus the focus of the weekend should be on Caleb, Giovanni, and the newest addition to their family, Sarah.

The ceremony was emotional for everyone and there wasn't a dry eye in the house as little Sarah smiled up at the two men who had promised to love her unconditionally for the rest of her life. Sarah was a beautiful four-year-old girl who had been tossed around the system ever since the day she was born. Her parents as well as the many foster care parents she had been placed with weren't prepared for the responsibilities that came with raising a child with Downs syndrome.

It took someone special to open their home and their hearts to a child that the rest of the world had written off and I couldn't have been prouder of Caleb and Giovanni. Although, I knew if you asked them they would say that they were the lucky ones. I thought they were all pretty fortunate to have found each other and I was so happy for them.

I caught Micah's eye during the ceremony and was pleasantly surprised when he gave me a small smile and tilted his head towards the new family. He obviously was as thrilled for his best friend as I was for my brother and I was glad that he had assigned his men with keeping an eye on Carter and Ryan while we were at home so that he could relax and spend some time with Giovanni.

After the adoption ceremony, everyone headed back to our parents' house for a celebratory cookout. I smiled as I saw my sisters and my mother cooing over Sarah and the pretty dress her fathers had picked for the occasion. *What is it about young children that turn grown women into puddles of goo?* I shook my head as I made my way through the backyard, enjoying the feel of the warm sun on my face.

My mother was born with a green thumb and it was never more evident than when you looked at the carefully cultivated gardens spread throughout the property. Neat paths had been cut in the grass to allow a person the opportunity to walk among the blooms, enjoying nature in all of its colorful bounty.

As I turned down one of the paths, I heard voices. My mom and Micah were talking quietly as they walked through the foliage. They stopped suddenly and I watched them from behind a large fern, curious about what they were discussing.

"Micah, I asked you out here for a specific reason," my mother said.

"I figured as much. What is it you wanted to ask me?" he asked, smiling at her kindly.

"Giovanni told me that you two have been friends for many years."

"Yes, he's like a brother to me," he responded.

Mom chewed on her bottom lip and I wondered what had her so worried. "He also told me that you have your own security firm. That you have been specially trained as a SEAL to protect people."

Micah let out a careful breath. "Yes."

"I won't ask you for details because I trust each of my son's judgement and if Carter and Landon don't want us to know what's going on, I have no choice but to trust that they know what they're doing. However, the fact that you've been travelling with them is very telling. Not to mention the other two men who stayed here last night."

The look she gave him was familiar to me because I had been on the receiving end of it many times growing up. It was a look that said, "I already know what you're up to so there's no point in lying to me about it." I wasn't surprised to see Micah's eyes widen. My siblings and I had all wilted at one point or another under the dreaded *Mom Look*.

"Yes, ma'am," he said quietly, lowering his eyes. His eyes sprang back up in shock as she grabbed onto his arm.

"Please, please keep my boys safe, Micah. Promise me," she pleaded.

"I promise, Mrs. Greene," he swore. I felt something tighten in my chest at the determination etched on his face.

"Please, call me Kathy."

"There you guys are," I said as I stepped out from behind the fern. Mom turned to me with a smile and Micah gave me a knowing look as if he had known I was there all along, which given his training was entirely possible.

"Hi, baby!" Mom exclaimed happily. "I was just showing Micah my gardens. Why don't you join us?" I glanced over the top of her head and smothered a laugh when I saw the relief on Micah's face. My mother meant well, but she could be a bit overbearing at times, especially when it came to the well-being of her family.

We wound our way through the gardens as we slowly made our way back towards the house and the tantalizing smell of meat cooking on the grill. We had almost reached the end when Micah suddenly stopped walking.

"What are those flowers called?" he asked.

Mom looked delighted that someone was showing an interest in her masterpiece, but I felt the tension in the man beside me so I leaned around him to see where he was pointing. I recognized the little blue flowers right away as being the same ones stamped onto each of the letters.

"Oh, those are one of my favorites. Their proper name is Myosotis, but most people call them forget-me-nots. Aren't they beautiful?" Mom crooned. My sister Michelle called out to her just then and she excused herself to go join the party.

Micah shared a look with me and I knew he was thinking the same thing. Forget-me-nots. It was a blatant message that whomever was sending the letters would not be ignored. I could feel my heart beating wildly in my chest and a shiver of dread went up my spine. My breathing increased and then Micah was there, in my space.

His hand rested on my lower back and I concentrated on the warmth of his palm soaking through my shirt. He leaned in, his warm breath ghosting across my cheek. "You're not alone, I'm right here, Landon. Concentrate on the sound of my voice and breathe with me."

I listened to the soothing timber of his voice and soon my heart returned to its normal staccato. I lifted my head, my nose brushing against his jaw. I wanted him to pull me in and hold me, but he sprang back quickly as we heard someone approaching. He chuckled as two of my younger cousins went running past us, but the smile slid away when he saw the look on my face.

"Landon," he said, an apology in his eyes.

"Fuck you, Micah," I growled out, interrupting him. Shock registered across his face as I turned and walked back to the house. From the night we met, he had done nothing but pull me in, only to turn around and push me away and I was sick and tired of it.

I maneuvered my way through the crowd and grabbed a bottle of beer out of a cooler on the deck, guzzling half of it down before I stopped for a breath. I needed to calm down before someone noticed how upset I was. I was nowhere near ready to explain to anyone in my family the effect Micah Hamilton had on me.

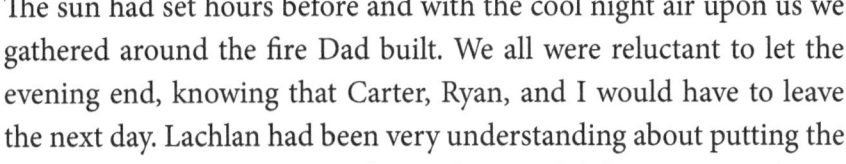

The sun had set hours before and with the cool night air upon us we gathered around the fire Dad built. We all were reluctant to let the evening end, knowing that Carter, Ryan, and I would have to leave the next day. Lachlan had been very understanding about putting the tour on hold while we came home, but we didn't want to push our luck.

After months of living out of a suitcase, it felt good to be home again if only for a little while. The food was delicious, but the company was even better. My family had always been extremely close and I had missed them terribly. Michelle and Emma took turns telling funny stories about taking Lamaze classes with their husbands. Jason and Mark were good sports though and they took the teasing well. Mark explained the reason why his doll's head had popped off as he practiced bathing the baby.

"You guys weren't there; you don't know how slippery those things get when they have soap on them."

Jason jumped to his friend's defense. "I caught the head as it flew across the room and we had it back on the baby within seconds. No harm, no foul." Everyone roared with laughter and their wives rolled their eyes when the two men bumped fists in a show of solidarity.

I was still chuckling when I felt someone settle in beside me. I turned, smiling warmly at my younger brother. "Hey, Caleb, where have you been?"

"I was checking on Sarah," he said with a dreamy smile on his face.

"Where is she?"

He gave me a wry look. "Where do you think?"

"Mom!" we said in unison.

"How are you feeling, Daddy?" I said playfully, smiling at the goofy grin that threatened to split his face.

"Man, I don't think I'll ever get tired of being called that. I have never been happier in my life. I have everything I could ever need." He gestured to the people gathered around the fire. "I have a loving family, I'm married to the world's most incredible man, and now I have a perfect little daughter who I love with all of my heart. Life doesn't get any better than that, Landon."

I tossed my arm around his shoulder and pulled him towards me, kissing the top of his head. "I'm so happy for you. You're one of the very best men I know and you deserve to be happy."

"Thanks, Landon." He pulled back so he could look at me. "What about you? Are you happy?"

I shrugged. "You know me, I'm always happy," I answered flippantly.

His brows drew in as he continued to stare at me. "But that's not really true, is it?" he said.

"What do you mean?"

Caleb leaned into me, speaking quietly enough that we wouldn't be overheard. "Landon, you haven't introduced us to any of your boyfriends since you brought that guy home with you your first year of college. What was his name?"

"Noah," I mumbled.

"Why is that?"

"Because there hasn't been anyone since then that was special enough to meet all of you," I told him honestly.

Caleb looked at me with concern. "I know something's been bothering you for a while now. I noticed you seemed upset about something at the wedding and Carter told me you haven't been eating or sleeping well."

"Are you two keeping tabs on me?" I bumped his shoulder so he would know I was kidding. I actually thought it was very sweet that my brothers cared so much about me.

"Just because you're older doesn't mean we can't take care of you just as well as you take care of us," he replied softly.

"That's true and I appreciate it."

"I mean it, Landon, you can call me day or night and I'll always be there for you."

I reached between us and squeezed his hand. "Thank you, Caleb. I'm very lucky to have a brother like you."

"Ditto," he said with a grin then sighed as he glanced around the fire. "Sooo…"

"Oh no," I groaned.

"What?" he asked innocently.

"That was a loaded *so* if I ever heard one," I snickered.

"It's just that I've noticed the looks you and a certain sexy ex-Navy SEAL have been exchanging all night. Care to tell me what that's about?" He fluttered his eyes at me hopefully.

"I have no idea what you're talking about," I insisted.

"Really?" Caleb leaned in close so he could whisper in my ear. "So you have no clue why he's staring at you right now like he's a starving man and you're a steak dinner?"

"What?" I yelped. My eyes darted up to look at Micah where he sat directly across the fire from me. He seemed to be having a deep discussion with Giovanni and he was staring at the ground, not at me as Caleb had claimed.

"Shut up, jerk." I elbowed Caleb in the side as he began cackling at my reaction.

"Okay, I'm sorry," he said, wiping his eyes. "That was funny though."

"Are you finished yet?" I asked when he had finally gotten himself under control.

"Yeah, I think so." He took a deep breath, clearing away his laughter. "Okay, I admit, I made that up so I could see your reaction. But he actually has been watching you all night and if we're really being honest, you've been watching him too. So, is there something going on with you two?"

Caleb waited patiently for me to answer. My brothers were my best friends, but I had spent so many years keeping certain aspects of my life hidden that it had become habit to clam up about men I was interested in. Finally, I decided that I was being ridiculous. What happened in the past had been shameful and confusing and had left an indelible mark on me, but whatever was going on between Micah and myself was completely different from that.

"There's definitely chemistry between us," I admitted quietly. I felt guilty when I saw Caleb's shoulders relax and the look of joy that crossed his face when I decided to confide in him. I hadn't realized that I had been hurting my family by holding a part of myself back from them. Maybe it was time to change all of that. "But every time we start to get close, Micah pulls away. It's so frustrating!"

Caleb chuckled. "I know what you mean. When Gio and I first got together, trying to get him to admit that he had feelings for me was like pulling teeth." His smile slipped away as he continued. "He'd been hurt terribly by his ex-wife and also the loss of his parents, and he wasn't prepared to open his heart up to anyone ever again. It took a lot of time and patience for him to trust me enough to let me in. He and Micah are a lot alike that way."

"What do you mean?" I prodded.

Caleb leaned in, speaking quietly. "Gio's told me some stuff. Nothing too detailed because he'd never betray his best friend that way, but from what he's told me, Micah had a really bad childhood. His mom took off when he was young and his dad was a mean drunk who used to get pretty rough with him. Luckily, he ended up moving in with Gio and his parents and they were able to show him what being part of a family was all about."

My eyes flickered over in time to see Micah and Giovanni getting up and walking away from the group, still deep in conversation. It made my heart hurt to picture him as a young boy, being neglected and abused by the people who were supposed to love and protect him.

"Look, Landon, if you want to be with him and by the look on your face I'm pretty sure that you do, you can't let him push you away." I cocked my head at Caleb as I took in his advice. "I've gotten to know Micah pretty well and I've learned that while he can be stubborn and withdrawn at times, he's also extremely intelligent, honest, and fiercely loyal. I have a feeling that when Micah falls in love with someone, it will be for life."

Caleb patted my leg and then left me to my thoughts. I stared at the glowing embers of the fire as I mulled over his words. I admit my breath had caught when he talked about Micah falling in love. My brothers had been very fortunate to find their soulmates and a part of me wondered if I would ever do the same, but it seemed highly unlikely. No one in their right mind would want me and all of the baggage I carried around.

So maybe I wouldn't be the person Micah fell in love with and wanted to keep, but that didn't mean we couldn't enjoy each other in the meantime. Maybe Caleb was right, maybe it was time to confront Micah and then refuse to let him back away.

CHAPTER
Eight

Landon

A S MUCH AS I LOVED BEING WITH MY FAMILY, I HAD BEEN gone a long time and I needed to go home and take care of a few things before hitting the road again. I made my rounds, hugging everyone and congratulating Caleb and Giovanni once again on their new daughter, then I grabbed my bag from my room and walked out to the driveway. I pulled my phone from my pocket to call for a taxi when I saw someone walking between the parked cars. I could tell it was Micah by the stiff way he carried himself and I wondered idly if someone with his military background was ever able to fully relax.

"Micah!" I called out. He turned and my heart stuttered as the moonlight spilled over his face, accentuating his high cheekbones and strong jawline. He really was an exquisite man.

"Is something wrong, Landon?" His concern was evident and I realized I had been staring at him for several minutes without speaking.

"Everything's fine," I assured him. "I haven't had a chance to talk to you since we came home."

"Well, I'm tired so I was just leaving." He turned to walk to his Jeep, but I refused to let the opportunity pass me by.

"Great! Do you mind giving me a ride? It's much better than sitting in a smelly cab," I said cheerfully as I walked over to the Jeep and opened the passenger's side door without waiting for his reply. He gave me an odd look and mumbled something that sounded like, "Guess I don't have a choice, do I?" I ignored him and tossed my bag in the back seat before climbing in and buckling up my seatbelt.

My heart was racing as he climbed in next to me. I had never behaved so boldly with a man before, but Caleb was right; if I wanted to see what could happen between us, I couldn't let him push me away any more.

"Where exactly am I taking you?" Micah carefully pulled out of my parents' drive.

"My house, please."

"You'll have to remind me where it is."

"You don't remember?" I asked in surprise.

"I was a little distracted on the way there that night." He looked at me out of the corner of his eye so I kept my expression neutral, even though inside I was pumping my fist in the air. "And I didn't pay any attention on the cab ride home either; too much on my mind I suppose," he admitted gruffly. "So how far out are you? All I remember is that you don't live within the city limits."

"About twenty minutes away, I hope you don't mind." I had to fight the urge to laugh at the disbelieving look he shot me. I almost felt bad that I was making him go so far out of his way to take me home, but when I thought about the twenty uninterrupted minutes, I couldn't feel anything but happy.

He turned his glare back on the road ahead of him, his tight grip on the steering wheel turning his knuckles white. I took a deep breath, searching my mind for a topic of discussion. I needed him to relax if I was going to have any hope of talking to him about us.

"Caleb and Giovanni seemed very happy, didn't they?"

"Uh huh," he answered noncommittally.

"Sarah's an adorable little girl." He grunted in response. This was going to be a little harder than I thought.

"Dinner was good."

"What are you doing, Landon?" he said sharply.

"What do you mean?" I asked, feigning innocence. "I'm just trying to make conversation."

"Fine," he grumbled. "Why did you move so far away from your family?"

"Twenty minutes isn't that far away, but it's enough to give me some space when I need it. I'm not sure if you noticed, but my family can be a bit overbearing sometimes." Micah chuckled his agreement and I paused to listen to the sound of it. I rarely saw him when he wasn't in fiercely protective work mode and the change made him even more endearing.

"Anyway, I searched around and found the place that was perfect for me."

"Tell me about it."

"Excuse me?" I looked over at him, enjoying the view of his perfect profile.

"What does the perfect place for Landon Greene looks like? I mean, I really only saw the bedroom, right?" I smiled, taking it as a good sign that he wanted to know more about me and pleased that he was teasing me about our first night together instead of ignoring it all together like he usually did.

The rest of the drive was spent with me describing my home, from the beautiful hardwood floors that I had lovingly stripped and applied polyurethane until they gleamed, to the home theater I had installed. Micah seemed impressed that I had splurged on leather reclining theater seats and a professional grade projector.

"You must be a real movie buff," he said with a smile.

"Oh yeah," I said with a happy sigh. "Growing up, we didn't have a lot of money. I mean, it's expensive to raise five kids, right?" I waited until Micah nodded.

"Anyway, my uncle ran a movie theater about an hour away and once in a while our whole family would make the trip there and he would let us watch a movie for free. He also gave us popcorn and candy." I smiled at the memory. "Ever since then, when I watch a movie, it brings back those great memories."

"I bet you have one of those old-fashioned popcorn machines too, don't you?" I looked over in time to see Micah smiling at me and I responded with my own.

"As a matter of fact, I do."

"I'm glad you had that growing up," he said quietly. I instantly felt terrible. How could I ramble on and on about how great my childhood was when Caleb had just told me how Micah's had been the complete opposite?

"Micah…"

"It was nice seeing the way you and your family interact. I think the trip home has been good for you. I haven't seen you that relaxed since…" His words trailed off and he swallowed hard. "You'll have to let me know when to turn," he reminded me, changing the subject.

"Hang a left here. My house isn't too much further." I gave him directions until he pulled into my driveway.

"Micah, what were…"

"You better get some sleep, we have to be at the airport early," he interrupted, keeping his eyes focused straight ahead.

"I'm not tired! Look at me, Micah!" His head swiveled to look at me and I wasn't sure which of the two of us was more surprised by the forcefulness of my tone, but I had to get his attention somehow. "Finish what you were going to say." I turned in my seat, leaning against the door so I could look directly at him.

Micah looked at me with exasperation. "I was going to say that I hadn't seen you that relaxed since I made you come. Can I leave now? Did you get what you wanted?"

"No, I haven't. Not by a long shot." Heat sparked in his eyes as he picked up on my meaning.

His voice sounded pained when he spoke. "Landon, I already told you, you need time to think things through."

I squeezed my eyes shut and ran my hands through my hair, yanking on the strands as I released a groan of frustration. "You are so infuriatingly stubborn!"

I opened my eyes in time to see a small twitch of his lips and I almost faltered, wanting to see him smile. However, I had things that needed to be said and I was going to make damn sure he listened to me. I quickly reached over and plucked the keys from the ignition.

"Hey!" he objected, reaching for them, but I slid them into my pocket before he could get them.

"I have listened to everything you've said, but it's my turn to talk and you're not leaving until you hear me out." I held my breath waiting for his response. I wasn't a fool, I knew Micah could easily get his keys back and leave if he wanted to, he was an ex-United States Navy SEAL for crying out loud.

"Give me back my keys, Landon." He levelled me with a stare, challenging me and it pissed me off.

"Just stop it, alright?" I hissed.

"Stop what? You're the one who made me drive all the way out here and now you're holding my keys hostage." I ignored his rant and pushed on, knowing that if I didn't say what I wanted to right then, I might never get the chance again.

"You said you wanted to make decisions, to control things in the bedroom, so quit trying to decide what's best for me outside of it. *I* decide what's best for me and as far as I'm concerned, that's *you*." I held my hand up when he started to object.

"My entire life, I have been the one to take care of things. I watched over my siblings, making sure people treated them right and that they were happy, I started a business where I make decisions that could alter people's lives. I put together a worldwide concert tour and on top of it all, my baby brother has a crazy stalker sending him threatening letters." I paused to breathe, looking down at my hands that were folded in my lap. I appreciated that Micah kept quiet, allowing me to get it all out.

"I love my family and I love my job, but sometimes it all gets a little overwhelming," I whispered. I raised my eyes to look at him, his expression was tight, unreadable. "The anxiety's been getting worse, especially with each new letter; you saw what it did to me the last time. I know you're taking care of the stalker situation and that's helped a lot, but I need more. I'm so tired of shouldering the responsibility all of the time." I looked at him, pleading with him to understand.

"What do you need?" His eyes never wavered from mine and I felt lightheaded with hope.

"I need someone who can take me out of my own mind. Someone who will take control so I don't have to make any decisions even just for one night. I need you, Micah."

He was out of his seat and opening my door before I realized what was happening and then he pulled me from the vehicle. He backed me up against the side of the Jeep and leaned in until I could feel his breath on my lips. His hand snaked around to grip the back of my neck and his other fisted my jacket so I couldn't get away; as if I'd want to. His voice was gravelly when he spoke and it sent chills along my skin.

"Give me your house key." I reached into my left pocket and handed him the key without question. My breath hitched when he reached into my right pocket without asking and withdrew the keys to his Jeep, his knuckles running along my length through the thin material.

"You live in a nice neighborhood," Micah whispered, tracing his tongue along the shell of my ear and then breathing warm air over it. My response was guttural as a shudder wracked my body. My cock was rock solid and begging to be let out to play.

"I assume you want to continue living here, right?" I tried to concentrate on his words, but my head swirled as the stubble on his cheek scraped along mine making a delicious scratching sound. I lost the ability to speak when his lips ghosted across mine so I nodded my agreement instead. A wicked grin appeared on his face and the moonlight glinted across his perfect teeth making him seem like the Devil himself. "Then I suggest we take this inside."

—· ———⟩•⟨——— ·—

Micah stepped back and I nearly sprinted across the yard to get to the front door. I heard him chuckling behind me, but I didn't care. My body was shaking with my need for him. He crowded in behind me as he leaned around to unlock the door and I reached for the handle, but he stopped me, placing his hand over mine. I turned to face him, wondering why in the hell we weren't inside my house and naked already.

"Are you sure? Because once I open this door, I'm in charge." He studied my face closely for any sign of hesitation.

"I'm sure. Please, Micah, I need this." Normally, I would feel embarrassed about the desperation in my voice, but there was something about Micah that let me know it was okay; that I could do anything, say anything and he would never judge me for it.

With a single nod, he opened the door. I walked through the living room and turned on a low lamp while Micah locked the door. My heart beat wildly in anticipation as he stalked towards me like a large feline hunting its prey. I doubted any prey had ever looked forward to being caught the way I did in that moment.

He stood close enough that I could feel the warmth emanating from his body and smell the same fresh rain scent that I had come to associate with Micah. He slid his thumb lazily across my bottom lip and his gray eyes turned a darker, almost slate color as I opened my mouth to nip at him.

I stood still as he slowly began unbuttoning my shirt. I had to clench my hands into fists because as much as I wanted to grab on to him and feel his smooth skin under my fingertips, I wanted him to do whatever he wanted to my body even more.

When the last button was released he used both hands to slide the material off my shoulders and down my arms, letting it drop to the floor. He slid his hands over my chest, tugging gently on the hairs that covered my pecs and groaned his approval. The sound nearly brought me to my knees, but I jolted instead when he pinched one of my nipples between his thumb and forefinger, twisting just enough to border somewhere between pleasure and pain, and causing a shock-wave of lust to roll through me.

"Take me to your bedroom." His voice held such command that I turned immediately and led him upstairs.

Micah's hands were on my waist as I entered my bedroom and he spun me around, making me gasp as his lips came down on mine in a passionate kiss. He held nothing back and his kiss demanded the same from me. I gave myself over to him fully, begging him to take me back to that place where nothing existed except the warm feel of his skin on mine.

We broke apart, each of us gasping for air. "Take my clothes off, Landon."

I quickly got to work divesting him of his clothes. When he had taken me in my hotel room that day, I had been so out of my mind with pent up desire that I could barely concentrate on anything but the glide of his hand over both of our cocks. I promised myself that I would take the time to admire his sculpted body and learn the feel of his powerful muscles as he moved above me.

I pulled his shirt off and nearly choked as I took in the smooth, golden skin over an impressive eight-pack and obliques that would take me years in the gym to achieve. He had several tattoos that I had only caught glimpses of before, but was now eager to explore. I looked at him through heavy lids and he must have read the question there because he nodded, seeming pleased that I had waited for his approval.

An intricately woven tribal tattoo flowed over the entire length of his right arm and on his right pectoral was an octopus curved around an anchor that I had often seen used by those in the navy. I traced it with my fingertips and then circled around behind him, smiling at the show of goose bumps that appeared on his skin with my touch.

I stopped when I noticed the cross on his right shoulder blade. It wasn't large, but it stood out because it was the only tattoo with color. What surprised me the most were the initials S.E. in the middle of the cross. I couldn't help the pang of jealousy that swept through me as I wondered who the tattoo was for. Who had made such a lasting impression on Micah that he would have their initials permanently etched into his skin? An ex-lover? Did he still love him? Then I felt guilty. Did the cross mean he had lost whoever it was? Was Micah still pining over a long-lost love and that was why he was so hesitant to let me in?

He must have felt my tension because he turned suddenly and kissed me, making my head spin until I had forgotten what it was I had been worrying about in the first place. We kissed until I was forced to turn my head away, my lungs burning for air.

"I believe you were supposed to be undressing me," he reminded me with a smirk and I licked at his lips as I fumbled with his belt. The sound of his zipper lowering seemed loud in the quiet room and my dick wept with joy that I was finally going to be with the man who had held my mind hostage for nearly a year.

I lowered Micah's pants over his hips and was reaching for the waistband of his briefs when he stopped me with his hands. I wanted to scream my frustration until I heard him say, "I want you to finish undressing me on your knees."

I dropped to my knees happily, my face directly in front of his groin. I didn't waste any time removing the rest of his clothes and then I stared, in awe at his beautiful cock surrounded by neatly trimmed hair. I wasn't small by any means, but he had me beat easily by at least two inches and he had more width on him too. The sheer size of it had me feeling dizzy as I wondered how I would be able to take him all in.

A milky pearl appeared at the tip of the fat mushroomed head and I licked my lips in anticipation. His groan pulled my attention to his face where he had his head tilted, staring down at me intently. His voice was shaky, almost hoarse as he spoke.

"Lick it, Landon. I want you to learn what I taste like."

I held his gaze as my tongue darted out, capturing the salty drop. I moaned as I savored the flavor of him and I felt him tremble beneath my hands that rested on each of his muscular thighs. I was suddenly overwhelmed with the urge to please him, to make him feel as much pleasure as I possibly could.

I used my tongue to bathe him, feeling the veins with each pass over his impressive length. His fingers ran through my hair as I stretched my lips around the head of his cock and lowered my mouth until I felt it tickling the back of my throat.

"That's it, just like that," Micah coaxed. I still had plenty to go so I pushed myself farther until my lungs began to burn and my eyes watered. He pulled his hips back and angled my chin up so I was looking at him.

"Take however much you can. Whatever you do to me will feel amazing." The look on his face echoed his sincerity and I swallowed hard.

My heart swelled with emotions that I tried to stuff back down, afraid that they would show in my eyes and cause him to turn away. His words had solidified for me that I was safe with him. With my submission, I had handed him the power to do as he wished. If he wanted to, he could have forced me to choke on him and I would have done it because I wanted to be with him that badly, but he had just proven that he would not abuse that power.

I went back to work on him, that time wrapping my hand around the base and gliding it up and down in tandem with my mouth. He was dripping with my saliva and my jaws were beginning to ache, but I wouldn't stop until I had wrenched every bit of pleasure from him that I could. Pre-cum splashed over my tongue and I applied more suction, trying to draw more of the sweet liquid from him.

I was disappointed when he grabbed me under the shoulders and lifted me off of the floor, but then he tossed me onto the foot of the bed and I was suddenly distracted by the movement of his hands as they worked to unbuckle my belt and open my pants. He quickly pulled my clothes off and I sighed with relief when the cool air hit my aching cock which stood proudly, begging for his attention.

Micah moved to the table beside my bed and pulled open the drawer. I felt completely exposed as I lay there naked, my legs sprawled over the end of the bed as I waited to see what he would do next. He tossed the bottle of lube and a condom on the bedspread as he moved to stand between my legs. "How long has it been, Landon?"

I felt my cheeks heat with embarrassment until he leaned over me, covering me with his warmth. His lips brushed over mine as he spoke quietly. "Answer me."

"Awhile," I rasped. I refused to tell him it had been since before we met because I knew he would read too much into that. The truth was, I just hadn't been interested in anyone else since then, content instead to torment myself on the fact that I had missed out on what I knew would have been an incredible night.

"I'll need to open you up slowly then." He must have noticed the look of surprise on my face and he seemed hurt by my reaction. "I won't hurt you," he said firmly.

He had misinterpreted my look. I was merely surprised because I hadn't expected him to be so gentle, so tender with me. I hated the thought of hurting his feelings though so I grabbed his neck when he went to pull away. "I know you would never hurt me. I trust you, Micah."

He stared at me for several moments and I held my breath waiting to see if he would decide to stay or leave. Apparently, my words convinced him because he kissed me again, swallowing my sigh of relief. Flames licked at my skin as he placed kisses over my face and jaw, trailing down my neck and across my collarbone.

His tongue flicked over my nipple and I arched my back, wanting more. I loved to have my nipples played with and Micah took note of my reaction, nibbling and sucking each one into the wet heat of his mouth. In the distance, I could hear the snick of the bottle of lube opening and I began to writhe under him, desperate for his touch.

Cool, slick fingers found my entrance and his tongue invaded my mouth at the same time he pressed into me. I moaned, it had been so long since I had felt the delicious burn which soon turned into pure need.

"Please," I stuttered and he hurried to accommodate me, adding a second finger. His mouth never left mine as he bent over me, opening me up, preparing me to take him in. I relaxed my body as best I could, desperate to feel him moving inside of me. I lost track of time as he continued scissoring his fingers and stretching me. The feeling was incredible and when his fingers grazed over that perfect spot inside me, I nearly levitated off the bed.

"Micah!" I cried out.

"Yes," he growled triumphantly. "I like hearing you call out my name. I'm going to need to hear more of that." He quickly sheathed himself with the condom and slathered a generous amount of lube to his shaft, adding more to my entrance. He lifted my legs over his shoulders and tapped his cock against my hole several times, sparking the nerves there.

"Are you ready?" His eyes met mine as he lined his body up with mine.

I nodded my head eagerly, not trusting myself to speak at that point. He pushed in slowly, but my breath whooshed out of my lungs as I was soon stretched farther than I had ever gone. I gripped the comforter tightly, suddenly doubtful that I would be able to take him. Pain rippled through me and I felt my cock go limp.

Micah held still above me. The strain of holding back was evident on his face and I knew that a lesser man would have lost control by then, unable to stop the primal urge to take. Micah was no ordinary man though and so he panted through clenched teeth until finally I relaxed underneath him, allowing him to slide in the rest of the way.

He looked down at where we were connected as he began to move slowly, testing me. That was all it took for the pain to be erased by something closely resembling bliss. His hand wrapped around my cock, bringing it back to life, and I lowered my legs to his waist, locking my ankles together and using them to pull him closer.

"Who's in charge here?" he barked.

"You are," I gasped as he drove deep into me.

"Put them back then," he ordered and I quickly placed my ankles on his shoulders again. He wrapped his hands around my legs, ensuring that I wouldn't move them again and I whimpered at the loss of his hand on my dick.

"I told you, I make the decisions in here, but you didn't listen so I'm going to have to hold your legs." I reached my hands down between us, but the sound he made had me halting. *Good God that was a sexy sound.* "I hope you can come without touching yourself because your hands are not allowed on your cock unless I say so."

My eyes widened in shock. I had never been able to reach orgasm without some sort of stimulation to my cock, but I folded my hands behind my head instead so I wouldn't be tempted. It never even occurred to me to argue with him or go against his orders; I didn't want to. I was exactly where I wanted to be.

Heat blazed in his eyes when he saw my acceptance and he began to piston in and out of me with renewed vigor. After a few minutes, he switched his angle so that he hit my prostate with every thrust. Stars burst behind my eyes and my cock began to drip as he continued to peg me relentlessly and I wondered if I might actually come that way.

I had just finished the thought when my orgasm rushed over me like a freight train. "Micah!" I screamed as cum shot out of me so hard I could feel it splashing on my neck and coating my chin. I was shaking, but still he continued to thrust into me and I watched as he arched above me, letting out a loud roar as he chased his own orgasm.

He lowered my legs gently and collapsed onto my chest, gulping in air. I trailed my fingers in soothing circles over his back with one hand while my other scratched gently at his scalp. Whatever I had envisioned sex with Micah would be like, it was nothing compared to the mind-blowing reality I had just experienced and I never wanted to let him go.

After several long minutes, he lifted his head. "That should have happened a long time ago," he whispered, his lips smoothing gently over mine.

"It's better that it didn't happen until now," I said between kisses.

"Why is that?"

"Because if it had happened the night we met, I never would've been able to let you go and then we would have been the talk of the wedding," I teased.

He pulled back, looking intently into my eyes as if he were searching for something. I wasn't sure if he found what he was looking for because he climbed out of bed and stalked to the bathroom without another word.

I cursed myself silently for exposing my feelings that way, worried that I had scared him off for good, but then he came back out with a warm washcloth which he used to clean me up. He didn't speak, but his movements were tender and I found the care he was lavishing on me almost more intimate than the sex itself. He got up to dispose of the washcloth and I admired his exquisite form as he walked away. When he came back out of the bathroom he turned off the light before lying down beside me.

"You're staying?" I asked with more than a hint of surprise.

"Is that alright?" he asked hesitantly.

"Of course!" I said in a rush.

"Good, because I'm too tired to drive the hour it would take to get back to the city."

"Quit whining, it was only twenty minutes," I scoffed. He chuckled as he pulled me close and curled his body around mine. I never would have taken him for a cuddler, but it made me smile as I drifted off to sleep.

The alarm sounded early the next morning and I slapped at it until it finally stopped its constant screeching. Yawning, I rolled over and let out a yelp of surprise when I came face to face with Micah who had his head propped in his hand and was staring down at me as he tried to hide a laugh.

"Did you forget I was here?"

"More like I forgot where I was. I guess it's a hazard of living on the road. God, it felt good to sleep in my own bed again." Micah leaned down to kiss me, but I turned my head at the last second.

"What's wrong?" he asked.

"I haven't brushed my teeth yet." My voice came out muffled behind my hand.

"Landon," Micah said softly, pulling my hand away. "Who's in charge when it comes to sex?"

"You are," I whispered.

He removed the sheet and rolled his body on top of mine as he continued. "That's right and as the person in charge there may be times where I want to stick my tongue in your ass. There may be times where you have your tongue in mine. Will you stop me then?"

"N…no," I stuttered. My eyes rolled into the back of my head as he swayed his hips, making our cocks rub together deliciously.

"Then I don't think a little morning breath is going to bother either one of us. Do you?" Without waiting for a reply, he slid his mouth over mine and just like that, I lost the ability to think. All I could do was feel Micah as he slid a condom on, slicked himself, and entered me slowly. I was still tender from the night before, but I was able to take him in easier and before I knew it he had bottomed out, his hips snug against my ass.

I tried to slide my hands around his back, but he reached for them and placed them above my head, holding them securely so I was pinned under him. Instead of feeling panicked by the inability to move, I felt safe and cared for. I knew Micah wouldn't let anything happen to me.

"We don't have much time, are you good?"

"Yes, you don't have to hold back," I assured him.

He drew back slowly and then thrust his hips forward, hitting my prostate with perfect accuracy. He did this several more times until I started to see stars. I could feel sweat slicking between our bodies as he worked to bring us both to the brink.

"Micah," I shouted out a warning.

"Come for me, baby."

With his words, I flew over the edge of the cliff and soared through the sky. As I floated gently back down, I heard his shout and I smiled, happy that he was able to find his pleasure with me. As I drifted, I realized that for the second time in my life, I had managed to come with no stimulation to my cock. *The man is a sex god!*

His lips trailed over my neck and shoulders as he slowly pulled out of me. As sore as I was, I immediately missed the feel of him inside of my body. The way things were going it didn't look like I would ever get tired of being with Micah and that was a slippery slope to be on. Between his military background and the nature of his job, Micah lived a very solitary life and I wasn't sure that he would be willing to share that life with someone else, but I planned on enjoying any time I had with him to the fullest.

He started to get up, but I grabbed his hand, pulling him back down beside me. He smiled at me in surprise. "Was there something else you needed?"

I bit my lower lip nervously, afraid that what I had to say might bring a halt to what was happening between us, but I would never know until I tried. Micah reached over with his thumb and pulled my lip from between my teeth. "Landon, say whatever you need to say."

I swallowed down my nerves. "Last night was incredible and I like you and I like being around you and..." I trailed off when I realized I was rambling. "The thing is, I want to get to know you better. Not just in the bedroom, but out of it as well." I held my breath as I waited to see what his response would be. My heart plummeted as I saw his forehead crease and he looked down at where our hands were still held together.

When he looked back up his eyes were wary, but there was also something else in their depths that gave me a glimmer of hope. "The more I get to know you the more I like you too and I agree, last night was pretty amazing, so was this morning." We shared a smile before he continued. "I'd like to spend more time with you, but this is new to me so I need to take things slow."

I glanced down at the cum drying on my chest then arched a brow at him as if to say "Seriously?" He smiled sheepishly and his look was so boyish, so completely sweet, that I melted; I simply melted into a puddle of goo and feelings.

"I can do the sex thing easy, it's the rest that scares the hell out of me."

I leaned over him and I heard his breath catch as he looked into my eyes. "You don't need to be scared. I promise to protect you, Micah." His eyes softened with my words. The kiss we exchanged was sweet and tender and filled me with hope.

After taking a quick shower, getting dressed, and throwing my bags together we rushed out the door so we wouldn't miss our flight. We pulled into the airport with moments to spare and I grabbed my bag out of the back seat. I turned around, surprised when Micah crowded in close to me.

"I got something for you," he said. I was curious because he wouldn't look me in the eyes. I held my hand out and he dropped something into it.

I looked down and my vision turned blurry with what I found. The bright green plastic mesh tube, no bigger than my pinky finger was stitched together, securing the marble inside. It was a simple concept, but for a person like myself with anxiety, I could keep it in my pocket and work the marble back and forth between my fingers, relieving stress and anxiousness. Micah had known that I'd been embarrassed by my panic attacks before and so he had made the effort to come up with a way to help me through those moments without drawing attention to myself. His thoughtfulness took my breath away.

"I know it's nothing big, I just thought it might help," he mumbled, shrugging his shoulders awkwardly.

Heedless of where we were or who might be watching, I stepped into his space and kissed him soundly for several minutes, hoping to convey how much his thoughtfulness had meant to me. "Thank you," I whispered when we broke apart.

His smile was triumphant as he grabbed my bag from me and led us towards the area where Lachlan's private plane was waiting. I was still wearing a goofy grin as we boarded the plane, causing

Carter to narrow his eyes at me.

"What's up with you?"

"It was just a great trip home," I shrugged.

"Yeah, it sure was," he agreed with a smile.

CHAPTER
Nine

Micah

THINGS WERE GOING WELL; ALMOST TOO WELL AND IT HAD ME on edge. We had returned to the tour where Carter and the rest of the band continued to take Europe by storm. The security system I had set in place was now running like a well-oiled machine.

My men had worked hard with the security guards already in place to teach them what their roles were in keeping the band safe and they had learned to execute those roles with precision. We travelled in and out of cities with very little disruption and just as Landon had hoped, Carter was able to put any worries aside and simply concentrate on the music end of things.

There hadn't been a new letter in over a month and that was what had me on edge. As a SEAL, I was used to going into dangerous situations and dealing with them head on. Most of the time we knew who our enemy was and we could target their location and put a stop to whatever they were doing, or put a stop to them.

The situation with the letters was completely different. We didn't know who was sending them and there was no way to determine when or where they would show up again. I had no choice but to sit still and wait for the enemy to make their next move. The only thing I was certain of was that it wasn't over so I kept constant vigil because I was determined to keep my promise to Landon and make sure that no harm came to his brother.

I couldn't help the grin that spread across my face as I thought of Landon. We had managed to spend quite a bit of time together since we'd come back and I'd been pleasantly surprised to find that we had a lot in common. We were both avid Cubs fans, voracious readers, and loved any and all horror flicks, no matter how cheesy. We shared similar tastes in music and agreed that we'd choose cooking at home over dining in the fanciest restaurant any day.

We were quickly becoming friends, but it was more than just all of the things we had in common; I simply liked being around him. He was extremely smart, honest and one of the nicest people I had ever met. The more time I spent with him, the more he relaxed around me and his wicked sense of humor came shining through. I hadn't had much occasion to laugh in my life, but I often found myself laughing along with whatever story he was telling at the time and it always left me feeling lighter than I had before.

Landon wasn't the only reason I had been feeling lighter though. During our trip home, I had finally gotten the opportunity to talk to Giovanni. I had promised him when I first moved back to Chicago that when I was ready, I would tell him why I had left the SEALs. I knew the curiosity had to have been killing him, but it wasn't in G's nature to push. He had always been good about letting me work things out in my head first, knowing that I would eventually open up to him.

We had been sitting by the fire at the Greens' house, everyone talking around me as I tried to hide the fact that I was staring at Landon when I heard Giovanni approach. With all of the excitement of the adoption, it was the first time we had been able to catch up all weekend. He sat down beside me and I turned to him, noting the smile on his face. It was the most content I had ever seen my best friend.

"So how does it feel being a dad?" I bumped his shoulder as his grin turned sappy.

"It's like every single birthday and Christmas all rolled into one." He turned to look at me, his eyes dancing happily in the firelight. "Sarah's amazing, isn't she? Have you ever seen a more beautiful girl?" he gushed.

"She's perfect. The three of you are very lucky to have each other and I know you and Caleb will be the best dads in the world," I answered sincerely. G had always wanted a family. When he met Caleb, I knew he had met his soulmate and now with Sarah, he had everything he'd ever dreamed of.

"Thanks, Micah. I can't tell you how much it means to me to have you here today."

"I wouldn't have missed it for the world." I grinned.

"I know, but there was a time when you wouldn't have had a choice." I knew he was referring to my time in the military. I'd hated the fact that when he was going through some of the most difficult times of his life, I was far away on some mission. Sure, I had been allowed to come home for his parents' funeral, but I was expected to return shortly after. It had killed me to have to leave him when he was in so much pain. That was just one of the reasons why I had decided to walk away from that life. Giovanni was my family and I was tired of not being there when he needed me.

"I know you're probably wondering why I left the navy."

"I know you didn't make the decision easily and I know you'll tell me when you're ready."

I stared into the dancing flames of the fire for several minutes. "I think I'm ready," I finally said.

"Let's take a walk then," he said easily, standing up.

"What, now? But this is your party," I argued.

He bent down to look directly at me. "No matter what is going on in my life, I will always have time for you. Got it?"

I nodded my head, not trusting myself to speak around the emotions that were clogging my throat. What did I ever do to deserve a friend like him? I followed him away from the rest of the group and out into the gardens where we would have some privacy.

We walked slowly and Giovanni listened without interruption, letting me get it all out. When I reached the end, he grabbed me in a protective hug and held me as I cried into his neck; I could feel the shaking of his shoulders which let me know he was crying too. We stood that way for a while until we both had calmed down and we stepped back, wiping our eyes, and taking a deep breath. Through an unspoken agreement, we resumed our walk, moving on to a lighter topic. There would be time for further discussion at a later date, but right then both of us were feeling too raw.

"So why are you covering security for Carter's Creed? I would have thought Golden Entertainment would have their own security in place for tours."

"There's been a few developments that needed special attention," I hedged. "Lachlan called me in because he thought I was the best person for the job."

"You are," Giovanni said confidently.

I chuckled. "You don't even know what the job is, how can you say that?"

"Because I know you," he said with a shrug of his shoulder like it was that easy.

"Thanks." I was humbled by his obvious faith in me.

He stopped suddenly, turning to me with a look of concern marring his handsome face. "You know I won't keep things from Caleb, especially if it has to do with a member of his family. Is there anything we *should be worried about?"*

I sighed. "So far there have only been a few letters, but I'm taking them very seriously and I've increased security to help minimize the risk. I promised Landon and I'll promise you too, I will do anything I need to in order to keep Carter safe, alright?"

"That's good enough for me," he said with a confident nod. I just wished I was as confident in my own abilities.

"Speaking of Landon..." Giovanni looked at me out of the corner of his eye.

"Were we speaking of him?" I responded innocently.

"Now we are," he said with a chuckle when he saw me roll my eyes. "I like to pride myself on being a fairly observant kind of guy."

"Do you now?" I asked flatly.

"Yes, like right now I'm observing how nervous I seem to be making you." The laughter was evident in his voice. The bastard was quite pleased with himself.

"Why don't you just ask whatever it is you want to know," I sighed my exasperation.

"Fine, what's going on with you two?"

"What makes you think something's going on?"

He turned, blocking my path and held up one hand as he began ticking things off with his fingers. "One, you've been making moon eyes at each other all night, two, you act weird around each other, three, you both disappeared around the same time during my bachelor party and then he looked crushed when you took off early during the reception. Do I need to keep going? Because I have more fingers left."

"I have a finger for you, you know," I said sarcastically.

"Aha! You didn't deny it which means there is something going on!" I watched in shock as he circled around me, doing some horrible form of victory dance.

"Are you finished, Sherlock?" I couldn't help the laugh that erupted from watching his antics.

"That depends, are you going to tell me what's going on?"

"Fine," I grumbled, causing him to laugh.

"We're attracted to each other, okay? We left together the night we met, but nothing ended up happening. I tried to fight it, but lately the pull has been getting stronger."

Giovanni cocked his head as he studied me intently. "Why would you try to fight it? Landon's a great guy."

I stared at the ground as I answered him. "You know what my childhood was like, G. My dad was an asshole who did everything he could to make me feel as small as he was. That kind of stuff can have a lasting effect on a person. Between that and the stuff I just told you about, I'm not the best choice for any man, especially not one as wonderful as Landon. Besides, if we tried and things didn't work out, I don't want to risk losing you."

"Lose me?" His confusion was apparent.

"Well, yeah. He's your family now. If things went south, I know who you'd have to side with."

Giovanni stared at me a moment, his lips pressed together like he was angry. "Listen to me, Micah. Yes, Landon is my brother now, but you've been my brother since we were seven years old and that's never going to change." His hand landed on my shoulder.

"Individually, you guys are two of the best people I know and I think you deserve to be happy, whether that's together or apart. There are no sides, I want whatever is best for each of you. As far as your dad goes, he was a piece of shit who never deserved a son like you, so please stop letting him hurt you. He's not worth wasting another one of your thoughts."

"I'm trying. Most days, I do pretty well, but sometimes I still feel like that kid, growing up in a shitty trailer with a drunk for a dad."

"I know you do," Giovanni said with a sad look. "But you're so much more than all of that. You can't help what situation you're born into. All you can do is fight to get out and become something better than what your parents were and you already did that, Micah." I bit down on my bottom lip, unable to form words.

"I am so proud of you and what you've done with your life. You are honest, brave, and compassionate. You're everything your father was not." He pulled me into a hug when he saw my eyes filling. "It's time to quit punishing yourself for things that weren't your fault. You deserve to be happy, you deserve to find love. And if that happens with Landon, I'll be thrilled for you so don't use me as an excuse to push him away."

He arched his brow as I opened my mouth to argue, but we both knew that's exactly what I had been doing. I nodded my head instead and we began making our way back to the party. I was glad I had finally come clean with my best friend about everything that was going on because I felt like a huge weight had been lifted from my shoulders.

I had taken Giovanni's advice and decided to give Landon a chance and so far, I had never been happier. I had no idea what would happen between the two of us, but Landon was unlike anyone I had ever met before and I wondered if it was possible that I had found the man who could accept me, despite all of the baggage I carried.

—· ⟫•⟨ ·—

I stepped into the dining hall and the smell of the food that the caterers had prepared made my mouth water so I walked through the line, quickly filling my plate. We had arrived in the last city on the European part of the tour that morning and I had skipped lunch because I wanted to make sure everything was secure for the show that night. The next day we would return to America and the excitement could be felt from everyone involved. Europe had been wonderful, but everyone was worn out and we were all ready to head home to finish up the last leg of the journey.

"Micah, over here!" I turned and saw Carter waving me over from where he sat, curled into Ryan's side. They were sitting with the rest of the band and as I walked over with my dinner, I saw Landon's head pop up, the smile that spread across his face made me feel warm all over.

"Hi!" I said to everyone at the table even though my eyes were on one man in particular. We had both been very busy the last few days and so we hadn't had any time to be together. He looked good though, the dark rings and the sallow complexion he had worn when I first joined the tour had almost completely disappeared and I couldn't help but wonder if my being there had made the difference in him being able to sleep better; I certainly hoped so. He squirmed under my intense gaze and I smirked, happy with the obvious effect my presence was having on him.

"Is everything ready for the show?" Carter asked, pulling my attention to him.

I nodded. "Yes, you're good to go."

I saw Ryan heave a sigh of relief and Carter grabbed his hand, squeezing it gently with his own. I couldn't imagine how hard it had been on him to know that some crazy person was after the man he loved and there was nothing he could do about it.

"Good. I'm ready to rock the house and then get laid one last time before we cross the pond again," Rocko announced, holding his hand up to Steve for a fist bump. Steve just shook his head at his friend.

"What's the flavor tonight, Rocko boy?" Tyler teased.

Rocko's face scrunched up as if he were thinking about the answer very hard. "Maybe a man and a woman this time," he finally concluded, nodding his head with a cocky smile. "You know I hate to limit myself in any way."

"That's why you know no limits," Kalia said as she stood up, kissing the top of his head to help soften the words. The concern the bandmates held for their friend could be seen on each of their faces, but they knew he was a grown man and had to decide things for himself.

The other members of the band stood and cleared their plates so they could get ready for the performance, leaving me sitting with Carter, Ryan, and Landon. "I'm so worried about him," Carter said when the door had shut.

Ryan kissed the side of his head. "I know you are, baby, we all are. You know there's nothing we can do though until he's ready to help himself. All we can do is be here for him when that time comes."

Carter let out a weary sigh. "Yeah, you're right."

A smile appeared on his face as he turned to me and I could see why so many of his fans swooned when they met him. There was no doubt that all three of the Greene brothers were stunningly gorgeous men although I personally preferred Landon's taller build and broad shoulders.

"How are you doing, Micah? Are you tired of life on the road yet?"

I chuckled as I wiped my mouth with a napkin. "I'm definitely not a fan of living out of a suitcase, but there have been good things about the trip, too." My eyes flickered over to Landon whose lips curved into a small smile as his cheeks pinked from my words.

Carter sat up straighter in his seat, his eyes darting back and forth between the two of us. "Wait a minute. I thought when I caught you two before that was just a one-time thing. Is there something…"

"Look at the time! Honey, you're going to be late for your sound check," Ryan warned. He grabbed Carter by his bicep and tugged him towards the door.

Ryan winked at me as his fiancé pointed his finger at his older brother. "This isn't over. You and I are going to have a long talk later, Landon."

"Oh boy, now I'm in trouble," Landon said with a chuckle after Carter was gone.

"I'm sorry about that." I frowned, hoping I hadn't put him in an awkward position.

"Don't be, he already had his suspicions even before he saw us together that day."

I tilted my head in question. "Since when?"

A sheepish grin spread across his face and it made me want to pull him close and kiss him all over. "Since before you started working here." My face must have registered my surprise because he continued to explain. "Apparently, Carter and Caleb noticed the way I looked at you at the wedding and they've been keeping tabs on me and comparing notes ever since. They gossip worse than two old ladies when they get together." I chuckled as he rolled his eyes dramatically.

"So, I haven't seen you much in the last few days. How have you been?" I asked.

Landon leaned back in his chair and clasped his hands over his head. My eyes darted down to where his shirt had ridden up, revealing golden skin and a sexy trail of dark hair that disappeared into the waistband of his pants. He was dressed more casually than his usual suit and tie which told me he was done working for the day.

I continued to ogle him, only halfway listening as he described how much work was involved with moving an entire entourage of people and equipment overseas. My eyes scrolled up his body, passed the broad chest and the strong jaw. My balls tingled when I saw his tongue dart out to wet his lips before landing on his hazel eyes which were staring back at me through hooded lids.

Despite the time we had spent together since we returned to the tour, we hadn't done anything more intimate than a few heavy make out sessions, each of us content with getting to know each other. We stared at each other, neither of us saying a word because the look we shared already said it all; we were tired of waiting.

"The way you're looking at me makes me think you've missed me," he teased.

"I have," I responded, surprising us both. I hadn't meant to expose my feelings so quickly, but when I saw his surprise turn into a pleased smile, I couldn't bring myself to take it back. I decided to downplay it instead. After all, he didn't need to know how many times I looked for him throughout the day or how often my thoughts strayed to him at night.

"Most of the people on the crew are from L.A. so they're Dodgers fans. How am I even supposed to talk to these people?" I said in mock exasperation. Landon threw his head back with a loud laugh and I watched him, loving the way his eyes crinkled at the edges when he smiled. He was a very outgoing, fun-loving person when he wasn't completely bogged down by his anxiety. I wanted to do everything I could to keep his anxiety at bay and to see more of the carefree, relaxed side of Landon.

"I can understand why you want to hang out with me then, since I'm clearly one of the few people with taste around here," he joked.

"That's true," I agreed with a smirk. "But there are other reasons why I like to be around you too." Without realizing it we had each been inching forward until we were leaning over the table and I cursed the fact that there was anything between us. Landon's voice was husky when he spoke and the sound of it made my dick tingle.

"What other reasons?" He stared at my lips hungrily.

"Because we like the same kinds of movies." He nodded his head, still staring at my lips. "And because of the way your body feels lying next to mine on the couch while we watch those movies." Landon swallowed hard and I knew I had his full attention so I decided to go for the kill.

"Mostly I like to be around you because I like the sounds you make when I..." We jerked away from each other in surprise as several of the stage hands filed in to get their dinner. A couple of them walked over to Landon with questions regarding the move back to America.

He was obviously busy and I had a few other things to take care of myself so I waved off his apologetic look and told him I'd find him later. My cock on the other hand wasn't as gracious about the interruption so I began slowly listing the presidents backwards in my head to help calm myself down as I walked down the hallway.

An hour later I walked through the front lobby of the hotel and rode the elevator up to my room. I had left Carter and Ryan under the careful watch of Greg and Carlos who would make sure everything ran smoothly both during the show and at the fan signing afterward.

It had been a long day and I was ready to work off some tension before bed so I changed my clothes quickly and headed down to the hotel gym where I was relieved to see that I had the place to myself. I popped my headphones in and started my workout. Before long I had worked up a cleansing sweat and I could feel the endorphins kicking in despite the burning in my muscles.

I climbed off of the treadmill and peeled my soaked tank top off, tossing it in the corner of the room. After adjusting the weights to give myself the best workout, I lay down on the bench and began lifting the heavy bar. Concentrating on the burning in my arms and the music pounding in my ears, I didn't notice someone had walked in until Landon leaned over me, startling me. He laughed as he grabbed the bar before I could drop it and helped me put it back on its stand.

"You scared the shit out of me," I said, sitting up and pulling the earbuds from my ears.

He chuckled quietly. "Sorry. In my defense, I did call out for you several times."

I held my earbuds up in answer. "Did you come here to work out or were you looking for me?"

"I decided to get a workout in before going to bed." Landon's lips quirked up sweetly. "Finding you here was just a perk."

"I'll say it was," I teased, running my index finger up his leg and teasing the skin along the back of his knee.

Landon shivered and then pulled away from me. "I did not come here for *that*, sir," he replied haughtily. I arched my brow at him as he walked over to the other bench press and lowered himself onto it gracefully. He may have acted like he only wanted to work out, but the definite bulge in the front of his shorts told a different story.

We finished lifting weights together and then we each moved to the floor to do some crunches. I watched Landon in the mirror as he did his crunches. Sweat dotted his brow and I could see the muscle play beneath the thin material of his shirt. As his body heated from exertion the intoxicating smell of clean sweat and man permeated the room. I breathed in the smell of him and felt my cock lengthen.

With a growl, I moved until I was hovering above him. I smirked at the look of surprise and excitement in his eyes. "Did you really think you could come in here smelling so good and looking like you do and I wouldn't pounce on you?"

"How do I look?" he asked playfully.

"Edible." I ran my tongue up his neck, tasting his sweat and making him writhe beneath me. "Lie still and don't move."

Landon stopped moving, responding immediately to the command in my voice. I let my eyes roam all over his face as my heart raced. The easy way he submitted all control to me, the way he trusted me with his body did funny things to my head and to my heart.

I lowered myself onto my forearms which caused our chests to brush, the soft cotton of his shirt brushing against my erect nipples. My hips swayed back and forth, grinding our cocks together. I could tell how hard it was for him to not move so I whispered into his ear, "Touch me."

He reached for me, running his hands up and down my sides and sliding around to glide over my sweat-slicked back. I bent my head and captured his bottom lip between my teeth, tugging gently, and eliciting a throaty moan from him.

"I keep remembering the night we had together. Do you think of that night too?" He nodded his head rapidly as I reached between us and slid my hand under the waistband of his shorts. My fingertips rubbed over the leaking head of his dick and he bucked up under me.

"What do you want, baby?" I whispered, tracing the outline

of his lips with my tongue. My hand reached around his shaft and tugged hard until he gasped.

"I...I want to feel you...everywhere. Above me, around me... inside of me," he said and whimpered as I worked his cock in my hand and rubbed my thumb over the cluster of nerves right under the head. His eyes rolled back in his head as I claimed his mouth with my own. I lost all sense of time and space as I devoured him and soon I was tugging on his shorts, working them over his hips, frantic to feel his warm skin against mine.

Through the haze of lust, I registered the sound of my phone ringing. With a loud groan, I shifted to one hip so I could pull it from my pocket. "This better be good, Tony," I snarled. I listened for a few seconds before responding. "We'll be right there."

I shoved my phone back in my pocket and started to get up. "What is it, Micah?" Landon looked at me worriedly.

I helped him to his feet and gave him one more kiss. "They caught some guy in Carter's dressing room. With any luck, he's the same guy that's been sending the letters. Come on, we need to hurry and change our clothes. I want to have a little chat with him before the police get ahold of him."

CHAPTER
Ten

Landon

I T WAS QUIET IN THE LIMOUSINE AS WE DROVE BACK TO THE concert venue. I looked at Micah who was clenching his jaw tightly as he stared out the window. I reached over and took hold of his hand that he held in a tight fist and opened it until I could thread my fingers through his. He glanced down at our hands and then at me, looking surprised to see me there.

"Are you okay?" I slid closer to him.

"I'm fine." His clipped answer told me otherwise.

"You know that when people say they're fine, that most of the time it means the complete opposite." I studied his face and I could see the worry there. I reached out and smoothed his eyebrows with my fingertips and I felt him relax under my touch.

"I fucked up…again." He sighed and it was a bone-weary sound that made my heart ache.

"What do you mean?"

He pulled his hand from mine and ran it over his short hair in agitation. "No one should have gotten past security who doesn't belong there and certainly not close enough to get into Carter's personal dressing room. I must have missed something, somewhere."

I hit the button that would raise the privacy screen between us and the driver and climbed on top of Micah, straddling his lap. His eyes widened in surprise, but instead of pushing me away, his hands slid up to rest on my hips. He let his head drop back against the seat as he stared up at me and I cupped his face tenderly in my hands.

"We don't know how the guy got in there so you shouldn't assume it was something you did wrong. I know you've tried to work each angle and plan for every eventuality, but, Micah, you can't think of everything."

"But I promised you and everyone else that I would keep Carter safe," he insisted.

"Carter is safe!" I insisted.

"Because he was on stage at the time," Micah growled back.

"With two of the world's most highly trained men watching over him; men *you* hired to guard him!" I refused to allow Micah to blame himself for the situation. "You have set up so much security that I'm surprised the Pentagon hasn't come searching for you to head up their team."

The slight twitch at the corners of his mouth told me that I was getting through to him. I leaned forward and rested my head against his. I closed my eyes and enjoyed the intimacy of the moment, so thankful that I was finally getting the opportunity to take care of him the way he always took care of me.

"You're a good man, Micah Hamilton, and I trust you." I shivered as I felt his hand cup the back of my neck and his mouth met mine. It wasn't his usual demanding kiss that told me in no uncertain terms who was in charge, but it left me just as breathless. The kiss he gave me in the back of that limo was one of want and need and so much tenderness that I knew no other man would ever make me feel that way. Micah was the one for me.

He slid his hands around my back and pulled me closer while I rested my face in the crook of his neck, breathing in his scent, and letting it settle over me. I felt exhilarated by the knowledge that I was in love with him, but I was also scared to death of getting my heart broken. It had happened to me before and I'd somehow managed to pick the broken pieces of myself back up and move on, but Micah was different; he had the power to destroy me and he didn't even know it.

I had to jog to keep up with Micah as he sprinted into the arena, shoving his way through the crowd of people leaving the concert. We showed our badges to a guard who let us backstage and we quickly found Tony.

"Where's Carter?" we asked at the same time.

"He's getting a shower in one of the other rooms. Ryan's with him and Greg is right outside their door," Tony assured us.

"Do they know what's happened?" I asked.

Tony turned sympathetic eyes on me. "Yes, we had to tell them why they couldn't go in Carter's dressing room." I nodded my understanding.

"Where is he?" I was shocked at the coldness I heard in Micah's voice as he asked about the man in question.

"Carlos is keeping an eye on him where we found him." Tony leaned in towards Micah and lowered his voice. "I'm waiting to call the police until you've gotten what you need from him."

Micah nodded at him and I felt a chill run through me as I watched the man I had just been kissing turn into a Navy SEAL before my eyes. His back went ramrod straight and his face became void of any emotion. It was unnerving to see how easily he switched gears, but I reminded myself that I was only seeing the armor he put on in order to protect someone, in this case, my little brother. Suddenly my skin was hot and my collar felt too tight. I changed my mind, Micah in protective mode was all kinds of sexy.

Carter, Ryan, and Greg met up with us as we walked to the dressing room. I squeezed Carter's hand as he passed and he gave me a nervous smile. Ryan had his arm wrapped protectively around Carter's shoulder and I was glad my brother had a strong man like Ryan to lean on. We started to file into the room, but Micah held his arm out to stop me.

"Are you sure you want to go in there? It's okay if you want to wait outside."

"I'm fine," I whispered.

His eyes narrowed. "You know that when people say they're fine, that most of the time it means the complete opposite," he said, throwing my words back at me.

"Except the times when they actually mean it," I quipped, ducking under his arm and entered the room. I appreciated his concern, but there was no way I was going to stay outside while they questioned the man who had been stalking my brother. I heard Micah sigh heavily before he followed me in, locking the door behind him.

Carter, Ryan, and I lined up along the wall, trying to stay out of the way. I looked at the man who was seated in a chair in the middle of the room. His hands were tied behind his back with what I assumed were plastic zip ties because I had seen Micah and his men handing them out to Lachlan's security crew in case they needed to subdue someone.

He looked like an ordinary man, one you would nod at as you passed by, but then forget a moment later. That surprised me because in my mind I had pictured him as some sort of larger-than-life monster, not someone who looked like an accountant. He was small in stature, probably around thirty-five years old, with white pasty skin that told me he didn't spend a lot of time outdoors. His mousy brown hair was receding and his belly hung over his trousers.

His eyes widened as he stared up at the formidable soldiers surrounding him. Sweat trickled down the side of his face and he was visibly shaking. Then he glanced behind the men and his entire demeanor changed as he caught sight of Carter for the first time. A huge grin split his face and he leaned forward as much as his restraints would allow.

"I knew you would come, my love. I knew you would want to be with me," he leered in a nasally voice.

My stomach roiled and Ryan moved forward and in front of Carter, blocking the man's view. The man let out a guttural wail as his eyes shot daggers towards Ryan. "You!" he snarled. "You're always trying to get in the way."

"Enough!" Micah shouted, startling us all. He knelt down in front of the man and I wanted to pull him back, but I reminded myself that he knew what he was doing. When he spoke again it was in a much calmer tone. "So you're the one, huh?"

The man looked confused as his eyes darted back and forth between Ryan and Micah. "What are you talking about?" he asked nervously.

"I'm talking about the fact that you're Carter's number one fan, right?" Micah's voice was smooth, almost like he was having a conversation with a friend.

The man gave Micah his full attention then, pleased with the fact that someone actually understood his importance in Carter's life. "Yes, I am," he preened.

"Is that the reason you sent all the letters? Because you wanted Carter to know how much you loved him?" Micah asked, his voice full of understanding. *Damn, he's good at this.*

"I didn't write any letters," the man murmured as he fidgeted in his seat.

Carlos pulled something out of his back pocket and handed it to Micah. "I found this on him when I was tying him up." My heart plummeted when I saw the familiar blue envelope. Micah opened it quickly, scanning the page before Ryan stepped forward to take it from his hands.

Carter and I leaned over his shoulder to read it too. *Can't you see that no one can give you what I can? I will prove it to you soon.* The words swam as tears filled my eyes. Panic started to seep in, but I pushed it back when I heard Carter gasp. He needed me right then and I would stay strong for him. Ryan grabbed him in a fierce hug, his larger body blocking him from the man who wanted to do him harm and I grabbed his hand, lending what strength I could.

"That is the same type of letter Carter received before; each claiming that he belongs to the person writing them." Micah remained calm, but I could hear the tension in his voice and I knew he was reaching the end of his rope. Sooner or later he was going to snap.

"No!" the man screeched. His face was dark red and spittle flew from his mouth as he launched into an angry tirade. He reminded me of a dog barking wildly against the restraints of his leash. "Carter is *mine*! I love him more than anyone, especially you," he snarled at Ryan. "He belongs with me, not the person who gave me the letter."

A cold chill swept over the entire room at his words. The man was obviously insane, but if what he was saying was true then we still didn't have the person that had been stalking Carter. I tried to hold myself steady as the panic ebbed in once more.

"If you didn't send the letters then how did you end up with one in your possession?" Micah asked him.

"Some guy saw me waiting outside. I was waiting for you, Carter, so I could take you home," he pleaded, trying to see around the men who were keeping him from the man he was obsessed with.

"So, a guy saw you outside and then what?" Micah prompted.

"He told me that he worked at the arena and could get me backstage to meet Carter, all I had to do was deliver that letter. He gave me a badge to use and everything."

"Where is the badge?" Tony asked.

"I put it in the garbage can in the hallway, just like the guy told me to. He said he'd pick it up later so he wouldn't lose his job." With a nod from Micah, Carlos left the room in search of the badge. I could tell the man was becoming annoyed with the line of questioning. "Look, I kept my end of the deal. You guys read the letter, now I want what I came for."

Micah stood to his full height, towering over the man. "And what exactly did you come for?" His tone was low, bordering on hostile and the man narrowed his eyes, suddenly unsure.

"I want Carter." He leaned around Micah and his eyes lit up as they connected with the object of his desire. "I can make you happy, Carter, you'll see. I'll need a few things from you of course, but I'll be as gentle as possible, I promise."

"What things?" I heard the tremor in Carter's voice as he spoke for the first time and I wanted to pound the man with my fists for making my brother feel afraid.

"Your teeth," the man whispered with a euphoric smile on his face. "You have such perfect teeth and they would look perfect as a necklace for me. Then when people see it, they'll know you belong to me."

With a loud roar, Ryan lunged for the man, but Greg stopped him before he could reach him and pushed him up against the wall. "I know you're pissed, man, we all are," Greg said steadily, looking Ryan in the eyes. "We're going to take care of the problem, but you need to focus on your man, he needs you."

Greg's words snapped Ryan out of his rage and he looked at Carter who had gone completely white and was staring blankly at the man. He nodded at Greg who released his hold and Ryan ran back to Carter, wrapping his arms around him and whispering soothingly into his ear, words meant only for the two of them. Carter slid his arms around his fiancé, crushing their bodies together and Ryan maneuvered them until he could open the door.

"I'm taking him back to our room." His eyes met mine and I nodded, swallowing around the lump in my throat.

"Nooooo!" the man wailed. "Come back here! Carter!"

"You find it?" Micah asked Carlos as he poked his head in the room.

Carlos held the badge up in answer. "I've got Brandon running a check on the guy."

"Great, can you go ahead and call the police, please?" Micah asked.

"Sure thing, Boss," Carlos responded, chuckling when Micah rolled his eyes.

"You have to get him back here," the man begged and Micah stood in front of him with his arms crossed. "You don't understand; Carter belongs with me."

"That's never going to happen," Micah stated coldly. The man stared at him in shock, most likely realizing that Micah had never been on his side and that Carter was never coming back.

"You son of a bitch! This isn't over!" the man screamed, thrashing his body against the chair and causing it to scoot across the floor. The plastic zip ties cut into his wrists, making them bleed, but he didn't seem to notice as he flailed wildly.

I felt my throat closing as the reality of what could have happened to my brother came crashing down on me. My body started to shake and I felt cold and hot all at the same time. I could feel my heart pounding against my chest and heard the blood whooshing through my ears. The light in the room narrowed until it was just a pinpoint and then there was nothing.

—·————⟫•⟨————·—

I gasped for air, feeling like I had been underwater too long and had finally reached the surface. I still couldn't see and so my arms shot out in front of me, connecting with something warm and solid. I clung to it and that's when I heard Micah's voice in my ear.

"It's okay, baby. I've got you and I'm not letting go." His words soothed me and I felt my pulse returning to normal. My arms and legs felt heavy so I slumped down in the safety of his embrace. My eyes fluttered open and I saw his beautiful face looming over me. His gray eyes were filled with concern and what looked like tenderness and his full lips were turned down in a frown.

I reached up and traced his lips with my fingertip. "You're so beautiful, why are you frowning?"

Micah chuckled. "I thought I caught you before you could hit your head, but you must have bumped it on something if you think I'm beautiful."

"You are beautiful and sexy and delicious," I slurred.

"Okay, time to get you to your room," he said with a laugh. He opened a door and got out and that's when I realized we were in a car. My cheeks filled with heat as I wondered if the driver had heard my words.

Micah held his hand out to me, helping me as I climbed from the back of the car. I swayed dizzily so he wrapped a solid arm around my waist, anchoring me against his firm body. He quickly ushered me inside the hotel and into a waiting elevator.

"How did we get back..." My words trailed off as flashes of everything that had happened came rushing back: the man screaming, Carter's stricken face, listening as he described what he had planned to do to my brother. I gasped, my chest feeling tight once again.

Micah pressed me against the wall of the elevator, crowding in around me so that there was no room for anything but the two of us. "Listen to me, Landon. You're away from that man, Carter is away from him. The police took him and he can't get to Carter any more. Your brother is safe."

Tears filled my eyes. I wanted to believe him, but I knew the truth. "It's not the same person though. There's someone else out there, the one who's been sending the letters and they're not going to stop," I wheezed out.

"Who is in charge, Landon?" he demanded. I stared at him blankly as I struggled to breathe. "Who, Landon?"

"You," I choked out as tears streamed down my face.

"Who's trained to keep your brother safe?" I watched the firm set of his jaw as he waited for my answer. The warmth of his body bled through his shirt and mine, soaking into my bones, and becoming part of me.

"You are," I said more strongly. I took a deep breath for the first time and I felt my head beginning to clear as I breathed back out.

"That's right, I am. I made you a promise and I will not break it. Do you still trust me, Landon?" My head swam for a different reason as his breath washed over my lips. I stared at his mouth hungrily.

"Yes," I answered honestly. I trusted Micah with my life and with my brother's life.

Micah must have noticed my change in demeanor because without another word, he slammed his mouth over mine. I opened up to him, wanting him to drink his fill of me. He groaned loudly as his tongue delved into my mouth, tasting every crevice, and tangling with my own in a sinful dance.

The elevator dinged loudly as it stopped on our floor. Micah barely waited for the doors to open before he grabbed my hand and pulled me down the hallway to his room. He swiped his card quickly and then yanked me into the room, locking the door behind us.

He pulled me back against his hard body. I could feel his erection pressing into the curve of my ass and I let my head fall back on his shoulder. He trailed a line of kisses up my neck and I tilted my head to give him better access. "Do you need me to help you get out of your head, baby?" His breath tickled my ear.

"Yes, I need…" I moaned as his hips started a slow grind.

"Tell me what you need, Landon." I jumped as his teeth nipped at my earlobe.

"You, Micah. I need you." A long sigh escaped me as he cupped my jaw, moving my face so that he could reach my lips. His tongue slid into my waiting mouth and I captured it, sucking on it like it was his cock. My dick ached behind my zipper and I reached down with my hand, wanting to free it, but he grabbed my wrist and brought it up to hold tightly against my chest. With his other hand, he reached down and cupped my groin, making me buck into his hand.

"Your cock belongs to me. You will not touch it unless I say so. Nod your head if you understand." The demanding tone he used sent a jolt of electricity straight to my balls and I nodded my head eagerly. "You will not touch me either unless I say so, do you understand?"

I whimpered at the thought of not being able to touch all of that silky skin over smooth rippling muscles, but he pinched my nipple hard between his thumb and finger and I almost came from that alone. I nodded my head, hoping he would touch my cock.

"Good," he said, slapping my ass hard enough to make it sting. "Get undressed and lie down on the bed." I hurried to do as he said, throwing my clothes onto a nearby chair. I pulled the comforter down the bed while Micah rummaged around in his bag and tossed a bottle of lube and a strip of condoms onto the side table. When I was naked, I crawled across the large bed and lay down, my hands resting on my stomach. I was surprised to see Micah standing at the foot of the bed, arms crossed and still fully dressed.

"Spread your arms out," he said. I unfolded my arms slowly and stretched them out to the sides. He grasped my ankles in his hands and spread my legs open wide. "That's better," he soothed. "Don't hide yourself, Landon. You're a sexy and desirable man and every part of you belongs to me to do with whatever I want."

"Yes!" I hissed. I should have felt embarrassed to be so exposed, especially since he was wearing clothes, but instead I just felt hot all over. Micah was giving me exactly what I wanted; he was taking me away from my own worries to a place where he made the decisions and all I had to do was feel. It was a beautiful gift he was giving to me and I hoped he got something out of it in return.

I watched as he moved around to stand at my side. His eyes roamed over my body and I felt his gaze like a caress leaving goose bumps on my skin. He ran his fingertips over my lips, down my chin, along my neck, and brushed over my collarbone before circling my peaked nipple. My breathing became more labored and I bit down on my lip to stop myself from pleading with him to hurry up and fuck me.

"So beautiful, so perfect," he murmured so quietly I wasn't sure he meant for me to hear it. "Can I trust you to keep your hands where they are or do I need to tie you up?" The glint in his eyes told me that the idea excited him and to be honest it had my blood racing too. I had never allowed someone to tie me up before, but I had never been with someone that I trusted as much as I trusted Micah.

"Tie me up, Micah. Please," I begged.

He smiled approvingly then walked to the closet, returning with several silk ties. They felt cool and smooth against my overheated skin as he tied each of my wrists and then attached the ends to either table at the sides of the bed. My eyes widened when he tied my ankles and attached the other ends to the legs of the bed. I was spread eagle, completely at his mercy and I had never felt more desired as I did when his eyes raked over me.

"Are you comfortable?" His eyes met mine and I could see the fire blazing in their depths.

"Yes," I panted.

"If at any time you feel uncomfortable or you want to quit, just tell me. No need for a safe word. I'll do whatever you need, alright?" If I hadn't been convinced that I was already in love with him, I would have known for sure in that moment. I wasn't sure he'd want to hear it though and I certainly didn't want to scare him off so I simply nodded my head instead.

Micah stood at the foot of the bed and slowly began to undress. My mouth watered as each inch of his delectable skin was revealed to me. He tossed his shirt to the floor and I let my eyes drink their fill as they wandered over his sculpted chest which sported the perfect amount of hair, the detailed tattoos, and washboard abs. The man was magnificent and I felt a surge of pride to know that for even a short amount of time, he was all mine.

I held my breath as he unbuckled his jeans and slowly lowered the zipper. He slid his pants down smoothly and I groaned when his cock sprang free, unrestrained by his lack of underwear. I wanted to lick him from head to toe. He kicked them aside and carefully climbed onto the bed, crawling up my body without touching me until we were face to face.

"I like you tied up, completely submissive. It makes me want to take my time and play with you." He chuckled at the whimper that escaped my lips. "Does that turn you on to know that you are completely at my mercy? That I can do whatever I want to you, for as long as I want and you can't escape." He nibbled along the edge of my jaw.

"Please..." I cried.

"Please what?" He smirked evilly.

"Touch me!"

"Mmmm...I do love the way you beg." He slammed his mouth over mine in a bruising kiss. The room was spinning when he finally pulled away and I sucked in some much needed oxygen. "Look at you," he whispered as he moved lower on the bed, dragging his tongue over my body. My back arched off the bed as he sucked hard on my nipple. He moved lower still, circling my navel with his tongue and then delving it in to taste.

I angled my head up so I wouldn't miss a thing as his head dipped further down to lick across the top of my pubic hair. He slid his body until he was resting between my legs and proceeded to bury his nose in the juncture of my thigh, inhaling deeply. He looked up and his eyes were the color of storm clouds over the sea.

"I love the way you smell, like soap and sweat and man." He kissed the sensitive skin then made me scream when he opened his mouth and sucked, hard. When he was done, he pulled back and admired his handiwork. It was bright red where the blood had rushed to the surface of my skin. He had marked me and I prayed that the proof of it would last for a long time.

"Mine," he growled as if he had heard my thoughts. I squeezed my eyes shut tightly so he couldn't see the emotion in them because as much as I wanted to belong to him, I was sure he didn't mean what he had said. He was simply caught up in the moment.

My eyes sprang open when I felt something wet on the head of my dick and I saw his tongue flicking across it, gathering the liquid that was leaking from my tip. "God, you taste as good as you smell." He flattened his tongue and let it sweep over my length from base to tip before he opened wide and took me all the way to the back of his throat. I let out a strangled cry and my head dropped back onto the pillow.

He bobbed up and down on my cock until I was a writhing mess underneath him and I groaned in frustration when his body lifted off of mine. I immediately missed his warmth and I turned my head to search for him. He came back to the bed and my eyes widened when I saw what he was carrying.

"Patience, baby. I want to play for a while," he explained as he opened the bottle of lube and poured a generous amount over my dick, making it jump in reaction to the cold.

I eyed him warily. "What do you mean by *a while*?"

He arched a brow at me and gave me the sexiest smirk I had ever seen. "Well, I guess that's my decision, isn't it?"

"Yes," I whimpered.

He leaned over me and licked across my lips while staring into my eyes. "Good boy," he whispered. His words did funny things to my belly and I had the sudden urge to laugh, but then something slid over the head of my cock, engulfing it and sliding down to the base. I jackknifed off the bed at the grip that was surrounding my dick.

He slid back down between my legs without breaking stride and I was able to get my first view of what he was doing to me. The object he was holding looked like a large plastic flashlight, but was filled with some sort of silicone material that was shaped to look like an ass. He pulled it off of me slowly then lined my tip with the tight opening and slid it down over me again. My eyes rolled back in my head as it squeezed my cock just right. I could feel each ridge in the perfectly designed toy as it slipped over my skin and my balls drew up tight against my body.

"Wha…No!" I cried, staring at him in shock as he stopped moving and his fist clamped around the base of my shaft until my orgasm retreated.

"I told you I wanted to play, Landon. Have you ever been edged before?" I knew he was referring to the practice of bringing someone to the edge of climax only to stop before they reach their goal. The idea was that the pressure would build and make the orgasm that much greater.

"No, but I've heard of it. I'm more of an instant gratification type of guy," I said through clenched teeth.

Micah laughed. "Too bad you're not making the decisions then, isn't it?"

I glared at him which only made him laugh harder. He slid the toy over my dripping cock and began his slow torture once again. After a few strokes he dipped his head between my spread legs and licked over my hole.

"Micaaaaahhh…" I moaned, my hands gripping the sheets tightly. His movements ceased and he squeezed the base of my cock. "Bastard," I growled.

"That's not very nice," he chuckled. "We can quit anytime, you just have to say the words," he reminded me. He looked at me intently, waiting to see what I would do.

"Continue," I grumbled. He presented me with a smug grin. He knew all along that I would never want him to stop; we both knew. He went through the cycle several more times until I had sweat dripping down my face and I was tossing my head from side to side on the pillow, delirious with my need to come. He added a finger to the mix and was stroking my prostate while simultaneously sliding the toy up and down my shaft.

"Please, please, please," I chanted mindlessly.

"Okay, baby. You can come," he conceded.

I wanted to weep at those words. I felt the burn that had lingered at the base of my spine shoot up throughout the rest of me. My balls were full and snug against my body, ready to unload their seed. Just as I was about to spill over he pulled the toy off, tossing it aside and covered my cock with his lips, sliding his mouth down until I was deep in his throat.

"Micah!" I screamed as I shot spurt after spurt of cum. I could feel him swallowing around me and then his fingers swept over my prostate one more time and I felt myself floating away.

Someone tugged on my arms and legs, freeing them. I heard his voice and it sounded as if it were far away. "Landon, come on, baby. Come back to me." He brushed gentle kisses over my cheeks, my forehead and the tip of my nose. I felt boneless and my eyelids were heavy as I pried them open to see his gorgeous face.

"My Micah," I slurred. A strange look flickered across his face, but was gone before I could read too much into it.

"How do you feel, baby?" He brushed my hair back from my face and smiled at me.

"I think I lost consciousness," I admitted.

"I think you're right," he agreed with a gentle laugh. We kissed lazily for several minutes until a thought occurred to me.

"Wait, what about you?"

His cheeks colored slightly as he grinned at me. "I already came. Watching you come apart so beautifully, hearing your cries and tasting you…it was all too much and it sent me over the edge with you."

I tilted my head up and kissed him again, wrapping my arms around his neck and deepening the kiss. He reached down and grabbed the blanket, pulling it over us and I sighed happily as our combined body heat seeped into my bones. Micah scooted over to lie next to me, but I smiled when he pulled me towards him and wrapped his arms around me. I tucked my head under his chin and let the sound of his heartbeat lull me to sleep. It didn't matter how far around the world I travelled; right there in the arms of the man I loved was my happy place.

CHAPTER
Eleven

Micah

"YES, THANK YOU FOR YOUR HELP." I HUNG UP THE PHONE and slid it into my pocket with a frustrated sigh.

"Everything okay?" I turned to see Landon walking out of the bathroom, a swirl of steam following him out from his shower. He wasn't looking at me as he absently ran a towel through his thick chestnut hair so I took a moment to admire him. Water dripped down his neck, through the soft hairs covering his pecs, and trailed over his abs before pooling in the towel that hung low on his hips.

"Micah?" I heard a deep chuckle and glanced up to find Landon watching me, a sexy smirk playing on his lips.

"I'd apologize, but I'm not sorry for ogling you. You're a gorgeous man, Landon." I stepped closer to him and placed my hands on his hips. He wore a pleased smile as I leaned in for a kiss. His arms came up to wrap around my neck as we deepened the kiss and my cock began to swell as I swallowed his soft moans.

"I want you," I told him as my fingers worked to untie the towel, letting it drop to the floor.

"Take me," he whispered as I bent down to lick one nipple. It peaked under my ministrations and I sucked it into my mouth, making him buck against me. He tasted clean, fresh, and manly and I couldn't get enough. I wanted to explore every single inch of him, taking the time to find each one of his pleasure zones. Unfortunately, we didn't have time for all of that because we had a flight to catch.

"This will have to be quick, baby." I licked my way up the side of his neck as he rutted against me.

"Quick is good," he said and I could hear the urgency in his voice. He wanted me as much as I wanted him.

The night before had been amazing. Landon had given himself to me beautifully; following my instructions and showing incredible restraint as I pushed him further and further to the edge. Then there was the moment when he was still on the cusp of unconsciousness when he had whispered, *My Micah* and my heart nearly stopped.

I had always been somewhat of a lone wolf. Growing up, I had to look out for myself because my father certainly wasn't going to do it. Then right after graduation, I enlisted with the navy where even though I had brothers watching my back, I was still ultimately responsible for my own safety.

Of course I had Giovanni, but I was never going to be the number one person in his life. Caleb and Sarah were, which was exactly as it should be. Lying there with Landon though and hearing his words, was the first time I had ever felt like I truly belonged to another person and I clung to that, desperately wanting it to be true.

However, in the harsh light of day I realized that it had most likely been the endorphins making him say that. There was no way a man as special as Landon, with so much love inside him, would ever choose to claim someone like me as his own. How could he when he was trusting me to keep his brother safe, all the while not knowing what a failure I was? I pushed the thoughts from my head as I pulled him towards the bed, determined to make the most of whatever time I had with him.

Landon lay down and I followed, quickly covering him with my body. We shared a passionate kiss, our hardened cocks rubbing against each other with each movement of our hips. I reached for the lube that was still on the nightstand and poured a liberal amount on my fingers before moving to kneel between his legs.

"Spread yourself wide for me, Landon. I want to see your pretty pink hole." I sat mesmerized as he grabbed his legs behind the knees and pulled them to his chest. The way he gave himself so freely to me every time, without question, was very humbling and I had to swallow hard around the sudden lump in my throat. If he only knew what he did to me, he would know that he was the one with all of the control because when I was with him, I could feel myself coming undone.

"Perfect," I whispered as I circled his opening with the tip of one finger. I watched as my finger breached him, sliding in to the second knuckle. He bucked against me and my eyes flew to his face, making sure I hadn't hurt him.

"Please, Micah. I need more." He groaned loudly as I added a second finger, twisting it to open him up and I reached for my cock and began rubbing my hand up and down it. I curved my fingers up, letting them graze over that special spot inside him and his hips lifted off the bed as he cried out.

"So responsive," I murmured. When his muscles had relaxed and he began to flex himself around my fingers, I pulled them out and grabbed a condom, quickly sheathing myself. I didn't want to wait another minute to be inside him. I lay down on the bed next to him and he looked at me questioningly.

"I want you to ride me," I told him as I stroked my dick. His usually golden eyes had darkened to a rich brown as he climbed up to straddle my waist.

I held the base of my shaft to help guide it in as he slowly lowered himself onto me. He fit around me like a glove, his smooth walls hugging my cock tightly. I was surrounded by his blazing heat and I watched his face, contorted in concentration as he struggled to fit all of me inside, taking me deeper in that position than he had ever done before.

Finally, he was fully seated, his ass resting on my groin. I grabbed onto his hips and squeezed them with my hands to hold him steady so that the moment wouldn't end before I had the chance to make it good for him. He reached down and ran his fingertips over my brow as he waited for me to gain control. I stared up at him and he gave me a gentle smile. I didn't want to read too much into the look, but it was getting harder and harder to hold onto my heart when he was near.

"I need you to move." I took a steadying breath as he lifted himself up and then slid back down slowly. His tight ring squeezed my cock perfectly and I had the strange notion that we had been made exactly for each other. He undulated his hips as I ran my hands over the expanse of his chest, threading my fingers through the downy hairs there. I slid my hand over his abs and down further to the juncture of his thighs. When he lifted up, I circled my cock with my fingers right at the point where we connected. He hovered there as I slid my finger around his slick opening and slowly pushed my finger in alongside my cock.

I felt him tense. "You can do it, baby. You'll take anything I give you because you know it will please me." He cried out at the added pressure to his already stretched hole, but soon I was in all of the way and his head slumped forward in relief.

"That was very good, Landon. Very good." He lifted his head and smiled dreamily. His eyes were unfocused and I knew he was completely blissed out. I gently removed my finger and gripped his hips.

"Lift up, baby. I'm going to finish us off."

He was shaky, but managed to raise himself and I began lifting my hips, thrusting into him with precision and aiming for his prostate. His cock bobbed as he met my thrusts enthusiastically and I grabbed it, stroking him up and down in sync with our movements.

"Micah, I'm going to come," he gasped.

"Do it. Cover me with it," I told him, my own orgasm creeping in.

I watched in awe as he threw his head back, screaming my name as he came, hot ribbons of cum landing on my chest and shooting up to my chin. He was glorious. My own orgasm swelled over me like a tidal wave, pulling me under and spinning me wildly until I finally surfaced, gasping for air.

As I struggled to fill my lungs, I noticed that Landon was cleaning me, licking his own cum from my chest. I pulled him up and crushed my mouth to his, groaning as I tasted his seed on his tongue. He lowered his head to my shoulder, nuzzling his way into the crook of my neck and I couldn't help but smile at how cute it was. I wrapped my arms around him protectively as he let out a contented sigh.

"I think I'm going to need another shower," he said with a yawn.

"Come on, sleepy head, I'll shower with you and then we need to get going." Wincing, he climbed from the bed. I chuckled as I saw the way he moved gingerly into the bathroom and he scowled at me over his shoulder.

"That's all your fault. Well, you and the anaconda between your legs," he grumbled. I couldn't help the laugh that escaped me at his pitiful face, but I slid my arms around his waist and kissed his pouting lips, sucking the bottom one into my mouth until I felt him relax in my arms. I glanced over my shoulder at the clock.

"If you don't mind missing breakfast, I can make it up to you in the shower," I offered.

"I'm not hungry for food anyway," he said, pulling me towards the shower.

—· ——⟫•⟨—— ·—

"So, who were you talking to earlier?" Landon asked me as we rode to the airport.

After another shower where I spent most of the time on my knees, we had gone to his room so he could gather his belongings while I checked in with Tony, Carlos, and Greg. They assured me that everything was running according to plan and they would be escorting Carter and the other members of the band to the airport where they would meet us for the long flight home. Fortunately, Lachlan had provided a company jet so we didn't have the hassle of going through a crowded security checkpoint.

"When?" I asked distractedly, as he threaded his fingers through mine. All night and into the morning we had been in our own intimate bubble and I dreaded the chaos and noise that would accompany us as we landed back in the United States. I couldn't imagine how difficult it must be for Carter and Ryan to always be in the public eye.

"When I got out of the shower the first time. You seemed upset." He looked at me directly and I was struck again with how gorgeous he was.

"Oh, yeah. I was speaking with the police. They questioned the man, but he didn't tell them anything new so they searched his apartment."

"And?" Landon prompted.

I sighed heavily. "It was about what I expected. He had a huge shrine made in Carter's honor. Magazine photos and articles plastered all over the walls along with other memorabilia he had collected along the way. No blue stationery though."

"So he wasn't the one sending the letters," he said and I pulled him closer, hating the look of disappointment in his eyes.

"It doesn't look like it, but they placed a restraining order against him and they're holding him while they look for the employee who gave him the badge. Apparently, the man skipped town and none of his friends have heard from him."

"So we're back at square one then," Landon said gloomily.

"Hey, we will find the person responsible and we'll stop them. I won't let anything happen to your brother," I assured him.

"I know you won't," he whispered, cupping my cheek with his hand and kissing me softly. With a contented sigh, he rested his head on my shoulder. I put my arm around him and stroked his hair absentmindedly as I stared out the window, not really seeing the scenery as it passed by. Landon had so much faith in me and I would rather die than let him down.

The flight home was long and most of us used the opportunity to recline the plush leather seats and catch up on sleep before all of the craziness of the tour picked back up again. When I woke, Landon's head was laying on my chest and he had pulled a blanket over the two of us.

I rubbed the sleep from my eyes, careful not to disturb the warm man cuddled against me and turned to find Carter watching us from the couch directly across from me. Ryan was sleeping with his head in Carter's lap and I noticed sheet music spread out on the space beside him. I stiffened, unsure what his reaction to seeing me with his brother would be, but he gave me a soft smile.

"Thank you," he whispered.

"What for?" I asked curiously.

He tilted his head towards Landon who continued to sleep peacefully. "I haven't seen my brother this relaxed in a long time, maybe ever." His eyes took on a faraway look as he spoke. "We've always been extremely close as far as siblings go, all of my siblings are. Something changed with Landon along the way, though. He still loves us, still would do anything for us, but he stopped sharing certain details about his life with us." He looked back at me and I could see the pain in his eyes.

"I know something happened that he doesn't want us to know

about and we've all worried about him. He became agitated, restless as if he couldn't get comfortable in his own skin. He quit eating the way he should and I knew he wasn't sleeping well." He smiled up at me. "Lately, he seems to be taking better care of himself, he's obviously sleeping better," he said with a chuckle.

"There's a light in his eyes again that I was afraid had burned out forever. I feel like I'm getting my old brother back again; the real one that laughs a lot and enjoys life instead of simply going through the motions."

"Why are you thanking me though?" I asked him, bewildered.

Dimples formed at the corners of his mouth as he smiled at me. "Because you're the reason he's finally happy again," he answered easily.

I stared at him blankly for a moment before gazing down at the man we were discussing. Could Carter be right? Was there any way that I had made Landon happy? Sure, I had helped him during his panic attacks by giving him something else to focus on, but could Landon actually feel for me even a fraction of what I felt for him?

I glanced back over at Carter to ask him something, but Ryan had woken up and the two of them were staring lovingly at each other. I looked away to give them some privacy. I concentrated on my breathing to slow my pounding heart. Regardless of what Landon did or did not feel for me, I needed to stay focused on the job at hand.

Just as I had predicted, chaos erupted as we landed in New York. People were screaming, women were fainting, and camera flashes blinded us as we climbed into the waiting limos. The band would be staying at a hotel in the city for a few nights as they did a series of interviews for local television and news programs. Then they would continue on with the concert schedule, making their way across several states before completing the tour in Chicago.

The schedule was an exhausting one, but I took comfort in knowing that I would be near Landon. Already it was becoming painful to think about when the tour ended and our jobs took us in different directions. Once the threat to Carter was behind us, I would return to work at *Hamilton Security* and I assumed Landon would leave on another tour, either with Carter's Creed again or one of the many other bands he managed.

After we had checked in at the hotel, Landon went with Carter and the rest of the band to do a few interviews. I sent my three men along with a couple of the security team members Lachlan had provided to accompany them. I knew it was probably overkill, but after what had happened in Europe, I wasn't taking any chances.

I hung up my dress shirts and slacks so they wouldn't get wrinkled and unpacked my toiletries then I called Mary to check on things at the office. She assured me that everything was fine and that the two new men I had hired to help out in our absence were doing a great job. I was pleased to hear that our case load had nearly doubled because it meant that my business was really taking off.

I hung up and looked around the large room. I felt antsy so I decided to go for a run. There was something about the letters that had been tickling the back of my mind, but so far had remained out of my reach. It was aggravating, like being unable to think of a person's name; you knew it was right there on the tip of your tongue, but you just couldn't say it.

I pulled on a pair of loose jogging pants and a hoodie because it was a bit cold outside and laced up my running shoes. Running had always allowed me to clear my mind and focus better. I hoped that it would work again to help me figure out what it was that I was missing. I stepped outside of the hotel and sent a quick text to Tony letting him know where I was going in case he needed to reach me. I plugged my headphones into my phone and scrolled to my favorite playlist. It was a beautiful day out and I enjoyed the fresh air and the sun on my face as I began a steady jog.

The sidewalks weren't terribly crowded, but I still had to weave in and out of people so when I saw a nearby park I decided to head over to where it was less populated to finish my run. Soon I had a steady pace going and I could feel sweat dripping down my back and soaking the front of my shirt. It was invigorating and I loved it.

Music filled my ears, cutting out the sounds of the city and I let my mind sift through all of the letters Carter had received so far. They had been arriving at different intervals over a period of months, and were gaining in intensity. The last letter had stated that the writer was going to prove that they could give Carter what no one else could, which had me on high alert because it sounded like the person was tired of waiting and may possibly be planning to make their move.

The writer had used the forget-me-not flower stamp on each letter which hinted that it was not a random person sending them, but perhaps someone Carter knew. The words themselves, I believed had been chosen just as carefully. The question was, what other message was the person trying to send him?

I heard the pounding of my heart echoing within the earbuds as my phone switched songs. The familiar beat of an old song filled my head and my steps faltered as the singer began the haunting lyrics until I eventually stopped moving all together. I doubled over, placing my hands on my knees as I gulped for air and let the words sink in.

Everything clicked into place like pieces of a jigsaw puzzle fitting together and a cold chill ran through me. The person sending the letters definitely had a hidden message and I had finally figured it out. I took off at a dead run back to the hotel. I knew what the message was, all that was left was figuring out what it meant to Carter. Then we would know who was sending the letters and I could put a stop to them before they hurt anyone.

CHAPTER
Twelve

Landon

I RODE BACK TO THE HOTEL WITH CARTER, RYAN, AND GREG. THE band had successfully pulled off three back to back interviews where my brother, being his usual self, charmed the pants off of everyone including the lovely Robin Roberts. The rest of the band had decided to explore the city and they took Carlos and Tony with them, but Carter was tired so he and Ryan decided to go back to the hotel and order in room service.

I told them that I was tired too, but the truth was, I was anxious to see Micah. The hours that I'd spent following the band around had been the longest I had been away from him in quite a while and I found myself missing him as the day dragged on.

We were laughing when we got off the elevator onto our floor as Carter told us what Robin had whispered to him during a commercial

136

break. The laughter died in my throat though when I saw Micah pacing back and forth through the hallway, his hands linked together over his head. My heart began to beat faster as I wondered what had happened and I rushed over to him.

"Micah, what's wrong?" He lowered his arms and I noticed some of the tension seeping out of his body when he saw us. He shared a look with Greg who was standing alert and ready for whatever his boss needed from him.

"We need to talk. All of us." He looked at each of us and I saw the concern I felt mirrored on both Carter and Ryan's faces.

"Do you want the rest of the band here?" Carter asked.

Micah shook his head as he led us to his room. "Not yet. I'd rather keep this as private as possible for as long as we can."

We filed into the room and Micah motioned for us to take a seat. Carter and Ryan sat together on the couch, holding hands, while Greg chose to remain standing. I perched on the edge of a chair, following Micah with my eyes as he moved around the room to his briefcase where he pulled out a file and highlighter.

He walked back over, holding the file up for us to see. "These are copies of each of the letters we've received so far."

He sat down across from me, using the coffee table to spread the letters out in order. We watched quietly as he bent over the papers, highlighting certain sentences and phrases. When he was finished, he shuffled the papers around and spread them out in an alternate order then he looked up at us, his expression grim.

"There's been something about these letters that continued to nag at me. I couldn't put my finger on what it was exactly, but I felt like the sender was trying to tell us something."

"You mean something other than the fact that they're a total wackjob?" Carter asked.

"Yes," Micah answered with a smirk. "Something other than that. I kept feeling like there was a hidden message, something only Carter would understand."

"Wait a minute. Are you saying that the person may actually be someone Carter knows and not just some obsessed fan?" Ryan asked, pulling Carter tighter to his side.

"That's exactly what I think and I've figured out what the hidden message was," Micah replied, looking at us levelly. I held my breath, waiting to hear what he had discovered.

"While you guys were gone, I decided to go for a run to help clear my head. I was thinking about the letters and listening to music as I ran. When the song changed, it all became clear." He looked to Carter. "I need you to listen to this and tell me if it means anything to you, okay?"

Carter nodded his head and Micah hit play on his phone. As the song began to play he pointed out the words he had highlighted from the letters. Carter and Ryan bent over to see the words Micah was pointing to, but I couldn't move because I was suddenly frozen to my seat.

I read a study once that claimed that memories are stimulated by high levels of emotions. For most of us, music brings about emotions, therefore music, at least certain songs from our past, can trigger memories. From the very first note, memories began to flood my system; memories that I had spent years pushing down into a box. By the time Sting started crooning "Every Breath You Take," I was shaking and my teeth began to chatter.

Micah sounded like he was talking underwater as he pointed out the words. From the first letter: "You are more beautiful, *every single day*," and the second letter: "When I close my eyes, *I can only see your face*. You are my forever." With each letter, I could feel the box opening more, releasing the ugliness I had tried to keep hidden. I wanted to slam the lid on it, lock it tight, and throw away the key, but I couldn't make my body move.

My eyes moved to Carter and I could suddenly breathe easier as a new thought occurred to me. I needed to tell them what had happened; it was time to be honest about my shameful past. I looked at each of their faces and I knew that once I had told them everything, they probably wouldn't look at me the same way, they may even hate me as much as I hated myself for what I'd done. As much as it would kill me if that happened, none of it mattered. The only thing that mattered was letting them know that my brother was safe.

"Turn the music off." Micah's head shot up and he frowned at me. "Please, Micah. I need you to turn it off." He must have seen the seriousness in my eyes because he reached for his phone and hit stop. "We had it all wrong, the person sending the letters isn't after Carter."

"What are you talking about?" Micah asked.

"He was never after Carter; it's me he wants," I explained with a smile.

"I'm going to need you to explain, Landon. And while you're at it maybe you can explain why the fuck you're smiling." I was shocked by the anger in Micah's voice; I'd never seen him so furious. His face was red and his hands were fisted. He looked like he'd been wound too tight and was ready to explode at any minute.

"Don't you understand? Carter's safe!" I turned to look at my brother. "You can go wherever you want. You can tour the whole world and not have to constantly check over your shoulder to see who's following. That's all I've ever wanted for you; to be able to play your music, live your life, and be happy."

I looked at each of their faces in confusion. Micah had stood and was pacing the floor behind the couch. Carter had tears streaming down his face as he came over to me and wrapped his arms around me. I held him as he sobbed onto my shoulder, rubbing my hands over his back soothingly. I looked to Ryan for an answer, but he just gave me a sad smile and nodded his head like he understood.

When his tears had slowed, Carter looked at me. "You are the most amazing big brother anyone could ever ask for. You made sure no one ever picked on me for being smaller or for being gay. You drove me to my music lessons before I got my license and you came to all of my performances when I was playing in dive bars. You've managed my band, making sure I was never taken advantage of and that I got the best deals possible. You have spent your whole life making sure I was safe and happy, but, Landon…" He paused to take a warbled breath as more tears filled his eyes. "Landon, you have to know that *your* safety and *your* happiness is just as important to me, to all of us."

"He's right," Micah exclaimed vehemently. Carter made room as Micah stormed back over and sat on the edge of the coffee table in front of me, taking my hands in his. His voice was softer as he spoke to me. "We're all glad that Carter's safe, but your safety is important too." He squeezed my hands. "It's everything," he whispered.

My eyes widened as I looked into his eyes. The emotions I saw swirling there had my heart flipping inside my chest. Was it possible that Micah felt the same way about me that I felt about him? I pushed the hope that was starting to swell back down before I could let it take over. I still had to tell them about my past and I knew that my words would probably change everything.

"Landon, you said it's you he wants. You know who's sending the letters?" Micah asked. His eyes narrowed as I pulled my hands from his and stood. This was going to be difficult enough, I wasn't sure I could do it facing them. I walked over to the large window and stared out at the busy city below.

"I never had a boyfriend growing up. I kissed a few guys in high school, but I was too busy with basketball, the various clubs I was in, and making sure my grades stayed up to really get involved with someone. When I went away to college, I decided it was time to cut loose and have some fun. I made friends, went to a few parties and eventually I met Noah. Everyone on campus knew who he was; he was popular, gorgeous, quarterback of the football team, and for some unknown reason, I was the one he wanted."

I turned around when I heard Micah growl. He looked pissed off, but I continued, knowing he was just going to get angrier with me as my story unfolded. "We dated for a few months and I liked him a lot, I even brought him home for Thanksgiving to meet my family." I shoved my hands into my pockets and felt the little marble toy Micah had given me to use when I was feeling anxious. I grasped onto it like a lifeline and began to work it through my fingers and I watched Micah's expression soften when he saw what I was doing.

"By the time we got back to school, I had made the decision that Noah would be my first." I glanced around the room, sure that my face had turned pink, but they all just looked at me, waiting to hear the rest. "He had been asking since our second date and I had put him off, wanting to get to know him better first. I was surprised that he had been so patient with me, especially when he could have had any guy he wanted. After the weekend with my family, I felt like we had gotten to know each other well enough so I waited for a night when I knew his roommate usually was at work and I headed over to his dorm."

My eyes became unfocused as I remembered the scene I walked in on. "I got to his room and the door was unlocked so I went in. He didn't notice me at first because he was too busy being spit roasted by his roommate and another guy I had seen around campus," I ground out. "I figured out why he didn't mind waiting for me to put out, it was because he was already getting it on a regular basis."

"Landon, I'm so sorry that happened to you," Carter said as I walked over to the mini fridge and pulled out a bottle of water. My throat was dry from purging myself so I sucked down the entire bottle. I looked at Micah who looked like he wanted to crush something with his bare hands.

"Don't be," I told him. "At least I found out before I slept with him. Besides, that's not the worst part of my story." I walked back over to the chair and sank down tiredly. I stared at the bottle in my hands, picking at the label nervously. I wished I could stop right there and never have to see the disappointment and disgust on their faces that was sure to come, but I had already come that far. It was time to end it.

"I was devastated and I ended up pulling away from everyone. I turned down my friends' offers to go out until eventually they stopped asking. I quit going home as often because I knew everyone would know something was wrong and I didn't want to talk about it. My grades slipped so badly, I was in danger of failing all of my classes." I sucked in a deep breath.

"That's when Kyle, Professor Brooks, stepped in. He was my psychology professor and he asked me to stop by his office one day after class to talk about a paper that I had recently turned in. He said he was concerned with the changes he'd seen in me, both with my grades and physically. He'd always been very friendly, kind, easy to talk to, and I ended up pouring my heart out to him. I told him all about Noah and how I had almost let him be my first, but then he had hurt me."

I cleared my throat. *Time to rip the Band-Aid off.* "He listened to every word and then he wiped my tears away as he told me that I deserved so much better than someone like Noah. He told me that he had been watching me for some time and he thought I was brilliant and witty and stunning. I had been feeling so low about myself since Noah cheated on me. I thought that there was something wrong with me that drove him to find someone else. Kyle's words were exactly what I needed to hear. He made me feel desirable again, so I didn't stop him when he kissed me." I stared at the floor, refusing to meet their eyes as shame washed over me.

"I knew it was wrong and that he could get in trouble for dating a student, but I needed someone to *want* me so badly that I ignored all of that and dove right in. Kyle was much older than me, almost twenty years older, but I didn't care; he was sexy and mature and worldly. I fell in love with him and soon we were having sex. We had to sneak around so he wouldn't lose his job, but I thought it just added to the thrill. He told me he loved me and I believed him."

I took a deep breath. "This went on for a few months until one day I went to his office to see him. The door was open when I got there and I saw that he was with someone so I waited in the hallway. It was a woman and a little boy. I couldn't hear everything they were saying, but I heard the little boy call him Daddy. I was shocked because Kyle had never mentioned that he was bisexual and he certainly never told me that he had a child. I stood there in that hallway, praying that the woman was his ex and was just there to let him see his little boy, but then I watched as he kissed her."

I sucked in a shaky breath as tears poured down my cheeks. It was humiliating having to relive all of that in front of them so I was shocked then when Micah strode over, knelt down in front of my chair, and pulled me into his arms. He didn't say a word, just held me as I cried, letting all of the hurt, betrayal, and guilt flow out of me.

"Why didn't you tell any of us what you were going through back then, Landon?" I looked over Micah's shoulder at Carter. He had his arms wrapped around himself as if he were holding himself together and he had tears streaming down his face.

I hung my head, unable to look at him. "Because I was so ashamed of what I had done. Don't you see? I was the *other woman* so to speak. How could I look at Mom or Dad or any of the rest of you when I could barely stand to look at myself?"

Hands lifted my chin and I looked up into Micah's face. His eyes shown with compassion and it nearly did me in. "You didn't do anything wrong. You trusted the wrong man, a man who never deserved your trust and certainly not your love. *He* was the one who lied and didn't tell you that he was married and *he* was the one who betrayed his vows to his wife, not you." Micah looked so sure of the things he was saying and I wanted to believe him so badly, but I had spent years feeling guilty for my part in the betrayal and it was hard to just switch that off.

When I hesitated, he continued. "Tell me something, Landon. If Kyle had told you from the very beginning that he was married and had a child, would you have started a relationship with him?"

"Of course not," I said with a scowl. "I wouldn't have even kissed him."

"Why not?" he asked.

"Because I'm not like that," I said with disgust.

"Exactly," Micah said with a satisfied smirk. I glanced behind him when I heard Carter and Ryan start to chuckle. Even Greg looked like he was fighting back a laugh and that got me chuckling. Soon we were all laughing which did wonders for clearing some of the tension in the room.

"Landon," Carter said after a few minutes, sounding more serious. "I understand why you didn't tell the family at the time; your emotions were too raw, but I hope you realize now that there's nothing in the world you could tell us that would make us quit loving you or make you lose our respect."

I swallowed thickly. "Thank you. I'm very lucky to have you for a brother."

"I feel the same way. I've always wanted to be just like you, well, except for the whole terrible taste in men thing you've got going on," he teased, jumping back when I swatted at him.

"I think I've gotten much better at it actually." I sneaked a peek at Micah out of the corner of my eye, but he looked lost in thought so I wasn't sure he had heard me.

"Okay, if everyone will have a seat, we have a few other things to discuss," Micah said. We all sat down and I let out a long breath, feeling like the weight of the world had been lifted from my shoulders. I had finally come clean about my past and it seemed like everyone still cared about me. Nothing else mattered at that point.

CHAPTER
Thirteen

Micah

"LANDON, I KNOW THAT TELLING US ABOUT YOUR PAST WAS very difficult, but I need you to tell me a few more things." I could see how worn out he was and I felt bad for asking him to dredge up any more painful memories, but my first concern was and would always be, keeping him safe. If Kyle was going to come after him, I was going to be there to stop him.

"What do you want to know?" he asked wearily.

"What happened after you saw him kissing his wife? Did you confront him?"

Landon winced. "I felt like I was going to throw up actually, so I ran to the nearest bathroom. He didn't have a clue that I had seen him until a week later. He'd called, but I wasn't ready to face him yet so I lied and said I was sick."

"That's understandable," I told him.

"I never wanted to see him again so I dropped his class right away. When he got the notice from the college that I had officially withdrawn, that's when he started to lose it."

"What do you mean by lose it?" I asked.

Landon rubbed the back of his neck uncomfortably. "He started calling me constantly, all day and throughout the night. He left notes on my car windshield and even showed up at my dorm, which he had never done when we were dating for fear of being found out. I finally decided that the only way I would get him to go away was to confront him about what I saw."

"What did he have to say about that?" Carter growled. I could tell he was pissed off and it made me smile to see Landon's little brother jumping to his defense.

"He was shocked at first that I had seen them and I could see the regret in his eyes. He told me that his parents would never have approved of him being gay so he started dating a woman he met one night at a bar and eventually they got married and had a son. He said he tried to love her and in his own way he did care about her, but being with her intimately and always having to live a lie was torture. He confessed that he'd been with a few men during his marriage, but that he'd never felt about any of them the way he felt about me. He said he was completely in love with me."

I cleared my throat. I was having a hard time hearing about another man being in love with Landon, no matter what the end result had been. It took everything in me not to drag Landon into the bedroom so I could remind him who he really belonged to.

"I told him that I couldn't be with him anymore; that not only had he lied to me, but he was also using me to cheat on his wife and that I refused to be a part of it," Landon explained.

"How did he take it?" Ryan asked.

Landon shook his head sadly. "He cried, begged me to take him back, said he would leave his wife if it meant he could be with me. I told him that I didn't want to be the reason a marriage ended and that what we had was over for good. When he started to get angry, I left. I avoided areas where I knew he'd be and I stayed in my room as much as possible, often showing up to my classes at the last minute so that there would be plenty of students around if he tried to talk to me. It didn't matter though, he continued to harass me, sending flowers to my dorm room, calling non-stop. Then one morning I went out to my car and he had written all over my windows, *I'll be watching you*."

"Why that song?" I interrupted.

"He used to tell me that he knew he was going to fall in love with me from the very first time he saw me. He said he'd watch me sitting there in his class and wish that I was his, but I was with Noah at the time." Landon winced as his eyes darted over to me. "He said it was our song and he liked to play it during sex."

I ran my hands over my face, trying to get myself under control. The last thing I wanted was to add to his stress by letting him see how much this conversation bothered me, but the truth was, just the thought of some other man having his hands on Landon, touching his body, made me want to kill someone. Not just hurt them, kill them. I had never felt so much possessive rage before in my life.

"I'd eventually had enough. I couldn't file a complaint with the dean because I knew Kyle would probably lose his job which would hurt his wife and kid and I figured I'd already done enough damage to them." Landon held his hands up when we all started to protest. "That's how I felt about it at the time. Anyway, he wasn't letting me go and I didn't see any other option so I transferred to a different school and moved back home so I could commute. I told my parents that I was just homesick and wanted to be closer to the family."

"I feel really bad about giving you such a hard time because I had to give you back your old room. I was so pissed that I had to share a room with Caleb again," Carter said with a sheepish grin.

Landon laughed. "You weren't as mad as Caleb was. Carter used to have a lot of trouble picking up after himself," he explained.

"Used to? Sometimes I think we have carpet instead of hardwood floors because he has so many clothes laying around," Ryan chimed in, laughing when Carter elbowed him in the stomach.

"Have you ever heard from Kyle again?" I asked.

"He sent a few letters to the house right after I moved back, but eventually they stopped when I had them returned. Then one day out of the blue he sent me a note. I didn't recognize the address so I opened it. He said that I was his one true love and that he would never let go of me. I didn't respond of course and that was the last time I heard from him."

"How long ago was that?"

"I guess about two or three years ago." Landon covered his mouth as he yawned.

"Okay, I think that's enough for one night; we all need to get some rest." Everyone stood and I pulled Greg aside as Landon said goodnight to Carter and Ryan.

"I don't like this at all and I'm going to need some time to come up with a plan. The whole time I thought we were dealing with an obsessed fan, but this is something entirely different."

"Yeah, I agree," Greg said, his face showing how seriously he was taking the threats. "What do you want me to do?"

"Get the others up to date on what's changed and then I want you guys to continue watching over everyone. If this guy really wants to get to Landon, he may use his friends and family to do it." Greg nodded and started to leave, but I grabbed his arm to stop him. "Just tell the others as much as you absolutely have to. I don't want to make Landon feel any more uncomfortable than he already does, so the less people that know the details, the better."

Greg looked affronted. "I would never tell personal things about your man, you know me better than that." He rolled his eyes at the shocked look on my face. "Seriously, man? I was special forces just like you. I was trained to sniff out terrorists, I think I can figure out when my boss is in love."

"Shut up," I hissed, checking over my shoulder to make sure no one had heard. Luckily, they were in the middle of some type of three-way hug. I scowled at Greg who threw his head back in a laugh. I could still hear him laughing as he made his way down the hallway.

Carter and Ryan left after that and I shut the door behind them, turning to Landon. "I'm going to head to my room," he said.

"You're not going anywhere," I informed him.

"I'm sorry, Micah, but I'm exhausted. I just want to curl up in bed and forget about the entire day." I hated how hesitant he looked, like he wasn't sure if I'd be alright with the fact that he didn't want to have sex. Didn't he know that he meant so much more to me than just sex? The answer hit me hard. How could he know when I never told him?

"Landon, I want you to stay here…with me." I cleared my throat, shoving my hands into my pockets. "You've had a very rough day and I need to hold you while you go to sleep. I just want to hold you," I repeated. I had never voiced my feelings for another man before and it came out sounding awkward and lame, but the smile on Landon's face told me that I had done something right.

"I'd like that very much," he said quietly, his arm brushing mine as he walked around me and into the bedroom. I let out a long breath that I hadn't realized I'd been holding and turned to follow him.

Neither one of us spoke as we undressed. I got into bed and held the covers up for him to climb in next to me, but he lay on his own side instead. Landon seemed a little shy and I figured it was because we had never gone to bed together without me taking control and telling him what to do.

"You'll have to come closer if I'm going to hold you," I teased.

He bit down on the corner of his lip and smiled as he slid closer to me. I pulled him so that his back was pressed against my chest and wrapped my arm around his waist. It was dark in the room except for the lights from the city that made their way through the gauzy curtains. We were up high though so instead of being intrusive, they cast a soft, cozy glow in the room.

His skin was warm under my palm and I absentmindedly ran my fingers in circles around his navel, feeling the soft hairs of his happy trail. I breathed in the smell of his skin and laid gentle kisses along his shoulder, making him sigh happily. I pulled my hips back discreetly when I felt myself becoming aroused. I told him that I was just going to hold him and I meant it, but other parts of my body were protesting being that close to the beautiful man and not taking him.

"Are you disappointed in me?" Landon whispered so quietly I almost didn't hear him. I could feel the tension in his body as he waited for my response.

I shifted him until he was lying on his back and I could look down at him. I needed him to see my face so he would know that I was being completely honest with what I was about to say. "Absolutely not, Landon. I've known since I met you that you are a good man with a kind heart and a strong moral compass."

"But you heard what I did," he said, worrying his bottom lip with his teeth. I tugged it gently with my thumb and smoothed over the marks left behind.

"I listened to every word you said and it only confirmed what an outstanding man you are. Landon, it was not your fault that you opened your heart up to the wrong man. You needed him at the time and you trusted him. As soon as you found out the truth, you ended it. Even though it had to have broken your heart, you took the high road and placed his family's needs above your own. I think you're amazing."

We stared at each other for several moments until he reached up slowly, slid his hand around my neck, and pulled me down for a kiss. It wasn't full of passion and desperation as most of our kisses up to that point had been, instead it was slow and tender and I felt as if I were getting to know the real Landon for the very first time. He had finally lowered his walls and revealed everything about himself and it had only made me fall for him that much harder.

Landon was extremely close with his family and it had to have been very difficult to carry a secret like that around for so long, worrying that he would lose their love and respect if they knew the truth. I suspected that the guilt he had felt from that time in his life was at the root of his panic attacks and as much as I hoped that his anxiety would lessen now, I couldn't help but wonder what would happen when he no longer needed what I had to offer.

"Get some sleep, Landon. I'll keep you safe," I promised.

"I know you will, Micah. I trust you." My heart thrummed in my chest. I lay back and wrapped my arm around him as he settled his head on my chest. My fingers ran through his thick hair and I listened to his breaths even out as he drifted off to sleep.

I lay awake for several more hours, my mind turning wildly as I tried to plan the best course of action to ensure Landon's safety. I knew I needed to track down Kyle Brooks, locating him was a priority and I would use every resource available to do so. The problem I was having, was figuring out what to do with Landon until Kyle had been located. I thought long and hard about whether or not I should take him away somewhere. If Landon disappeared off the grid then it would make it harder for Kyle to find him, but I also knew that there was safety in numbers.

While the tour at times felt like a travelling circus, the truth was that the people involved had become an extended family of sorts. Those people would help serve as eyes and ears, making sure that no one was around who wasn't supposed to be there. Also, having Carter, Ryan, and my own security guys nearby seemed like a more logical choice than to take Landon away to some remote cabin in the woods. Although the thought of Landon lying naked on a bear skin rug in front of a roaring fire had the blood rushing to my cock. *Easy, boy, with any luck there will be time for that.* My first priority was getting the target off of his back.

I looked down at the man who slept peacefully in my arms. I couldn't understand how anyone could be lucky enough to have him in their life and then throw that opportunity away. Noah had been a selfish bastard and a complete idiot to not wait for Landon. Kyle on the other hand had the sense to realize how special Landon was and try to hold onto him, even if the way he went about it was completely wrong.

As much as I hated having anything in common with a stalker, I could understand how losing Landon would make a man go crazy. Just the thought of never getting to hold the man in my arms again made my chest ache and tied my stomach in knots. He was kinder and more giving than any man I had ever met before and it saddened me that he didn't see all of the wonderful things that I saw when I looked at him. I would have to work on changing that.

After everything he had been through and the people he had loved that had betrayed him, it surprised me that he would still be willing to put his trust in me and I didn't take that lightly. I refused to be just another man that let him down, so sooner or later I was going to have to tell him the truth about me. I knew that once he found out, he may decide that I wasn't the man he wanted there, protecting him. If that were the case, I would have to find a way to deal with it because his safety was the only thing that mattered to me. Failing him was not an option.

CHAPTER
Fourteen

Landon

I woke up as the sun was just beginning to rise and I could hear the sounds of the city outside my window as people rushed to their jobs. I stretched my arms over my head, smiling around a yawn. I'd had the best night of sleep I could remember in ages, which was weird if you considered that I had just learned that one of my exes was stalking me.

I knew it had more to do with the fact that I had fallen asleep in the arms of the man I loved. A man who now knew all of my ugly secrets and still wanted me in his bed. The question was, did he want me for anything more than that? The fact that he had held me all night without pressing me for sex left me feeling very hopeful.

I was also feeling hopeful that maybe we would have time to sneak in a little fun before our day started. I turned to him and was immediately disappointed when I discovered his side of the bed was empty. The sheets were cold which told me he had been gone for a while.

"Micah?" I called out. I frowned when there was no response and tossed the covers aside to go look for him. That's when I noticed the note on the side table.

Landon,

Sorry to leave without a proper goodbye, but I had a lot to take care of. Carlos is right outside the door, please don't go anywhere without him. Call me if you need anything.

Micah

I sighed as I set the note back down. I was disappointed not to see Micah before he left, but I appreciated the fact that he was working so hard to protect me. He had been hired to watch over Carter and since the threat to my brother was gone, he could have very easily headed back to Chicago. Especially given how busy he said his business had become. Not only had he stayed, but apparently, Carlos and the other men who worked for Micah had remained to watch over me too.

I got dressed and pulled my phone out of my pocket to check the time. I had three missed calls and a voicemail from Caleb, basically demanding that I call him back immediately. I rolled my eyes as I pulled my shoes on. As twins, it was very difficult for either of my brothers to keep secrets from the other. They shared a sixth sense, or as my mom called it, twintuition. Basically, their connection ran so deep that at times, they could feel what the other was feeling. Therefore, it only made sense that when Carter found out my secrets that Caleb would have picked up on his stress, even from miles away.

I couldn't bring myself to feel annoyed though because I had already decided that I would tell my family everything once I got back home. It had been a relief to finally tell someone else what had happened and to hear them say that it wasn't my fault. It would take time for me to fully believe that after all the years I'd spent feeling guilty, but I would continue to try. I was tired of feeling isolated and alone.

I had worn a mask in front of my family for so long, hoping they couldn't see how much pain I was in, but they had known something was wrong anyway. Then Micah came along and he was the first person to look hard enough to see the cracks in my carefully constructed façade. He knew what I needed even before I did and he had never failed me which was just one of the many reasons why I loved him.

I walked out of Micah's room and my cheeks flushed as I said hello to Carlos who gave me a nod, but I could see he was trying to hide his grin. He obviously had ideas about what had occurred in that room between me and his boss and I wondered how disappointed he'd be to find out that we had only cuddled. The thought had me grinning from ear to ear though as I walked down the hallway to my room.

Micah had been true to his word, not expecting anything from me. The way he had sheltered me in his arms, holding the rest of the world at bay, filled me with warmth. If I'd had any doubts before, the night before had proved that Micah was the right man for me. The hard part would be convincing him that we belonged together.

We stepped into my suite and I looked over the menu for room service while Carlos walked around, making sure nothing was out of place. I didn't want to seem rude so I offered to order something for Carlos as well. He assured me that he had already eaten breakfast after his routine ten-mile run and an hour in the gym. I simply nodded my head and told him that I preferred to eat *before* my twelve-mile run and hour and a half workout. He turned to me with a blank look, but I saw the twitch of his lips as his eyes swept over my body.

"Shut up," I grumbled.

"I'll just wait outside to give you some privacy," he said. Laughter filled the hallway as soon as the door shut. I quickly changed my order from a stack of pancakes to oatmeal and an apple. *Stupid, perfectly buff G.I. Joes.*

My phone started ringing as I walked into the bathroom. I knew

I wouldn't be able to hold Caleb off for much longer, but I needed a shower and coffee first. Lots of coffee.

—· ———⟫•⟨——— ·—

I got out of the shower and pulled on my robe just as there was a knock on the door. Carlos swung the door open and pushed a cart into the room. "Switch jobs?" I joked.

"Switch breakfast?" he teased back, smiling when he lifted the silver dome and saw my healthy breakfast.

"Shut up," I mumbled, but I couldn't help the grin on my face as he chuckled.

"I like you, Landon. You're alright," he said as he went back out to the hallway.

My smile spread as I realized that I had just received the stamp of approval from one of Micah's friends. I ate my breakfast quickly, kicking myself the whole time for not just ordering the pancakes. When I was finished eating and had consumed two cups of coffee, I called my brother.

"Where the hell have you been? I've been trying to call you all morning," Caleb shouted.

"I just woke up and decided to get a shower first, is that alright with you?" I countered.

I heard him sigh through the phone. "I'm sorry, Landon. I got a bad feeling before bed and I was going to call, but then Sarah got sick and I was up all night with her. I didn't get any sleep all night, but I had to call and find out what was going on."

"First of all, what's wrong with Sarah?" I asked, concerned for my new niece.

"She had a fever and kept pulling on her ear, so I'm pretty sure it's an ear infection. I'm going to call and get her in to see the pediatrician as soon as they open," he explained.

I smiled. "Caleb, you sound like a dad."

"Yeah, I do, don't I?" I could hear the smile in his voice.

"I'm happy for you," I said sincerely. Pride swelled my chest for the amazing man he had grown up to be.

"Thanks. I never dreamed I could have so much in my life. Giovanni and Sarah, they're just…" I heard him swallow.

"They're your everything, I get it."

"Yeah, they are." He cleared his throat. "Talk to me, Landon. Tell me what's going on," he said, bringing the original conversation back around.

"What has Carter told you?" I asked.

"Wha…"

"I know the two of you have been talking about me and comparing notes," I interrupted. "I also know that you both did it because you love me and you were worried about me. I love you too, Caleb."

He blew out the breath he'd probably been holding for a while. "I really do love you, Landon. Are you ready to tell me?"

I sucked in a deep breath and then began pouring my heart out for the second time. It was actually easier that time and I wasn't sure if it was because I didn't have to see Caleb's face as I told him or what it was, all I knew was that I felt even lighter when I reached the end.

Caleb was quiet for a few moments and I glanced at my phone to see if the call had dropped at some point. I hoped not, because I didn't want to have to go through all of it again. I may feel better as I released my past, but it still took an emotional toll to have to relive all of the pain and guilt.

"Landon…I'm so sorry," Caleb finally said. His voice sounded strained, like he was trying not to cry.

"It's okay, I'm doing better now. It's helped a lot to finally get it off of my chest."

"I'm glad. It kills me that you never came to any of us and told us how much pain you were in. That's what a family is for, to support and comfort each other. We love you and we would never judge you." I could hear the hurt in his voice.

Another wave of guilt washed over me, but that time it was because I hadn't trusted the people that loved me the most and in doing so, I had hurt them. "I'm sorry, Caleb, I should have trusted you all with what was going on. I guess I was so caught up in my own shame that I assumed everyone else would be ashamed of me too."

"I could never be ashamed of you, Landon. You're my big brother and I will always be proud of you and look up to you. You're one of the very finest men I know."

I closed my eyes as tears threatened to spill over. I was humbled by his words even if I didn't feel worthy of them. I promised myself that I was going to start changing that though. If everyone else was able to see good in me, then perhaps it was time I started seeing it in myself.

"Thank you, Caleb. You have no idea what that means to me," I choked out.

"Just don't keep things from us anymore, okay? You have always been the strong one, looking out for the rest of your siblings, but we're all grown up and we can help look out for you too."

"I promise, no more secrets."

"Good," he said, sounding mollified. "So do you really think it's Kyle that's been sending the letters? Do you think he's going to come after you? What do you think he wants?" I chuckled at Caleb's familiar way of tossing out question after question without waiting for an answer. *Maybe he should have been a lawyer instead of a chef.*

"I don't know who else it could be, especially using that particular song in the messages. He obviously hasn't given up, even after all the years since I saw him last and the letters sound as if he's getting more and more agitated. As for what he wants, I have no idea. I mean, I know he wants me, but what for? I made it abundantly clear that things between us were over," I explained.

"I don't like you being alone while a crazy man is targeting you. Maybe you should come home so you have all of us around to watch out for you," Caleb suggested.

I chuckled. "Caleb, I'm constantly surrounded by members of the crew, the band, and Carter and Ryan; I'm never alone. Besides that, I have Lachlan's security team at my disposal, not to mention Micah and the other three former special forces agents that he brought in to help. Seriously, there's a man standing guard outside my door that I think was a Green Beret. He's built like a tank; no one could get past him."

"I'm glad to hear it. I just have one more question."

"What?" I knew he was just worried, so I refrained from rolling my eyes.

"Does Micah do a good job of…guarding your body?"

I laughed. "I am not answering that, you little shit."

"I'll take that as a yes. I knew he'd be good at that, he's extremely good looking. Although, he's not as good looking as my husband, but not everyone can be as lucky as me," he teased.

"Poor guy, I think you're delirious from sleep deprivation. You better take a nap," I retorted.

Caleb laughed. "Maybe I will as soon as I get back from taking Sarah to the doctor. Oh, crap, I better call and get her an appointment before they fill up for the day. I've got to go, love you!"

I chuckled as I hung up. I was glad that Caleb was so happy with his life and I was relieved that both of my brothers had forgiven me for not telling them my secrets long ago. Eventually, I knew I would need to tell my sisters and my parents, but that would have to wait until I was back home and safe from Kyle.

I spent most of the day working from my room. Carter and the rest of the band had another full day of interviews, but I figured they were probably safer if they weren't around me given the fact that I was the one with a target on my back.

My mind wandered to Micah throughout the day. I wondered

where he was and what he was doing. I knew he was working hard to track down Kyle, but I missed him and I would have rather had him there with me. I sighed loudly. If I was having trouble dealing with being away from him for a few hours, what was I going to do when it was all over and we had to go our separate ways? Just the thought had my stomached tied in knots.

Micah had taken my breath away from the moment I laid eyes on him. There was no denying how masculine and gorgeous he was, but I had learned that there was so much more to him than just that. He was also incredibly kind, devoted, honest, and made me laugh again. He was the best lover I'd ever had, but he had also become my best friend too. I found myself opening up to him more and more as we spent time together and I knew I could tell him anything and he wouldn't judge me.

I knew there were parts of himself, painful parts, that he was still holding back from me, but the closer we became, the more hopeful I was that he would eventually trust me enough to share those parts. He had waited patiently for me to open up and I would do the same for him. Whenever he decided he was ready, I would be there. I didn't know what would happen in the future, if we even had a future together or if Micah even wanted that. All I knew was that I was completely head over heels in love with him and I wanted anything he wanted to give me for as long as he was willing to give it.

A knock at the door tore me from my thoughts and I realized I had been daydreaming for over an hour. My heart flipped over in my chest as Micah poked his head around the door. He smiled back at me as he walked in, but he looked tired and I could see the worry lines around his eyes. I felt bad that I was causing him so much stress. I stood up from the table as he came near and held my arms open to him. He hesitated for a second, looking a little surprised, but then he stepped into my arms and allowed me to wrap my arms around his back. He was tense at first and then I heard him sigh and his body relaxed against mine. I rubbed my hands soothingly up and down his back, our bodies swaying slightly as if we were slow dancing.

Micah nuzzled into the crook of my neck, making me shiver and then began placing soft kisses up the column of my throat and over my chin before kissing the corners of my mouth. I licked out at him and he captured my tongue between his lips, sucking on it. He hadn't been in the room more than a few minutes and already I was lost to him. I whimpered as he pulled away and tried to follow him with my lips, but he placed his hands on my chest, kneading my pectorals with his fingers.

"Carlos said you hadn't eaten since breakfast so I figured I'd take you to get something to eat," he offered.

"I am starved, now that you mention it." I hooked my fingers through his belt loops and tugged him towards me so he could feel my arousal against his own.

He dropped his head back with a groan, but then stepped away from me with a determined look. "Later, I promise, but I'm going to take care of your other needs first." I started to protest, but my stomach chose that moment to rumble embarrassingly. He laughed loudly. "See, he's in agreement; dinner first, then…dessert." I laughed as he waggled his eyebrows at me playfully. I was glad to see him looking more relaxed than when he first came in.

I grabbed my jacket because the temperature had dropped considerably throughout the day and smiled shyly when Micah held the door open for me. *I guess chivalry's not dead after all.* We rode the elevator in silence and then strode through the elegant hotel lobby side by side. The sounds of the city hit me full force when we stepped outside and I smiled because it reminded me of home. Even though I lived outside of the city limits, I spent most of my days at my office, in the heart of Chicago and I'd missed it.

Micah cupped his hand around my elbow and pulled me towards the curb as he hailed a cab. I looked at him in surprise. "We'll blend in better if we're not in a stretch limo," he explained. I nodded because it made sense. If you wanted to go undetected in the city, what better way than inside one of the thousands of yellow taxis. Micah gave the driver the name of a restaurant then leaned back in the seat as we took off, weaving in and out of traffic. His shoulder brushed with mine and the contact sent a wave of pleasure down my arm.

I turned my head to look at him and was surprised to see him staring back at me. He opened his mouth to say something, but shut it right away as if he'd changed his mind. His gray eyes flitted through many emotions, too quickly for me to make any sense of. I wasn't sure what was going on with him, but he seemed to be on edge so I decided to ease into conversation and then maybe he would relax enough to tell me whatever it was he wanted to say.

"Where are we going?" I asked him. I watched some of the tension bleed from his shoulders at the simple topic.

"To my favorite Mexican restaurant. Giovanni and I came to New York for a week after we graduated high school. His parents knew that after I joined the navy and he took off to college we wouldn't have as much time together so they gave us the trip as a graduation present." I watched him as he smiled at the happy memory and it made me smile too. "Anyway, we went out one night, each of us too young to get into most of the clubs and we found this little hole in the wall Mexican restaurant. Luckily, we didn't let the look of the place scare us off because it ended up being the best food I'd ever put in my mouth, with the exception of Mama Romero's cooking of course."

"Of course," I cut in, still smiling. It was rare to see Micah so relaxed and happy and I was determined to keep him that way for as long as possible.

"They make really authentic Mexican cuisine, not that knock-off Tex-Mex stuff. I'm talking hand-made tortillas, salsa that will leave your eyes watering, and fajitas that'll make you want to sing." I laughed at his impassioned description.

"You've sold me on it already, I can't wait to try it."

The cab slowed and I reached for my wallet to pay the driver, but Micah waved me away. "I wanted to treat you tonight, so I've got this.

And dinner."

My breath caught in my throat and I felt butterflies in my stomach. Was Micah taking me on a date? Because that's exactly what the night was beginning to feel like. I tucked my wallet back in my pocket as Micah climbed out of the cab and leaned back in, holding his hand out to me. I got out of the car and was surprised when instead of letting go as I had expected, Micah threaded his fingers through mine and led us to the front door.

I looked up at the plain gray brick building. There was nothing that made it stand out amongst the other businesses on that block except perhaps the garish red flashing sign over the metal door that read *Bello's*. Recalling the limited amount of Spanish I had learned in high school, I knew that the name meant beautiful which was quite ironic given the exterior of the establishment, but I trusted Micah so I followed him through the door.

As soon as we walked in, my senses were assaulted with the tantalizing smell of peppers and onions as they blended with chicken and juicy steaks over an open flame. My mouth began to water as I looked around the restaurant. The walls were adorned with colorfully handcrafted items such as painted clay masks and beaded handbags and a mariachi band weaved through the tables, serenading the patrons with their lively music. The entire place was warm and welcoming and I finally understood the reason for the name.

I turned to Micah who had been watching for my reaction and gave him a slow smile. "You didn't tell me how beautiful it was inside."

He smiled back and his eyes sparkled. "Just wait until you taste the food."

A robust man with a thick moustache and a broad smile walked towards us, reaching his hand out to shake each of ours. "Buenas noches, me llamo; Juan. Bienvenidos a *Bello's*." Micah and I stared at him blankly and he let out a boisterous laugh. "Good evening, my name is John. Welcome to *Bello's*."

"Thank you," I murmured, wishing I had paid better attention to my Spanish teacher. He led us to a table in the corner with a green cloth spread over it and a small candle placed in the middle, giving it a cozy, intimate feel.

We were quiet as we decided what to order, but our eyes were drawn to each other over the tops of our menus on several occasions. I felt like a shy teenager out with a guy I liked for the very first time instead of two grown men who already knew each other intimately. I felt my cock stir as I remembered just how intimately we knew each other and I shifted in my seat. Micah arched his brow knowingly and chuckled before turning his attention back to his menu.

Everything had felt different since the moment he'd arrived in my hotel room. Over the months of the tour we had spent countless hours eating burgers or pizza while watching baseball and getting to know each other. This was something altogether different though. It felt more special and the word *date* floated around in my head again, leaving me feeling lightheaded.

I had never been on a date before. Noah and I used to hang out with mutual friends either at parties or one of our dorm rooms; we'd never gone on an actual date. Then of course there was Kyle, but we always had to sneak around so going to dinner or a movie was off limits. After getting burned twice, I hadn't been very interested in having another relationship so I threw myself into my work and family.

We placed our orders and then made small talk while we waited for our food to arrive. Micah listened as I told him about my conversation with Caleb and he seemed genuinely happy for me that it had gone well.

"You're very lucky to have a family you're so close to," he said wistfully.

"I know I am. I get along really well with all of my siblings and our parents are great, a little crazy sometimes, but great nonetheless."

"They seemed pretty normal to me. How are they crazy?" he asked.

I waited until the waitress had set down our food, taking a moment to breathe in the aroma of the sizzling fajitas before answering his question. I regaled him with stories of my parents, including the time I came home early from a class to find my mom seated at the dining room table dressed in a fur coat and my dad serving her food, wearing nothing but an apron. "To this day aprons still creep me out... and fur coats." Micah stared at me wide eyed then began laughing when I gave a full-bodied shudder at the memory.

I chuckled along as he wiped tears from his eyes. "Okay, I'll admit, that is a little crazy...and disturbing." He grinned at me. "But at least they love each other. It's important that parents love each other so they can pass that love on to their kids."

He was still smiling at me, but I felt my heart shatter for him, knowing the hurt that was behind those few words. "Yeah, I was very fortunate," I murmured. I wasn't sure what to say; I wanted to know more about Micah. Hell, I wanted to know *everything* about the man seated across from me, but I also didn't want to bring up unpleasant memories. I only knew what Caleb had told me and that wasn't very much.

"I didn't have that growing up," he said in a matter of fact way. He leaned back in his chair and picked up his bottle of beer, picking at the label absentmindedly. "My mom took off when I was little and my dad who had always been a mean drunk became even meaner and I became his sole target."

His eyes darted to mine and I tried to school my expression so he wouldn't see how upset I was. The thought of anyone hurting him, especially the people who were supposed to love him the most, had me seeing red. Micah didn't need my anger then, he needed for me to listen so that's what I did.

"At first, he would just call me names and say hateful things to me, but then he found out I was gay and it got worse. He started hitting me, broke my arm a couple of times, and my leg once when he kicked me too hard. I missed so much school because I didn't want my teachers to see the bruises that I should have failed and I would have if it hadn't been for Giovanni."

A smile played at his lips as he thought of his best friend and I felt a surge of love for my brother-in-law. "One time, he kept calling over and over and I kept telling him that I didn't feel well and he should stay away so he wouldn't catch it, but he was stubborn so he waited until my dad left for work and he showed up at my door with a stack of books. He stayed up with me all night, helping me catch up on all my work."

Micah took a drink of his beer and then let out a long breath. "Looking back, I'm sure he knew what was going on, but he never said a word. He just showed up and helped me the only way he could. I started spending as much time as possible away from home just to avoid running into my dad. I got in with a rough crowd and ended up getting picked up by the cops one night when another guy and I were caught trying to break into a convenience store." His eyes darted to mine again to judge my reaction and I gave him a little smile. Conversation stopped when the waitress brought us another round of beers.

"Anyway, they dragged me into the station and since it was my first offense, they let me off with a warning. Then they said they were going to call my dad and I kind of lost it. I mean, if the guy broke my bones when I hadn't even done anything, what the hell was he going to do to me when I had?" My hands fisted at my sides as anger coursed through me.

"I was terrified so I begged them to call Mr. Romero instead. Of course, they wanted to know why I was so upset and everything just kind of spilled out. Mr. Romero said he wanted me to live with them and I agreed that I wanted to, so the cops paid my dad a visit and basically told him that they knew what all he'd done and if he didn't let me go then they'd have no choice but to press charges. That was that, I moved in with the *Romeros* and stayed there until I graduated and went off to the navy. I haven't seen my dad since. I don't even know if he's still alive and frankly, I don't care."

I cleared my throat, but my voice still sounded raspy when I spoke. "I'm so sorry you went through all of that. You deserved better."

Micah shrugged, not yet looking at me. "It is what it is. I eventually got to see what a normal family looked like; it just wasn't my own."

"Is that why you need control? Because you didn't have it growing up?" I asked cautiously.

Micah looked at me sharply at first and then his expression softened when he saw my genuine concern. "Yeah, that's part of it." I wanted to ask him what the other part was, but the waitress brought our bill to the table and Micah scooped it up and was standing before I could say any more.

Micah hailed another taxi and held the door for me while I climbed in. I reached for his hand as the driver took off and he clasped it in his own. "Thanks for dinner, I had a really nice time."

It was dark outside, but I was able to make out his smile with the help of the streetlights passing by. "Thank you for going with me. I've been wanting to take you there ever since I saw we were stopping in New York." I smiled at the fact that the restaurant had been a happy memory for him and that he had chosen to share it with me. He pulled me into his side and I rested my head on his shoulder with a sigh of contentment.

I'd heard somewhere that every once in a while, the stars and universe would align and you could be exactly where you were supposed to be at that moment in time. In the back of that cab, driving down the busy streets of New York with Micah by my side, I knew that that was my perfect moment. There was nowhere else I'd rather be.

CHAPTER
Fifteen

Micah

THE NIGHT HAD GONE BETTER THAN I'D HOPED. LANDON seemed to like *Bello's* and the food was even better than I remembered it being. I hadn't planned on telling Landon about my childhood over dinner, but as usual I felt so at ease around him that the words had just poured out of me.

After spilling my guts to Mr. Romero that night at the police station, I had only ever spoken to one other person about the way my father had treated me and that was Giovanni. He'd already seen the evidence and I was going to be living with him so I thought it was only fair that he knew the whole truth. After that, I didn't see any reason to hash it out again and so I had buried it along with the other part of my life I'd rather forget.

Things with Landon were different though, I trusted him and I had finally accepted that I was in love with him. For the very first time in my life I was in love with someone and I wanted to know everything about him, but that would only work if I was willing to share everything about myself. Telling Landon about my dad had been easier than I thought and I appreciated the fact that he listened quietly, letting me tell the story in my own way. I saw the emotion in his eyes when I finished and it nearly took my breath away. I was used to being the one in charge, the one who protected others. I'd never had anyone look at me quite the way Landon had, like he wanted to hold me close and shield me from everything that might hurt me.

I had always thought that falling in love would be scary, it would mean giving up some of the control I had fought so hard to gain in order to treat the other person like an equal partner. I had never considered what it would be like to fall in love with a man like Landon though. I had no doubt that loving him would be the best thing to ever happen to me and I trusted him and knew that he would never mistreat me or take away my dignity like the people in my past.

I wanted a relationship with him, but Landon had already had two other men in his past that hurt him badly by lying to him and I refused to hurt him further by not telling him the truth about me. I just hoped he could forgive me because the thought of him walking away nearly brought me to my knees.

We arrived back at the hotel and held hands as we rode the elevator up to our floor. When the doors opened, Landon gave me a questioning look. "Do you want to come back to my room?"

"The answer to that will always be yes," I said with a smile and Landon responded with one of his own. He pulled the key card from his pocket and I held my hand out. "Let me go in and have a look around first, okay?" After doing a quick sweep of the room, I told him it was safe to come in.

Landon locked the door and I watched as he walked towards me. He slid his arms around my waist and leaned in, brushing his lips against mine. My hands itched to touch him, but I couldn't put it off any longer. I needed to tell him the truth and with any luck he would let me touch him after.

"Landon," I said hoarsely as his lips ghosted over the side of my neck. "Landon!" I said again more forcefully. That captured his attention and he leaned back, looking at me with surprise.

"What's wrong?"

"We need to talk," I told him, stepping out of his arms in order to clear my head.

"That doesn't sound like a good thing." He cocked his head at me and his eyes showed his worry.

I cleared my throat. "Can we sit down please? I need to tell you something and it may take a while to explain." He nodded and took a seat on the couch. I sat down next to him and folded my hands together. I looked up into his eyes as he reached over and covered my hands with his own.

"Whatever it is, you can tell me, Micah," he said so sweetly that I wanted to forget the whole thing and just take him to bed, but I couldn't do that.

"I lied to you, Landon." The words rushed out of me before I could change my mind. I felt the loss immediately as his hands pulled away from mine.

"Explain please," he whispered. I dared to look at him and immediately wished I hadn't. The wary look he had on his face hit me like a ton of bricks. *Please don't let him hate me.*

"I will, but I need to start at the beginning," I said quietly.

"I'm listening." He leaned back into his seat and crossed his arms. I recognized the defensive position easily because I had used it throughout my entire life. It looked all wrong on a man like him.

"I told you I had fallen behind a lot in school, even with Giovanni's help. He got me to the point where I could graduate, but my grades had suffered enough that I was in no position to go to college. I discussed my options with Mr. Romero and finally decided to enlist in the navy." I smiled as I pictured my first few years as a sailor.

"They kicked my ass from the very beginning, but instead of beating me down the way my dad had done, they lifted me up and turned me into a better, stronger version of myself. After a lifetime of never knowing what was going to happen next, I finally had rules and a routine that I could count on and I thrived. After a couple of years, I made it into the SEAL program and that's when I really began to shine. My CO convinced me to become a career SEAL, said he saw a lot of potential in me and believed I would move up quickly through the ranks. Then we were sent to Iraq." I was too antsy to sit so I stood up and walked to the window, looking out at the lights from nearby buildings.

"We'd been there for a few months when we were called to do a hostage recovery. It was supposed to be an easy job; get in, get out. I'm still not sure what went wrong since everything's classified, but somebody somewhere fucked up royally and the next thing I knew we were surrounded by hostiles." I heard Landon's sharp intake of breath, but I knew if I looked at him I'd never get through the rest of my story so I kept my eyes glued to the window.

"I can't really tell you how long I was there, because the days blended together after a while. I was held in a cell that was too small to stand up or turn around in. It was pitch black except for a slit at the base which they used whenever they would deem it necessary to hose out the waste. The only time I saw any light was when they would take me out to torture me into answering questions that I had no knowledge about." I could hear the bitterness in my voice and when I looked at Landon's reflection in the window, I saw his hand in front of his mouth as if he were holding back a sob.

"One night a voice spoke to me through the small opening. I hadn't even been aware that there was someone on the other side. I'd heard screaming and crying in the distance, but I didn't realize anyone was that close. He told me his name was Spencer. He was twenty-one and was a member of the Royal Air Force. He'd been captured along with his team and just like me, he hadn't seen them since.

We talked constantly, sharing stories about ourselves and our hometowns; we talked until our voices gave out. We couldn't see each other, but just that small amount of human contact helped us keep our sanity in an otherwise maddening situation. They would pull us out one at a time for routine beatings and when we would return, bruised and broken, we'd reach our fingers through that little slit and comfort the other.

"One time, they hurt me so badly I didn't know if I would survive and part of me thought that would be better because at least then I'd escape their torture, but then I thought about Giovanni. His parents had passed away at that point and he was the only person I had left in the world that cared about me. I didn't want him to be left wondering what had happened to me, so Spencer and I made a promise to each other that if something happened and only one of us lived, the surviving one would find their family and tell them."

I turned around when I heard a strangled sound and when I saw the look on Landon's face I rushed to his side. I sat down next to him and reached out a shaky hand to wipe the tears from his cheeks, relieved when he didn't push me away. He reached over and grabbed my hand in his, squeezing it in a show of support.

"Then one time, they came and got Spencer," I stared down at Landon's hand in mine and tears made my vision swim. "It was different that time. I could hear him screaming which wasn't unusual, they were sick bastards who had made torture into a fine art form." I wiped my tears away angrily.

"What was different was the sound of his screams. Whatever they were doing to him, must have been pure hell. I never knew a person could sound like that. I could hear him begging them to kill him, to please just end it. When I heard that, I lost it. I started screaming and banging on the walls of my cell. I could barely move in the small space, but I hit and kicked until my hands and feet were bloodied. They were killing my friend and there was absolutely nothing I could do to stop them. Once again, I was completely powerless."

Landon wrapped his arms around me and held me as I cried.

I'd been required to relay everything that had happened to the U.S Embassy during their investigation and I had done so stoically, dealing only with facts. Then I'd given Giovanni a watered-down version, telling him the basic story, but still I didn't delve too deep. I wasn't ready to open old wounds. With Landon though, I wanted, needed, him to know everything. I trusted him enough to bare my soul and as much as it hurt to relive that pain, it was also healing. He ran his fingers through my hair, whispering soothing words as he rocked us back and forth. When my tears had slowed, I took a deep cleansing breath and blew it out. I sat up, determined to finish.

"I continued fighting until I eventually lost consciousness. I don't know how long I was out, but when I came to, everything was quiet. My throat was raw from screaming and the blood on my hands and feet felt sticky. I reached my fingers under the tiny slit and whispered for him, but of course there was no answer, he was gone. I'd heard his cries cut off before I passed out so I already knew, but I didn't want to accept it. Spencer had been my friend, my lifeline and then all of a sudden he was gone and I was all alone."

Landon got up and brought me a bottle of water from the mini fridge. My hands were shaking as I took it, but I drank it down gratefully. I leaned my elbows on my knees and stared at the bottle, rolling it back and forth between my hands.

"One day…one *fucking* day later, I was rescued. I should have been ecstatic when I heard the gunfight going on outside my cell. I should have felt relief that I would be getting out of there, but all I could think about was that if Spencer had held on for one more day…" I squeezed my eyes shut and put my fist to my mouth to hold back a sob. I could feel Landon's hand on my back, rubbing in soothing circles.

"I found out later that they had captured fourteen men between the British and American squadrons. Five made it out alive and only two of us were American; we'd been held hostage for about two months. I spent three weeks in the hospital where they had to re-break several of my bones so that they would heal properly. I was also severely dehydrated and malnourished. It took another three months of physical therapy to get me back into proper physical shape, but at that point I was done. I was proud of the work I'd done as a SEAL, but I was ready to come home. I wanted to reconnect with G and hopefully start my own business, so that's what I did. The navy gave me an honorable discharge and I moved back to Chicago."

"Did you ever talk to Spencer's family?" I looked up at Landon and the compassion in his eyes stunned me for a minute. I gave him a wry smile.

"Yes, I did. Spencer had told me that his parents were deceased, but he had an older brother. I went to see him and he cried when I told him, but he was so grateful to know what had happened so he could have closure. He thanked me for being there for Spencer and making sure he wasn't alone during that nightmare. He said if I ever needed anything in the world, he would give it to me; he even offered to buy me a house."

"I'm glad you were able to do that for him, but a *house*?" Landon asked in disbelief.

I chuckled. "Yeah well, he's rich, extremely rich. I refused his offer, but we've remained pretty close ever since. Maybe it's because I was the last one with him, but I think when he sees me he feels a little closer to his brother."

"I'd love to meet him someday," Landon said quietly.

"You already have; it's Lachlan Edwards."

Landon gasped. "That's your connection to Lachlan?" His shoulders slumped at the realization. "Poor Lachlan, I had no idea he'd lost his brother that way." His eyes widened and he cocked his head at me. His voice was filled with sadness. "Spencer Edwards…S.E. That's the cross tattoo you have on your back."

"Yeah, I got that in memory of him right after I got out of the hospital. It's my way of showing that I'll never forget my friend."

"Of course you won't," Landon said, wrapping his arms around me and pulling me close. The angle was awkward since we both were sitting on the couch, but I didn't care. My hands slid around his waist and I hugged him tightly, letting his warmth soak into my chilled bones. I breathed in his familiar scent and let it soothe the frayed nerves left behind from my tale.

After a while he pulled back so he could look in my eyes. "I don't understand though, why did you say you'd lied to me?"

I swallowed thickly. "I couldn't stop my dad from doing the things he did and I had no control whatsoever when those animals were torturing me or when they were killing Spencer. Kyle's out there somewhere and I feel powerless to stop him. My lie was that I promised you that I would keep Carter safe and now you, but the truth is, I don't know if I can and just the thought of something happening to you…" I trailed off as a shudder wracked my body.

Landon pushed me back into the couch and climbed over me, straddling my hips. He cupped my face in his hands and lifted until I was looking into his beautiful hazel eyes. "Micah, you were just a kid when your father did those things, but you still found the strength to tell someone and get the help you needed. What happened to Spencer was horrible and I know if there had been anything you could have done, you would have, but they were barbarians and they made sure you couldn't touch them. You said yourself that you wanted to give up, but you didn't. You held on until help could come. That only happened because of the strength inside you." His eyes were full of emotion as he traced his fingers down the side of my face.

"Don't you see? You are the strongest, fiercest, most loyal man I know. I've trusted you to keep me safe when I was at my most vulnerable. During my panic attacks, I've let you see a side of me that no one else knows and you took care of me each and every time. You never lied to me because I know that no matter what happens, you'll do everything within your power to keep me safe." He smiled gently. "I trust you, Micah, and I love you."

I gasped and my heart pounded wildly in my chest. My fingers gripped his hips as if I were afraid he'd disappear. "Do you mean that?" I searched his face for any sign that he regretted his words, but pure love was the only thing I saw staring back at me.

He closed his eyes and he leaned his forehead against mine. I could feel his breath on my lips when he spoke. "I absolutely mean it. I love you; I'm *in* love with you, Micah. I have been for a long time, but I was too afraid to tell you."

"Why would you be afraid to tell me?" I asked.

"Because I wasn't sure that's what you wanted," he whispered.

I pulled back so I could see him; he looked vulnerable. "It is what I want. I love you, Landon, and I want you in my life for as long as you'll have me."

He nodded his head as a smile spread across his face. "In that case, I hope you can deal with forever because once you're mine, I'm never letting you go."

"I'm already yours and you are most definitely mine," I growled as I cupped his head and pulled him in for a kiss. I slid my tongue between his parted lips and swept it through his mouth, feasting on his sweet flavor.

After a few minutes, he pulled back gasping for air. "What do you want me to do?"

I stared at him for a moment. I'd told Landon everything about me, there were no secrets between us anymore. He knew the things that had happened to me and he understood the reasons why I needed to feel in control. He was offering to give himself to me so that I would have that control and I loved him even more for it, but I wanted something different. I loved the man in my arms and I wanted something more with him. I wanted to give more of myself to him than I'd ever given anyone else; he deserved no less.

I shook my head at him and his brow furrowed in question. "Not this time," I told him. "There will still be times when I need to control you, but right now, I want us to be equal partners. I want to make love to you, Landon."

CHAPTER
Sixteen

Micah

WITHOUT A WORD, LANDON SHUFFLED OFF OF MY LAP and held his hand out to me. I placed my hand in his and let him help me to my feet. He led us to the bedroom and turned to face me. "I can't wait to show you how much I love you," he whispered.

He traced the shell of my ear with his tongue then moved down to the sensitive spot below the ear and sucked. My hands flew to his biceps and I grabbed on as my knees went weak. His hands landed on my hips, helping to steady me. He worked the back of my shirt from my pants and I groaned at the first touch of his hands on my skin. His tongue plunged into my mouth as his fingers raked down my back.

I was shaking with the need to throw him onto the bed and plunge my cock into his delectable heat, but I wanted the moment to be special. I breathed deeply through my nose as he pulled my shirt over my head and began placing wet kisses down my neck. He licked a path around one of my nipples and then latched onto it with his teeth, nipping it sharply and then soothing it with a swipe of his tongue.

My cock was raging hard and begging to be a part of the action. "Micah, I need you to touch me," Landon whispered breathlessly.

He didn't need to ask me twice. I had his shirt off and his belt undone in a matter of seconds. "Eager?" He chuckled as I worked the button of his pants open and began to lower his zipper.

"You have no idea," I growled and he responded with goose bumps across his skin.

"I think I have some...Ooooohhhh," he groaned as I freed his cock and wrapped my hand around it.

My mouth sealed over his while my hand pumped his rigid member. I could feel him dripping onto my fingers and it added fuel to the fire. I was delirious with my need for him. His hands found my shoulders and pressed down in a silent plea. I was more than happy to oblige and I dropped quickly to my knees.

His cock was long and thick and the mushroomed head was slick with his excitement. I leaned in and buried my nose in the crease where his leg met his groin. It was warm and held his smell the strongest and my head swam as I breathed in his musky, masculine scent. "Landon." The sound coming from me was full of want, need, and reverence. I was in love with the man and I wanted to spend the rest of my life worshiping his body.

My hand grasped his leaking cock and I swiped my tongue over the purple head. His flavor burst on my tongue and I became ravenous. I kissed the tip of his shaft and then wrapped my lips around him and slid down until my nose was buried in his soft hairs and I could feel the broad head of his cock hitting the back of my throat. I had never been happier to not have a gag reflex when I heard his cry of pleasure.

Beads of sweat formed above my eyes and my body shook with desire. I kept my mouth on him as I worked my pants open, sighing in relief when my cock bounced free. My thumb slid through the liquid dripping from me and I used it to make the glide easier. My head bobbed up and down on his rod several times and then I flattened my tongue and licked up one side and down the other, feeling every vein in his thick cock.

I reached down and began playing with my balls, lifting them and rolling them around in my warm palm. Landon bent down, wrapping his body around my head and over my back as I continued to pleasure him. I felt his hands on my ass, gripping it then spreading it open, and I moaned in delight when his finger slid through my crease and tapped at my puckered hole, awakening every nerve there. It had been years since anyone had touched me there and the fact that it was Landon, had me racing to the edge of the cliff. I squeezed the base of my shaft in a punishing grip until the blood retreated and I had some control over myself.

I pulled off of Landon's cock and wet my finger. I reached around his legs, spreading him open, and circled his tight entrance with my slick digit. I sucked his dick back down my throat and breached his hole at the same time his finger slid into me. My head swirled with how good it felt to have him touching me there, but my focus shifted when he suddenly stiffened and cried out. His hole quivered around my finger and I swallowed quickly, not wanting to lose one bit of the delicious cum shooting down my throat. His finger slid out of me, leaving me empty and missing his touch. I removed my finger from him and licked his cock until it was completely clean. I sat back on my heels and caught him as he sank wearily to the floor. I felt a surge of pride for putting that dreamy, faraway look on his face.

His head fell back on the bed and he opened one eye to peer at me with a lazy smile. "That was amazing. Give me a few minutes and I'll return the favor."

"We have all the time in the world." I smiled and kissed his forehead.

I sank down next to him, leaning my head back, and we turned to look at each other. The love I saw shining in his eyes was the same look I had been seeing for a while, I just hadn't recognized it for what it was. Landon loved me, he wanted to be with me, and he wanted to be mine. I couldn't remember a time when I was happier.

"I've never had someone to call mine," I whispered.

Landon's hand reached for my jaw, cupping it. His thumb stroked over my cheek. "I've been yours from the moment we met." He looked at me adoringly. "Can I ask you something?"

"Of course," I answered, curious about what could possibly have him acting so shy after everything we'd done together.

"Well, it's just that this was the first time that I was free to explore and so I just went with it and I was wondering if you minded when…" His voice trailed off.

"You mean; did I mind when you stuck your finger inside of me?" My voice was husky as I remembered the feel of him breaching me. He nodded once, licking his lips and I could see the desire springing back to life in his eyes. Talking about it was turning us both on.

"I've enjoyed some ass play in the past, but it's been a long time since I let anyone get that close." He bit the corner of his lip and I could see that he had other questions. "No more secrets, Landon. You can ask me anything you want."

"Have you ever bottomed before?" He looked like he wasn't sure if he wanted the answer to that or not and I was relieved that I could ease his mind.

"No, baby. I've only ever topped."

"Is that something you think you might want to try?" he asked tentatively.

"Honestly, the thought never occurred to me. I topped from the very first time and that's just all I've ever done," I said with a shrug.

"Oh," he replied.

"Landon, I love you. I've never said that to a man before and I don't take it lightly. I love you and I'm yours. My heart and my soul and my body belong to you. There is no part of me you can't have so if you want to top me sometime that's fine."

His eyes widened a bit then his lips lifted in a smile. "I prefer bottoming actually, but I want to know what it feels like to be buried deep inside of you, touching you where no one else has been. When you're ready, I'd like to try that."

His words were like a match to gasoline, lighting me up from the inside out. I hauled him to his feet and then pushed him back, making his body bounce on the bed from the force. He threw his head back with a laugh as I knelt above him and spread his legs wide. Landon's laughter died off when he caught my feral gaze and he reached for my cock, sliding his fingers up and down it with a feather light touch. My hips punched forward, begging for more and he wriggled out from under me. He got on his knees and leaned down on his forearms, capturing my weeping cock in his mouth.

I linked my hands together on the back of his head and held him still as I hit the back of his throat. "Landon!" I cried as he swallowed around me. He pulled back, his tongue swirling around my tip before sliding back down. His lips wrapped tightly around my base and his nose tickled the short hairs that surrounded my cock. His nostrils flared as he held that position for a few seconds, finally pulling off of me and gasping for air.

He sucked me in again and I spread my hands over his back, sliding them down his sleek body and over his pert ass. I licked my finger and slid it over his crease until I felt his hole. My finger had already loosened him a bit before so I dipped it in without any hesitation. Landon wailed his pleasure around my cock and wiggled his ass, letting me know he wanted more. I was more than happy to give him what he wanted and soon I was working two fingers in and out of his eager hole.

181

His mouth was working magic on my dick and my balls began to draw up tight. When he started riding my fingers wantonly, I knew it was time. I pulled my cock out of his mouth and pushed him back on the bed. He sprawled across the bed and I let my eyes feast on every inch of his perfect body. I reached towards the bedside table and grabbed a condom and lube.

His eyes were heavy with lust and he reached for his cock, pumping it in his hand as he watched me prepare for him. When I was properly suited up and slick with lube, I lined my cock up at his entrance. His eyes held mine as I entered him and we both gasped at the connection between us. We knew that it was different from all the times before. It was more than two bodies coming together, it was about two souls merging into one.

I slid in slowly until my hips were nestled snuggly against his ass then I leaned down on my forearms, bracketing his body with mine. Our sweat-soaked chests glided against each other as I plunged in and out of him with a steady rhythm. His fingers smoothed up the sides of my ribs and back down, loving me with his touch. Our mouths fused together and we poured everything we had into the other.

Landon hooked his legs together around my waist and lifted his hips and I slid impossibly deeper inside him, making us both cry out. Our movements became more urgent and I lifted myself onto my hands, adjusting my angle so I could hit his prostate with each plunge of my hips. Landon tossed his head back and forth in wild abandon as I pumped into him, faster and faster, each of us searching for something just outside our grasp.

I felt him stiffen beneath me and his back arched off the bed as his orgasm took over, a fountain of warm cum spurting from his tip. I dipped my head and licked a ribbon of milky seed from the hollow of his throat. With his flavor on my tongue and his hole clamping down on my cock, I let the orgasm I'd been holding back rip through my body. I threw my head back with a howl, taken by surprise by the sheer power behind my release. Lights flashed behind my closed lids and my arms felt shaky and weak, unable to hold me up any longer.

I dropped down onto my lover, gasping for air and completely spent. I felt his hands smoothing over my back and his lips pressed to my temple as he whispered words of love to me. After a few minutes, I lifted my head and looked at him.

"That just keeps getting better and better," he said with a satisfied grin.

"I don't know, I think it needs some work," I deadpanned.

"Oh, you think so, huh?" he said, catching on to my teasing.

I shrugged my shoulders innocently. "Yep. It's going to take lots of practice; maybe even a lifetime."

"I can live with that," he whispered right before I sealed my mouth over his.

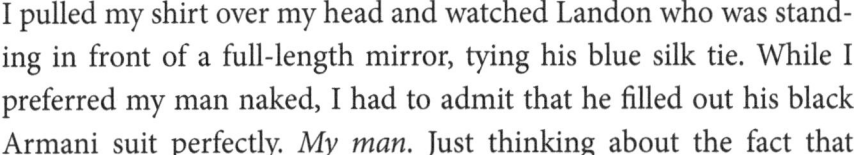

I pulled my shirt over my head and watched Landon who was standing in front of a full-length mirror, tying his blue silk tie. While I preferred my man naked, I had to admit that he filled out his black Armani suit perfectly. *My man.* Just thinking about the fact that Landon loved me and wanted to be with me had put a permanent smile on my face.

"I'm not ready to leave." I looked at his bottom lip which was pushed out in an adorable pout.

"What do you mean?" I put my hands on his hips and pulled him until his back was flush with my chest. My chin rested on his shoulder as we looked at ourselves in the mirror. No doubt about it, we were a handsome couple.

He shrugged and my head bobbed up and down with his movements. "I don't know, it's just that we've kind of been in our own little bubble. We've been able to shut out the rest of the world and this is where you told me you loved me."

ANNABELLA MICHAELS

"I know what you mean. It's been great having the time alone while the band was off doing interviews, but just because we'll be leaving New York doesn't mean what's happening between us is over. I love you and I will tell you that in each and every city we stop at."

"Really?" he asked with a lopsided grin.

"Yes, really. I love you, Landon, and that's not going to change no matter where we are," I assured him.

He turned in my arms and linked his arms around my neck. My hands slid up his back as we shared a lingering kiss. "I love you too."

"I will never get tired of hearing that," I said.

"Why can't you come with me to the concert?" He backed away and grabbed his watch off of the side table and slipped it onto his wrist.

"I need to run down to my room and pack my stuff, then I'm going to check in with Brandon to see if he's located Kyle yet. Once that's done, I'll head over to the arena." I slid my gun into the waistband of my jeans and then pulled my jacket on, covering it up.

"Maybe from now on we don't need to get two rooms," Landon suggested quietly.

"I think you may be right," I agreed with what I knew had to be a sappy grin. I kissed Landon one more time and then held the door open for him. We held hands as we rode the elevator down to the lobby where Tony was waiting to escort Landon to the concert arena.

He stepped out of the elevator, but I pulled him back and cupped his chin. "Stay with Tony until I get there okay? I don't want anything to happen to you." I couldn't put my finger on why I was suddenly feeling nervous, but figured it probably had to do with our new relationship. Landon was mine and that meant I had even more reason to want to keep him safe.

"I will, but you should still hurry. I tend to miss you when you're gone," he admitted softly.

"Are you ready to go?" Tony's deep baritone voice interrupted as he walked up to us. He must have noticed my hesitation because he put a hand on my shoulder. "I'll keep a close eye on him, Boss. I won't let that guy get anywhere near him," he assured me.

"Thanks, Tony. I'll be there as soon as I can." I watched as the man I loved walked out of the hotel and climbed into the back of a stretch limo. My chest felt tight and I rubbed at it with my hand. Just the fact that I loved Landon meant that I would always worry about him when we were apart, but factor in a crazed ex-lover who wanted him back for God knows what and I was going to lose my mind. With a shake of my head, I turned to ride the elevator back up to my room. The sooner I got everything done, the sooner I could be with Landon again.

I packed my bags and did a quick sweep of the room to make sure I hadn't forgotten anything. Satisfied that I had everything, I sat down and got ready to call my office, but my phone rang in my hand before I could. I was surprised to see Brandon's name on the screen.

"Hey, I was just getting ready to call you. Did you find Kyle?"

"Well, sort of," came his response.

"What the hell does that mean?" I growled. I wanted the whole thing to be over and to know that Landon was truly safe. If Kyle had somehow found out that we were on to him and had managed to slip away, then Landon would have to continue to look over his shoulder.

"He was no longer listed with the staff at the college and he didn't live in the house that was listed as his last known residence. It was like the guy had just disappeared, so I started searching archives of the local papers to see if there was any clue where he might have gone."

"What did you find?" A feeling of dread had settled in my stomach.

"His obituary," Brandon stated.

"You mean..."

"Yep. Kyle's dead. The obituary didn't give any information about how he died, just told about his work at the college and that he was survived by a wife and kid. I'm sorry, Micah, but he's not our guy."

Blood swooshed through my ears as I tried to digest everything Brandon had said. How could we have been so wrong about Kyle and if it wasn't him then who the hell was sending the letters? I mumbled a quick thanks to Brandon who assured me that he was going to keep looking into it.

"Fuck!" I yelled after I had hung up. I paced the floor as I figured out what my next move would be. I dreaded having to tell Landon that we were back to having no clue who the stalker was or what they wanted.

I gathered my bags and left my room. I was lost in my own thoughts as I walked down the hall, opened Landon's door and placed my bags near the bed. It wasn't until I turned to leave that I noticed the blue envelope on the floor and my heart began to race. Someone must have slipped it under the door after we left that morning. I picked it up, not caring about fingerprints at that point since the other letters had come back negative for prints.

The envelope was thicker than the previous ones and my hands were shaking as I slid it open. The blood turned to ice in my veins as I looked over the contents. *Every breath you take; I'll be watching you. Don't say I didn't warn you.* The hair on the back of my neck stood up as I sifted through the photos included with the letter. The pictures had been taken recently and were of me and Landon together. There was one of us from when we had gone for a run one early morning in England, one of us getting into the limo together, and one of us smiling at each other outside of *Bello's*. The stalker was serious and they were obviously ready to make their move.

I was already calling Tony as I raced down the hallway and to the stairwell, deciding it would be faster to take them than to wait for the elevator. Tony picked up just as I was sprinting through the lobby and outside to hail a cab. I had forgotten my jacket, but I barely felt the brisk night air as adrenaline pumped through my bloodstream.

"Tell me you're with Landon," I nearly shouted as I jumped into the back seat of the cab and gave the driver the name of the arena.

"Yeah, I'm with him. What's going on, Boss?" I could hear the concern in his voice immediately.

"Is he close enough to hear what we're talking about? I'll tell him what's happened, but I want to do it face to face," I explained.

"He won't hear anything, he's in the dressing room doing an interview," Tony informed me.

"Wait, Landon's doing an interview? With who? And where are you?" I rubbed my forehead as we sped down the city streets. I had a crashing headache that would continue to get worse until I could see my man with my own eyes.

"A lady came in and said she wanted to do an interview with Landon for some woman's magazine. Something about famous people and their families who work for them. I don't know, I wasn't really listening." I could practically hear Tony's eyes rolling and I would have laughed if I wasn't so worried. "Anyway, Greg called just as the lady got here and said that they had a bunch of crazy fans trying to sneak backstage and he and Carlos needed help keeping an eye out around the dressing rooms so I decided to wait in the hallway where I could help them and also watch over Landon."

I wasn't sure what it was, maybe just leftover adrenaline from before, but I couldn't shake the feeling that something wasn't right. "Tony, do me a favor and check on Landon, please."

"Okay, but I already checked everything before I left him. The back door was locked up tight so no one could get in and everything was secure in the room."

I held my breath as I heard Tony opening the door. "Landon, I'm sorry to interrupt, bu…what the hell? Where'd they go?" My vision blurred as I heard Tony say the words I'd never wanted to hear. "Shit, Micah, I'm so sorry; they're gone."

CHAPTER
Seventeen

Landon

I SMILED AS I TALKED TO MY SISTER MICHELLE ON THE PHONE. She and my other sister Emma had each gotten pregnant at the same time and the whole family was looking forward to the birth of its two newest members. They only had about a month left to go and apparently, things at home were getting crazy as each of their husbands tried to outdo the other when it came to decorating the nursery.

She told me how Emma's husband, Mark, had turned her simple idea of doing a pink nursery for their daughter into a princess extravaganza that rivaled the Disneyland theme park. I laughed when she said Emma had to veto his idea of turning the crib into a replica of Cinderella's carriage, complete with life-sized horse statues to pull it.

Not to be outdone, Michelle's husband, Jason, had taken the idea of an under the sea themed nursery for their son and had wanted to install a built-in aquarium into the wall right next to the crib. I told her that sounded really nice until she explained that the aquarium he planned on using was twelve feet long. I howled with laughter when she said she walked into their room one night and he was googling *How to care for your pet shark.* They finally agreed on a nice thirty-gallon tank with colorful salt water fish inside with the promise that they would take the baby to the aquarium for regular visits.

I was still chuckling as I hung up the phone. My family was crazy at times, but I missed them terribly. I couldn't wait for the tour to end so that I could go home and see everyone again and of course things would be different because I would have Micah by my side. I would no longer be the only one in my family who hadn't found love.

A knock on the door pulled me from my thoughts and I smiled at Tony as he stuck his head in. "You busy?"

"No, I just got off the phone. What's up?" I slid my phone into my pocket as he opened the door further and a woman walked in. "This lady is here to do an interview, is that alright?"

"I'm sorry, but Carter's going to be gone for a while. I didn't realize he had an interview scheduled." I pulled my phone out to check my calendar, embarrassed that I must have made some mix up in the schedule.

"You've misunderstood, I'm here to interview you." She laughed as my head shot up in surprise. "We're interviewing young entrepreneurs like yourself who just happen to work with their family members. We're hoping to put the spotlight on families that help each other reach their dreams and with everything I've heard about the way you've watched over your brother; I thought you'd be perfect for the article."

I studied her as she explained what all she needed from me. I wasn't sure what it was exactly, but there was something very familiar about her. She was a strikingly beautiful woman with long chestnut hair, eyes the color of the ocean, and curves that would probably make me behave stupidly if I were a straight man. She was shorter than me, but tall for a woman and had a very delicate bone structure.

"Umm, okay. Come on in, Ms.?" I held my hand out to her as Tony shut the door.

"Please, call me Cindy," she said as she shook my hand.

"Would you like anything to drink?"

"Water would be great, thank you." I turned to get a bottle of water from the fridge.

"I've sat in on many interviews with my brother, but I've never been asked to do one of my own so I'm quite flattered. Which magazine did you say…" My voice trailed off as I turned to face her, not understanding what I was seeing. Cindy had stood and was pointing a small handgun at me.

"Cindy? What are you doing?" I asked in confusion.

"Shut up and listen." Her beautiful face had morphed into a snarl. "We're going to go out the back door and get in the car that's waiting for us."

My eyes were wide and I felt hysterical laughter bubbling up my throat. "Is this some sort of joke?"

"Do I look like I'm joking?" she hissed. "Get moving and don't make any noise. I'd hate to have to hurt the sexy soldier in the hallway, but I will if he comes in here and tries to stop me."

She poked the tip of the gun into my chest and gave me a nudge which had me backing towards the door quickly. We slipped outside without a sound and I breathed a sigh of relief when Tony didn't come running. I would have felt horrible if he'd gotten hurt because of me. My eyes darted frantically around the dark parking lot, hoping someone would be there to see what was happening and could call for help. Unfortunately, that particular portion of the concert facility was used mainly for deliveries and employees to park their cars. With a sold-out concert being held there; the employees were probably all inside doing their jobs and most deliveries had been made during daytime work hours. My shoulders slumped when I realized I was on my own.

"Get in," Cindy ordered as she opened the passenger door. "Oh, and in case you were planning something dumb like jumping out and trying to run away, I should warn you that I'm an excellent marksman. I've spent many hours at the shooting range and I. Never. Miss." She whispered the last part in my ear and then laughed when I gave an involuntary shudder. "This is going to be fun," she gloated, clapping her hands together with delight.

I sank down into the passenger seat, my eyes frozen to the gun in her hand. "Wh…why are you d…doing this?" I stuttered.

"Don't worry, I'll answer all of your questions when we reach our destination." She started to shut the door, but stopped right before it could close. "Silly me, I almost forgot. Hand over your phone." She held her hand out and waited patiently for me to dig it out of my pocket. I placed it in her hand and watched as she tossed it carelessly over her shoulder. She slammed the door with a loud bang that rang in the small space and I felt my head swirl. I was breathing hard as my mind struggled to come to grips with what was happening. Who the hell was she and what did she want with me?

I watched as she rounded the front of the car, holding the gun up so it was still visible, as if I could forget she had it. My hands were shaking and my breath increased as I started to hyperventilate. I could feel myself gearing up for the mother of all panic attacks. I slammed my eyes closed, squeezing them tightly, and fisted my hands in my lap. I knew I needed to find a way to calm down and regain focus if I wanted to make it out of the situation alive. I took a deep breath in through my nose and held it there as I forced myself to block everything else out. I blew my breath out slowly through pursed lips then drew in another. Images of Micah holding me down, commanding me with his words and his body to hand over all control to him flickered through my mind and I felt myself beginning to calm. I did that for what seemed like a long time and eventually, my heart returned to a somewhat normal rate of speed and I was able to unclench my fists.

I was surprised to see that we were already moving. I wasn't sure where we were at, but I could see the lights in my side mirror as we left the city behind. The highway ahead of us contained only a few cars in the distance, giving me no opportunity to try and get someone's attention. Perhaps I could find out who she was and what she wanted and then put a stop to it.

I cleared my throat nervously as I glanced down at the gun which she had lowered to her lap. "You look very familiar, have we met before?"

"I thought you'd be much smarter considering your college education," she responded snidely. When I continued to stare at her blankly, she rolled her eyes as if she couldn't believe she had to deal with someone so dumb. "You really don't remember me?"

"No, I'm sorry." My eyes flickered back and forth between her face and the gun. Apparently my lack of memory had irritated her, because she picked the gun up and held it tightly in her hand. Her lips had turned back into an angry snarl and she let out a small growl that sent chills up my spine. Since she'd first walked into the dressing room, her behavior had been erratic, switching quickly from an almost childlike giddiness to inexplicable anger in the blink of an eye. My head spun as I tried to keep up with her moods.

"I was told you had seen me before. I would have thought I'd make a bigger impression on the man who was fucking. My. Husband," she shouted.

"You...you're..." I tilted my head and stared at her as the pieces of the puzzle began to click into place.

"Cynthia Brooks. Mrs. Kyle Brooks, or at least I used to be." I felt all of the blood drain from my face and I heard a loud buzzing noise in my ears. I barely noticed as she exited the highway and made her way down several long and winding roads.

"I did see you once, in his office. I had no idea, I'm so sorry..."

"Don't you dare apologize!" she cut me off with a wild shriek. She turned her head to glare at me. "It's all lies anyway. You're not sorry about what you did, you never were and that's why I had to find you."

I put a hand up on the dashboard, glancing back and forth between her and the road. She was no longer paying attention to the road because she was too busy shooting daggers at me. The car started to veer off to the right and I knew I needed to get her calmed down so that she didn't wreck the car and kill us both.

"Okay, okay," I said, trying to keep my voice neutral. "You said you had to find me. Tell me how you did it; how did you manage to send all of those letters and not get caught?" The change of subject worked because she turned her eyes back to the road and straightened the car with a pompous smirk.

"It's amazing what men will do for a pretty face," she purred. "I made some very interesting friends online that were willing to do whatever I asked in exchange for some provocative photos of myself. It was easy really; I just followed the tour schedule, found someone from my group chats that lived in that city, and began working my magic on him. One man was so enamored with the pictures I sent that he offered to hurt you if he could meet me in person." She laughed as if she were telling a funny story while having coffee with a friend instead of describing how she had sold herself to men just to exact her revenge on me.

"And the man that was caught? The one who was obsessed with my brother?" She had calmed down a lot and so I wanted to keep her talking.

She shook her head, looking contrite. "That one was my fault. I trusted the man I was talking to when he said he'd deliver the note. Instead, he chickened out and handed it off to the first groupie he found. The whole thing could have blown up in my face. Luckily for me, the guy he gave the letter to ended up being a complete nutcase and so it took some of the attention off of me."

The car slowed down as she pulled onto a narrow, one-lane road. Trees lined the sides of the lane, blocking the view of the moon and choking out our only source of light. It was eerily dark as we continued driving for several more minutes until suddenly the trees thinned out a little and a bit of light began to shine through.

Cynthia parked the car along the side of the road and told me to sit still while she came around to get me. My heart sped up as my body instinctively went into fight or flight mode. I looked around at my surroundings, trying to find a place where I could possibly run to for some help. As far as I could see there were no houses in the vicinity, but I supposed being lost in the woods would be better than staying near a woman with a gun in her hand and revenge on her mind. Before I could formulate a plan, she was around the side of the car and opening my door. I sat there stubbornly glaring at her until, with a sigh, she placed the gun to my forehead and cocked it. She laughed when I flinched and it was the sound of a person who had lost all touch with reality.

"Come take a walk with me, Mr. Greene. I want to tell you a story," she said in a sing-song voice. I got out of the car and she slammed the door, the sound reverberating through the still night air. I felt the press of cold metal at my back as she pushed me forward and with no other choice, I began to walk.

"Kyle and I met one night at a bar," she began. "We each had gone there with friends to get a beer after work. We headed up to order another drink at the same time and got to talking." Cynthia grabbed my elbow and led me off of the path and through the trees. The foliage was thick and I held my arms up as branches slapped at my face.

"He was charming and funny and very handsome," she said wistfully. "Of course, I don't have to convince you of that, do I?" My muscles tensed as she pressed the gun into my back painfully, but seconds later she pulled back and continued talking. "He asked me out for the next night and that was that. We dated about two years and then he asked me to marry him." She was quiet for a few minutes, lost in her memories. The only sounds were our labored breathing as we made our way up a steep incline and I wondered where in the hell she was leading me.

"My friends would complain about their husbands not showing them enough attention or spending all of their time drinking beer and watching football. They were jealous of the way Kyle treated me. We loved spending our weekends going on picnics, hiking, and visiting museums. I thought he was the perfect husband and I loved him very much." My stomach rolled as a sharp pang of guilt hit me.

"The only thing keeping our lives from being complete was my need to have a child. I had always dreamed of being a mother, but Kyle wasn't so sure about becoming a father. It took a lot of convincing, but eventually he agreed and within months I was pregnant. I gave birth to our son and..." Her voice cut off suddenly and I was surprised to hear sniffling behind me.

"Anyway, I finally had the family I had always dreamed of and we were happy. Kyle would come home every night after work, we'd eat dinner together and then we'd sit down to read. Kyle would hold our son and rock him back and forth as he read to him softly. More times than not, I'd end up setting my own book aside so I could watch the two of them together and listen to the sound of my husband's voice.

"Things went on like that for the first few years and then one night Kyle didn't come home right after work. He said he'd had a meeting with a student that had gone later than he'd expected. I didn't think anything about it, after all, he'd never given me any reason to doubt him. But soon he was having meetings and staff dinners and various other things he needed to attend until I noticed that he was gone more than he was home. I guess a part of me knew that something wasn't right, but I believed him when he would tell me that he needed to go out of town for a conference all weekend or that he was just too tired for sex. I suppose when you love someone, you tend to see what you want to see instead of looking at the harsh realities."

She stopped walking as the ground levelled off and we reached a clearing. Directly ahead of us was a set of tracks which led to an old train trestle which appeared as if it hadn't been used in over a decade. Ivy grew up and over the trestle which stood approximately 100 feet above a river. A cold wind whipped through my thin shirt and soon my teeth were chattering.

"Go on, you've almost reached the end." I turned to look at her sharply as she giggled like a deranged schoolgirl. Her eyes shone brightly with the reflection of the moon, making them look inky black.

"Cynthia, will you let me explain?" I spoke softly so I wouldn't spook her.

"Move!" she shouted as she pointed the gun at my head. My jaw clenched tightly as I fought a frustrated scream, but then I turned grudgingly and began walking down the tracks.

"Like I was saying, I had my suspicions, but no concrete evidence. The only real difference was the fact that he was gone more and how happy he was. I'd always thought Kyle was happy, but then things changed and he was like a whole new man. He smiled more easily, he laughed more often, and I often caught him whistling when he finally walked in the door after a long day. I had almost convinced myself that he was happy because of me and the life we shared, but then one day it all came crashing down around us." She stopped me when we were nearly halfway across the trestle and I wrapped my arms around myself to try and ward off the cold as I turned to face her.

"Cynthia, I never..."

"Shut up! I'm telling the story and you need to listen." She paced back and forth over the rickety wooden beams in obvious agitation and I wondered if I had any chance of wrestling the gun away from her, but before I could take a step forward she raised the gun and walked forward until it was pressed to my chest, directly over my heart.

"Kyle came home from work one night and he looked upset, like he'd been crying. I asked him what was wrong, but he said he didn't want to talk about it. He locked himself in his study and stayed up all night drinking and listening to that wretched song over and over again. Kyle had never been much of a drinker, but whatever had upset him had been bad enough to send him straight to the bottle. I sat outside his office door all night long, hoping he would open the door and tell me what was going on, but he never did. I could hear him crying through the walls, it was a lonely sound, like someone who'd had their heart broken." Her words caused me to wince which only served to anger her more.

"It's your fault things turned out the way they did. It wasn't enough for you to swoop in and take a man who didn't belong to you, you had to make him fall in love with you and then crush his heart, leaving nothing behind but an empty shell." Her hands shook with her anger and I stared down at the gun warily as she waved it in front of me.

"He finally admitted everything to me one night when he was too drunk to realize what he was saying. I listened while he told me about the gorgeous, intelligent, kind young man he'd fallen in love with. He explained that he'd wanted to leave me and spend the rest of his life with the man, but that he'd messed up and his lover had turned away from him. I never spoke a word as he confessed his sins to me and shredded my soul in the process. By the next morning, he had no memory of having told me and I had what I needed, a name: *Landon Greene.*"

My name dripped from her lips like acid and my stomach roiled wildly. I wasn't stupid enough to believe she had taken me up there just to talk, but I wasn't sure what I could do to get out of the situation. It had become very obvious that there would be no calming her down. I looked between the wooden slats of the train tracks and I wondered if I would be able to survive a fall into the churning water below. I shook off the idea quickly, realizing that even if I lived through the fall, the water had to be several degrees below freezing; hypothermia would set in before I even had a chance to swim to the edge.

"Things continued to get worse. Kyle was drunk more than he was sober and I'm pretty sure he started using drugs. He missed a lot of work because he couldn't get out of bed after his binges and he was put on probation. Eventually he was fired. I tried everything I could to pull him from the depression he was drowning in, but it was like he could no longer hear me when I spoke." Her head had lowered and her voice rang with sadness, but then her head shot up and she glared at me, her lip curling back in a vicious snarl.

"We lost our home and had to move in with my sister. I took a second job, working nights as a waitress in a diner. Then one day, I came home and found my husband hanging in the garage. He'd left a note saying that he didn't want to live any more after losing the only person he'd ever truly loved." I gasped as her words cut through me like knives. I had spent years feeling hurt and angry over what Kyle had done, but I had never allowed myself to consider the pain our breakup had caused him. Regardless of how things had ended between the two of us, there was a time in my life when we were happy and in love and it broke my heart to know that he had chosen to take his life.

"Do you have any idea what that felt like? I was his wife and we had a son, but all he wanted was *you*. It was because of you that I lost my husband and my son lost his father. You broke him until he felt like he had no choice but to end his life so I think it's only fair that you lose your life too," she screamed.

"Cynthia, I never meant to hurt you. I ended things as soon as I found out he was married *because* I didn't want to hurt you." My words came out in a rush, but I needed to make her understand. A cold sweat broke out all over me at the icy determination in her eyes. She cocked the hammer of the gun and lifted her other arm to take aim. I held my hands up in front of me. "Cynthia, please…"

"Stop! Drop the gun and raise your hands in the air!" My head swiveled at the sound of Micah's voice and I prayed that I wasn't imagining it, but Cynthia had turned too.

I heard her scream in outrage when she saw him and then everything happened all at once. Micah yelled again for her to drop her weapon, but she turned her attention back on me with a manic smile as she took aim once again. The sound of a gun going off rang through the quiet night, followed closely by a second louder blast. Fire burst through me at the same time that I began to fall.

CHAPTER
Eighteen

Micah

M Y HEART WAS RACING AS I RAN THROUGH THE CROWDED concert arena, pushing people out of my way as I went. My sole focus was on getting to Landon as quickly as possible. I rounded a corner and held my badge up to the guards as I sprinted past them and down the long hallway that would take me to the backstage dressing rooms. It felt a lot like the time I had raced behind stage when the guy broke into Carter's dressing room, the big difference then was, Landon had been at my side.

I saw Tony as I neared Carter's room and I slowed to a fast-paced walk. He gave me a look full of regret and opened his mouth to apologize, but I cut him off. "We'll talk about it later, right now we need to find Landon." He nodded his head and within seconds, had pulled his shoulders back straight and was in full military mode. "Tell me what you know," I said as I walked into the dressing room.

My eyes scanned the room as Tony began talking. "I'm not sure how long they've been gone, but they were only in here about twenty minutes before you called and had me check on them. None of the employees that parked back there saw anything, but Greg is getting the security feed from outside the building and I've already called the police."

I opened the back door, my eyes scanning the dark parking lot. There were cars parked all around, but no sign of people. My eyes zeroed in on an object on the ground near the wall. My stomach sank as I bent down over it. It was Landon's phone. I knew better than to touch it because there could be fingerprints on it. The screen was cracked, but when I used a pen to hit the button it still turned on and a lump formed in my throat when I saw his screen saver. I remember, we had been watching a movie together on the couch in his hotel room. We were stretched out and I was lying half on top of him with my head on his chest. The picture was of Landon kissing my forehead while I slept. My eyes burned and I had to blink a few times to clear my vision. I would be no help to Landon if I didn't remain focused.

I cleared my throat as I dialed Brandon in Chicago. "Where are you?" I asked gruffly.

"I'm at the office, what do you need?" he replied, my tone alerting him to the fact that something serious was going on.

"What's Kyle Brooks' wife's name?"

"Hang on a second." I could hear him shuffling through papers as he searched. "Here it is, Cynthia Brooks."

"Do you have a picture of her?" I asked.

"Yes, sir."

"Send it to all of our phones and then I need you to put a trace on the tracking device I put in Landon's watch. I'll call you back in a few minutes when we're ready to move." I turned to Tony who was hanging up his phone.

"They're bringing a car around for you."

"Thanks. I need to take your headset so I can communicate with Brandon." Tony handed it over and I put it on at the same time Carter and Ryan came rushing into the room. I saw the terrified look in their eyes so I placed my hand on Carter's shoulder to reassure him. I stiffened in surprise as he brushed my hand off and crushed his body into mine, wrapping me up in a tight hug.

"Please find my brother, Micah." His voice warbled and I put my arms around him, patting his back in what I hoped was a soothing gesture. I had never received many hugs in my life until I met Landon, but since then I had learned that the entire Greene family was a touchy-feely group of people. I had also learned that I didn't mind it as much as I thought I would.

"I will, Carter. I'm not going to stop until I bring him back," I vowed.

His head bumped my chin when he nodded, but then he stepped back and moved into Ryan's waiting arms. Greg rushed through the door along with the police at the same time our phones pinged. We all looked down as the image of Cynthia Brooks filled our screens. My jaw clenched and I looked up at Tony questioningly.

He nodded. "That's her."

A car pulled up just then and I raced to it as Greg called out that they'd be right behind me. I looked over in surprise as the doors swung open and Carter jumped in the passenger seat at the same time as Ryan and Carlos slid into the back.

"Hurry up, we have to find my brother." He waved his hand in a let's get moving gesture and I dialed up Brandon as we peeled out of the parking lot.

--· ⟫•⟪ ·--

"Okay, it looks like they headed east out of the city," Brandon said through the headset. My hands gripped the steering wheel tightly as I weaved in and out of traffic. Horns blared at me as I cut drivers off, but I didn't care.

"How far ahead are they?"

"They have about a thirty-minute lead on you. They're moving at a normal rate of speed, probably trying not to draw any attention to themselves, so you should be able to narrow that gap as soon as you get out of the city." I followed his directions until we reached the highway and I released a tense breath as traffic finally opened up. My foot pressed down on the gas as I began to cut down on the distance between Landon and myself.

We all jumped when Carter's phone rang and he glanced at the screen before letting out a curse. His head dropped back on the headrest as he answered. "Hey, Caleb."

I tuned Carter out as he attempted to calm down his frantic twin. I had been running on pure adrenaline ever since I found out Landon had been taken, but with nothing but the dark open road stretched ahead of me, my mind began to wander. Images of my father coming at me, belt in hand as I cowered on my bedroom floor flashed through my head. No matter how much I begged and pleaded with him not to hurt me, he would just laugh and then I would feel the sting of the leather across my back and my thighs, the metal of the buckle cutting into my flesh and making me bleed. The memories switched over to my bloodied fists pounding on the cell door as I begged for the monsters to spare Spencer's life.

None of it had mattered though because both my father and my kidnappers had held all the power and they wielded that power over me until I could no longer see any hope. My need for control had stemmed from those experiences and Landon had given me that gift, letting me feel stronger and more in control of my life than I ever had. But once again, I was left feeling powerless, only this time was worse because the person being hurt was the man I loved, the man I would gladly give my own life for.

My heart constricted in my chest as I pictured Landon's face the first time we moved beyond simply having sex and actually made love. He hadn't held anything back and I felt like I was able to look into his soul and see all of the love and trust he felt for me. No one had ever given themselves to me so freely, but then again, I had never allowed anyone to get that close before. It had been the single most precious moment in my life and I swore to myself that I would do whatever it took to keep him looking at me just like that for the rest of our lives.

I sniffed back the tears that were threatening to pour and sat up straighter in my seat with a renewed determination. I loved Landon and I wasn't going to waste any more time feeling helpless. I was going to find him and stop Cynthia from following through on whatever sick plan she had. I refused to fail again.

I slowed down as Brandon directed us down a one-lane road and into the woods. According to my calculations, Landon wasn't more than ten minutes ahead of us and that made me feel a lot more confident that I might get to him in time.

"Were you able to calm him down?" Ryan asked as Carter ended his call with Caleb.

Carter sighed tiredly. "As much as I could. I told him I'd let him know something as soon as I can. I feel bad for him, being so far away and knowing there's nothing he can do to help."

"We'll find Landon soon and then you can call and let Caleb know that everything's alright." Ryan laid a reassuring hand on his fiancé's shoulder and Carter reached up, twining their fingers together.

The trees finally started to thin out ahead of us and something shown in the headlights of our car. I slowed down as we approached a vehicle parked off to the side and my gut told me it was Cynthia's car. I ordered Carter and Ryan to wait while Carlos and I had a look.

I pulled my gun from the waistband of my pants then nodded to Carlos who was also holding his gun. My heart hammered in my chest as we crept up slowly. Carlos moved around the right side of the vehicle while I took the left. I released the breath I'd been holding when I saw that it was empty.

"It looks like they're on foot," I informed Brandon. "I'm going to need you to direct me."

"You got it," he responded confidently.

I looked back at our car where Carter and Ryan were already climbing out. "I'm following the rest of the way on foot. You two should wait in the car for the police to get here," I suggested.

The glare Carter gave me had me stopping in my tracks. "He's my brother; I'm going with you."

I glanced at Ryan who pointed at Carter. "I go wherever he goes."

I wasn't going to waste time arguing so I just nodded at them and turned, moving further into the woods. Branches hung down low and I held them back for Carter as he followed closely behind. We started climbing uphill with Brandon leading me as best he could. Finally, we reached the top of the incline. I held my hand up to silence the others when I heard voices up ahead. I moved carefully so I wouldn't give away my position until finally I was able to make out two people standing in the distance.

I continued creeping forward until I could clearly see Landon and my heart dropped down to my toes. They were standing on a train trestle and Cynthia had a gun in her hands, her full attention on Landon as she screamed at him. I slinked closer and heard him speaking to her, the fear in his voice evident. I wanted to get closer, but when I saw Cynthia take aim and Landon raise his hands up in defense, I knew time had run out.

"Stop! Drop the gun and raise your hands in the air!" I shouted and they both turned to look at me.

I had been hoping to throw her off guard enough that I could get the upper hand, but instead she let out a cry full of rage and turned back to Landon. She raised her gun once again and I ordered her for a second time to drop her weapon. When I saw her smile at Landon, I knew I had no other choice. I fired at her and saw it hit at the same time her gun went off.

I watched in horrified slow motion as blood burst from Landon's chest and he disappeared over the side of the trestle. I took off running and sank to my knees, searching the current for him, but I was too high up to see clearly. A pained cry rang out over the night and echoed off the surrounding hillsides. It wasn't until Carlos reached my side and pulled me to my feet, shaking me in his grip that I realized the sound was coming from me.

I barely registered Cynthia's lifeless form lying on the tracks as Carlos grabbed my hand and dragged me back over to solid ground. I felt numb everywhere and I just wanted to lie on the ground and close my eyes. There was no point in trying any more. Without Landon, there was no point to anything.

—·———⟫•⟪———·—

Carlos was saying something, but his words weren't making any sense. "Micah! Listen to me, man!" His loud scream tore through the haze and my mind cleared long enough to focus on what he was telling me. "Landon could have survived that fall and if he did, he needs us to get to him as quickly as possible. He's been shot and that water is below freezing. Ryan and Carter are going down there to look for him, but they need our help."

Adrenaline surged through my body and before I knew it I was down the steep embankment and running alongside the river, my eyes searching the water for any sign of the man I loved. I heard Carter and Ryan calling out to him and I joined in. I followed the flow of the current and tried to get ahead of it, knowing it would have already carried him far beyond the trestle.

I stumbled over a large rock in my haste to find him and landed on my knees. I felt blood on my hands as sharp rocks tore my skin, but I ignored the pain and moved on. A few seconds later I spotted something white in the water. It was up against something big and dark and didn't appear to be moving. I ran a little closer until I could see that the large dark shape was actually a tree that had fallen into the water. I heard a soft groan and the white object lifted and then fell back into the water.

I screamed for help and then without further thought, leapt into the icy water. It stole my breath for a few seconds as the cold seeped into my bones, but soon my SEAL training kicked in and I began slicing through the water. The current pulled and tugged, wanting to take me away from Landon, but I fought with everything I had until finally, I reached his side. He had lost consciousness, but luckily, he had become tangled in the branches of the tree and they held him secure. I worked quickly to untangle him and then wrapped my arm around his chest, making sure to keep his head above the water as I used my other arm and my legs to pull us to the edge of the riverbank.

Carlos and Carter helped to drag Landon's battered body out of the water and then Ryan took over CPR when his wound began to bleed heavily. I dropped down next to his body, my tired limbs giving out. My chest rose and fell as I slowly reached my hand over to find his. A loud tha-wumping noise filled the air and I watched as a flight care helicopter appeared over the ridge and circled around for several minutes before landing gently in a nearby clearing.

Emergency personnel suddenly rushed forward and loaded Landon onto a stretcher. They placed an oxygen mask over his face and then they were saying something to me. I finally understood that they needed to take him and they wanted me to let go of his hand, but I couldn't so I stood as Ryan helped lift the stretcher and held Landon's hand tightly in mine as we made our way over to the helicopter. I wasn't ever leaving his side again and so I was ready for a fight as they loaded him and prepared for takeoff, but Ryan said something to one of them and soon they pushed me into a seat, wrapped a warm blanket around my shoulders, and strapped a belt across me. I mouthed thank you to Ryan as he waved at me and then darted out of the way as the helicopter lifted off of the ground.

We raised up high in the air and I could see lots of red and blue lights dotting the area. As we rushed back to the city, I turned my attention to Landon. He still hadn't opened his eyes and he had a nasty gash above his right eye that had already started to bruise. His bottom lip was split and his skin was a waxy gray color that scared the shit out of me. I rubbed my thumb back and forth over his hand and closed my eyes in a silent prayer.

Soon we were landing on the rooftop of the hospital where a team of doctors and nurses were waiting to take him to surgery. As they prepared to transport him, I leaned down next to his ear and whispered to him. "I love you, Landon. Don't you dare leave me when I just found you."

They pulled the stretcher out and attached it to a gurney and then they were on the move, shouting instructions that I couldn't make any sense of. I ran after them, but was stopped when they reached a door that said authorized personnel only. A nurse said something to me, but her words didn't seem to make any sense. Finally, she took hold of my arm and pulled me into an empty room where she helped me out of my wet clothes and into a dry pair of scrubs. I mumbled my thanks, at least I thought I did and then she led me back out to the waiting area. I sank down wearily into the nearest chair and let my head drop back against the wall as I waited to find out if the doctors would be able to put the man who owned my heart back together again.

I had no idea how much time had passed as I stared blankly at the wall, lost in my own thoughts. I relived each moment I had spent with Landon and I thought of all the things I still wanted to do with him. I felt like I had just gotten a taste of what it would be like to be loved by Landon Greene and I wanted, needed, more of that in my life. No one else had ever loved me so completely before and now that I'd experienced that, I knew I wouldn't be able to live without it. *God, please don't take him from me.*

Someone knelt down in front of me and tears filled my eyes. I tried to blink them back, but they spilled over instead, dripping down my cheeks and soaking into my shirt. Giovanni reached for me and I sank into his arms with a choked cry. I didn't know how he had managed to get there so quick, but I was so grateful to have him there with me. The dam inside me burst and I twisted the back of his shirt in my fists as I sobbed all of my fear and grief into my best friend's neck.

Giovanni rocked me gently in his arms, his big hand rubbing over the back of my head as he whispered that he was there and he wasn't going to leave. He held me until my tears had run dry and then he sat back on his heels, his eyes full of sympathy and understanding. Someone handed me a tissue and I looked up startled into the face of Landon's father. I glanced around the room and saw Landon's mother and Caleb talking quietly with Carter and Ryan and my face flushed with embarrassment.

"Don't!" Rick Greene told me as he sank into the chair next to me. "Don't ever feel embarrassed for showing your vulnerability, son. Nobody can be strong all of the time and when you're not, well, that's when you need your friends and family around you to lend you their strength."

"You're right, sir. I'm very grateful to have Giovanni here." Giovanni squeezed my knee and I gave him a shaky smile.

Rick tilted his head and stared at me for a moment. "I know my son well enough to know that he's in love with you. Do you feel the same way about him?"

"I love him more than I ever thought possible," I answered truthfully.

Rick gestured to the others in the room and then looked back at me. "Then you have more than just Giovanni. We're your family too."

"Thank you, sir," I whispered. He patted my leg and then left to join his wife who was sobbing quietly as Carter explained everything that had happened. "They're nice people," I said.

Giovanni stood and then sank down into the seat that Rick had just vacated. "Yeah, they are." He looked over at them with a small smile then turned back to me. "They're also not the type of people to say things they don't mean. If they say that you're a part of the family, then that's that."

I smiled wider. "I guess I can live with that." I chuckled as Giovanni bumped my shoulder with his own. "How did you guys get here so fast?" I asked him.

"Carter called Lachlan who sent his private jet to pick us up. Emma and Michelle were upset they couldn't come, but their doctors said they can't fly so close to their due dates so they agreed to keep Sarah for us. We had to promise about three hundred times that we would update them as soon as we heard anything."

Just then the door swung open and a doctor walked out. I jumped to my feet and was in front of him so fast he took a surprised step back. "I'm looking for the family of Landon Greene," he said warily.

"I'm his family," I stated.

His eyes swept over me, sizing me up. "It's true," I heard Rick say. "Micah is his fiancé and we're his parents. The rest of these people are his brothers." I looked over at Rick and gave him a grateful smile. The doctor nodded and gestured for us all to have a seat so he could go over Landon's condition. Rick winked at me as he sat down and I smiled back.

"Landon is out of surgery and in critical but stable condition. The bullet nicked his heart which caused a lot of internal damage." Kathy gasped and I felt like I was going to throw up at the thought of how close the bullet had come to ending Landon's life. I breathed in and out through my nose and then realized the doctor was still talking.

"I think in Landon's case, hypothermia ended up being a good thing. Without the cold water lowering his body temperature significantly, he most likely would have bled out. Instead, we were able to repair all of the damage. We'll watch him closely over the next few days, but I feel very confident that he'll make a full recovery."

Everyone began laughing and hugging each other and then Rick asked when Landon would be allowed to have visitors. My head shot to the doctor as he explained that as soon as they got him into a room we could see him, but no more than two of us at a time and only for a few minutes. We nodded our agreement and then he disappeared behind the doors again with a gentle swoosh.

My legs felt like jelly and I sank back down into my chair. I lowered my head into my hands and said a quiet thanks to God, making a promise to Him that I would spend the rest of my days on earth, loving Landon to the best of my abilities.

CHAPTER
Nineteen

Landon

I WALKED THROUGH THE FRONT DOOR OF MY HOUSE AND LOCKED it before dropping my keys on the table by the door. It was good to be home. I grabbed a bottle of apple juice out of the fridge before heading into the living room where I sank down tiredly onto the couch. My doctor had warned me that it would take some time for me to get my strength back and he wasn't kidding. My heart had been strong and healthy and so it had healed rather quickly after the bullet nicked it, but the damage done to my chest muscles from both the gunshot wound and the surgery would take longer to heal. I'd been left with some vicious scars, but considering what the outcome could have been, I was just thankful to be alive.

Caleb and Giovanni had felt terrible that they couldn't stay longer than a day, but I told them that I completely understood their need to get back home to Sarah. She was young and they were still getting used to being a family; their priority needed to be her. Micah had hugged Giovanni before he left and whispered something to him that left both men a little misty eyed. I would forever be grateful to Giovanni for taking care of Micah when they were younger.

Carter had postponed his shows as long as he could, but once it became apparent that I was going to be all right, he returned to finish the tour. I was sad that I wouldn't be there with him to finish out the schedule, but Ryan assured me that he would watch over Carter and keep him safe. It hurt a little to know that my little brothers didn't need me as much as they used to, but it also filled me with pride to see how strong and independent they had become and that they had men who loved them and would move Heaven and Earth for them.

My parents had stayed in a hotel near the hospital for over a week until I insisted that they go back home. My sisters were nearing the end of their pregnancies and I didn't want my parents to miss it if one of them should deliver earlier than expected. I adored my mom and dad, but after having them hover over me constantly for more than a week, I was ready for some space. More than anything, I needed to be alone with Micah.

He stayed by my side the entire time, even throughout the night. I'd tried to talk him into sharing my bed with me, but he was worried that he might hurt me while we slept so he asked the nurse to bring a cot in instead and set it up beside me so he could reach through the metal slats of the hospital bed and hold my hand as I fell asleep. I'm sure the cot wasn't the most comfortable place to sleep, but after everything we'd been through neither one of us wanted to be away from the other.

The nurses thought we made an adorable couple and they were almost as enamored with Micah as I was, almost. I knew it was more than coincidence that had them stopping by my room more frequently than their other patients and I had smirked at him when they insisted on bringing him a tray of food along with mine each night for dinner and extra pillows for his bed. I couldn't blame them too much though; he was awfully pretty to look at. Micah just laughed it off, insisting that my attention was the only one he wanted. It never ceased to send a thrill straight through me to hear him say those words and I was pretty sure I had a goofy smile on my face most of the time.

After spending nearly three weeks in the hospital, the doctor had finally said that I was strong enough to go home. I was thrilled to be heading back to Chicago with Micah, but a part of me was scared to leave the hospital. Physically I was on the road to recovery, but mentally I felt like I had taken a giant step backwards. Ever since that night with Cynthia my anxiety had gotten worse. I became shaky when someone other than Micah was in the room with me and I jumped at loud noises. Micah was pretty sure I was also suffering from PTSD and he was worried that I didn't want to talk about what had happened.

The truth was, I couldn't talk about it because I wasn't exactly sure how I felt about it. I was pissed at Kyle for starting everything in the first place with his lies, but I was also sad that he had never been strong enough to be true to who he was in the first place, instead of dragging a wife and child through his pain. Despite everything he had put us all through, it killed me to think of him feeling so helpless that he would take his own life. I was angry at Cynthia, but I also felt incredibly guilty for the part I had played, even unknowingly, in the destruction of her marriage and for turning what I assumed was once a kind woman into the deranged monster who had tried to kill me. Mostly I was devastated to learn that the most innocent person in the whole thing, their son, had ended up losing both of his parents. Micah tried to comfort me by telling me that the boy had been taken in by his loving grandparents, but it was a small consolation.

My emotions were a jumbled-up mess and I wasn't sure what to do with it all, so I tried to push it all into a box and ignore it, but Micah refused to let me. He said he couldn't allow me to carry around that much pain ever again, especially over something he insisted hadn't been my fault. I could see how worried he was so as soon as we returned to Chicago I had agreed to start seeing a psychiatrist to get started on medications as well as a therapist to talk things out with and I had to admit that it was helping.

My therapist, Dr. Alberto, was a kind man with a calming way about him that immediately put me at ease. At my first appointment, I was too nervous to talk and so I spent most of that hour gazing at the various pictures he had hanging on the walls of his office. There was one photo in particular that captured my attention. It was a black and white picture of him cradling an infant in his hands while another man kissed her forehead. He'd caught me staring and explained that the picture was of him and his husband on the day they brought their daughter home. He asked me if that was something I would like to have one day. I was quiet for a minute as I tried to picture me and Micah in the future, holding a child that was ours to keep.

"Yes. Yes, it is," I whispered shakily.

"Then we have some work to do first, don't you think?" he'd replied softly. I'd nodded and with a new determination, I started talking.

He listened quietly as I spilled out everything that had happened and how I'd been feeling, then he patiently helped me to make sense of it all. Along with the anti-anxiety medications prescribed by my psychiatrist, Dr. Alberto also gave me coping mechanisms to use when I felt a panic attack coming on and he was helping me to determine what my triggers were that brought the anxiety on in the first place; that way I could limit the amount of stressful situations I found myself in and hopefully cut off any attacks before they occurred. He'd also diagnosed me with and was treating me for PTSD just as Micah had thought. I knew I had a long way to go, but I was proud of the progress I'd made and I was feeling stronger every day.

The sound of keys rattling in the door caused my heart to speed up, but instead of fear, it was excitement I was feeling, because I knew who was on the other side and suddenly, I didn't feel tired in the slightest. Micah walked in and locked the door behind him, before shrugging out of his jacket and hanging it on the hook. He hadn't noticed me yet and I took a moment to admire him. His hair had grown a bit while he was at the hospital with me, but he'd recently cut it short again and I loved to run my hands over the soft bristles. He was wearing a dark blue t-shirt which stretched tightly over his broad shoulders and revealed the beautiful designs tattooed down his arm.

His jeans hugged his perfectly shaped ass and I moaned as I pictured how that ass would taste on my tongue. He glanced over his shoulder when he heard me and turned with a cocky smirk on his face. "You know better than to do that to yourself, baby."

His eyes zeroed in on my hand pressing down against my growing erection as he stalked over to where I sat. We hadn't had sex since I'd been put in the hospital. I'd begged and pleaded for even a hand job, but he'd refused until I was properly healed. Given the fact that I could grow an erection from his scent alone, I often worried that I was going to suffer from a permanent case of blue balls.

"It doesn't look like I'm the only one affected," I commented, sending a pointed look to the prominent bulge in his pants.

"That's because just the sight of you does it for me." He leaned down to give me a kiss and I curled my hand around the back of his neck to deepen the kiss. He made a rumbling noise in the back of his throat that sent shockwaves throughout my entire body.

"Baby," he warned. He tried to pull away, but I fisted the front of his shirt and pulled him until we were both lying on the couch, him on top of me. "Landon, I want you too, more than you know, but I won't hurt you."

I threw my arms around his neck, refusing to let go and licked a line up his throat, over his chin, and across the seam of his mouth. "I guess it's a good thing the doctor gave me the all clear on sex today then, isn't it?" I whispered seductively as I pulled his bottom lip gently between my teeth.

His head pulled back and he stared directly in my eyes. "I'm on the edge as it is, Landon. Don't toy with me."

I chuckled. "I promise you, I'm telling the truth. He told me I was perfectly capable of withstanding sex again."

The cocky grin made an appearance once again and I had to fight the urge to devour his face. "Did you explain to him how energetic our sex usually gets?"

"Well, I didn't go into details, but he's seen you before so I'm sure he could imagine," I said, reaching around him to cup his ass. He pushed his hips into mine and we both groaned with pleasure. "Please, Micah," I whimpered.

"Tell me what you need." His voice was rough and the sound of it shot right to my balls.

"I need to feel your skin against mine. I want to feel you moving inside of me," I answered.

He slammed his mouth over mine and my head swirled from the passion behind his kiss. I groaned with frustration as he slowly backed away and stood up. "I'll be right back," he promised. My head slumped back as he started to walk away, but then he turned back to look at me with a fierce expression. "Be naked when I get back."

The command in his voice had my cock leaking and I sprang from the couch and began pulling my clothes off. Although the dynamic of our relationship had changed and neither of us required the need to dominate or in my case to be dominated, we each agreed that we enjoyed it and wanted to continue the role play from time to time. I was glad because seeing Micah in all of his dominant male splendor never failed to turn me inside out.

I stood completely naked in my living room and assumed a submissive stance by placing my hands behind my back and bowing my head. I heard his sharp intake of breath as he returned and saw me. I felt a surge of pride and my cock dripped onto the hardwood floor.

"That is the sexiest fucking thing I've ever seen," he growled. He stepped closer and I was pleased to see that he was naked as well. I heard him set the supplies down on the coffee table and then I stared at his feet as he approached, wondering idly when feet had become so erotic to me. I jolted when his hand landed on my shoulder, the feel of his skin burning me. It had been so long since I'd felt him touch me in a sensual way and I felt like I would lose my mind with my need for him.

His hand pressed against my shoulder in a silent command and I happily complied, dropping to my knees in front of him, still looking downward. His fingers dove into the hair on the back of my head and pulled gently, raising my head until my eyes met his. The look in his eyes was dominant, hungry, and possessive and I moaned in response. He grasped the base of his cock in his hand and held it up in front of me. The tip glistened with pre-cum and I licked my lips, my need to taste him overpowering.

"Wrap your lips around the head and suck." I leaned forward, but he pulled back. I glanced up at him in question. "Only the head. Don't go any farther until I give you permission." I nodded as best I could with him holding on to the back of my hair and then opened my mouth slightly, keeping my lips firm. He fed his cock into my mouth and I sucked the tip eagerly. Another burst of pre-cum was my reward and I hummed with joy as his flavor coated my tongue. I hollowed my cheeks and sucked harder, wanting to pull more of the salty goodness from him.

"Enough!" His breath was labored above me. My tongue swept defiantly over the bundle of nerves that lay just under the crown of his dick. His body trembled and before I knew it he had plunged his cock down my throat, making me gag at the sudden intrusion. My lips pulled up in a grin around his thick rod. As much as I loved his domination, I found it equally as thrilling when I was able to make him lose control.

He thrust his cock in and out of my mouth and saliva dripped from my chin as I swallowed him down to the root. I loved giving head to Micah; on my knees, pleasuring the man I loved was as close to paradise as I'd ever been. I could tell by the change in his breathing that he was getting close. Within seconds his movements faltered and hot streams of cum shot down my throat and coated my tongue. I drank greedily, not letting a single drop spill. When he had finished, I licked every inch of him clean and then sat back on my heels and gave him a satisfied grin.

He still looked dazed, but he smiled back at me. "I hope you're happy with yourself. That wasn't supposed to happen."

"I'm extremely happy, sir." I winked at him as I smacked my lips together loudly.

He shook his head with a chuckle then held his hand out to me. I took his hand and he pulled me to my feet in one swift movement. He leaned towards me and I sank into his kiss. The swift slap to my ass took me by surprise and I yelped into his mouth. Another stinging swat to the opposite cheek had me groaning and I wriggled my ass, inviting more of the same. He pulled back and held my chin firmly between his thumb and forefinger.

"I want you on the bed. Get on your hands and knees and present yourself to me. You will remain there until I am ready for you." The humor was gone from his voice, replaced with a deep command that made goose bumps break out across my skin.

When he stepped back I turned and made my way into the bedroom. I quickly crawled onto the bed and got on my hands and knees as directed. I dropped my head down so that I was able to see the doorway through my spread thighs. My cock was rock hard and I watched as a thin line of pre-cum stretched from its tip to the bed below, creating a pool of moisture on the sheet. I held my breath and listened for his arrival. I could hear him moving around in the kitchen, the sounds of water running and I bit my lip against a curse.

The anticipation grew as I waited for what seemed like an eternity. Finally, I heard his footsteps drawing nearer down the hallway and I wanted to weep with relief. My breathing increased and I was panting by the time he reached the doorway. He didn't cross over the threshold, but stood there instead and I could feel his eyes travelling over my body. After a few seconds, he stepped into the room and I gasped as his hand caressed the tender flesh of my ass.

"So perfect," he whispered. "I wish you could see how pretty my handprint looks on your skin." I felt something warm press against the abused area. I wasn't able to see him so I couldn't be sure, but it felt as if he'd kissed me.

More liquid dripped from my cock and I watched him lower himself to his knees on the floor behind me. I fisted the sheets in my hands as his thumbs spread my cheeks apart. I was in the most vulnerable position a person could be in and yet I had never felt safer. Warm breath glided over my hole and I wriggled my ass, needing more.

The first swipe of his tongue had me crying out and then he blew cool air over my then wet opening. He licked over the puckered skin again and then dove in, feasting on me as if he were a starving man. I began mumbling incoherently as his tongue joined in the action, snaking in and out of me and opening me up. He added a finger to the mix, working it in slowly and twisting his wrist so that it ran around my rim in a circular fashion.

Moments later, a second finger was added as he alternated between licking and sucking the sensitive skin of my inner thighs. His fingers continued to work their way in and out of me and I rocked my body forward and back on his hand. With his other hand, he reached between my legs and held my rigid shaft in his warm palm. He drew it back and flattened his tongue, licking me from the tip of my cock, all the way up to my balls. He swirled his tongue over my balls and sucked them one at a time into his mouth.

He released my balls and I breathed a sigh of relief. I was close to the edge and I needed a moment to gain control. Micah, however, had other plans and I soon felt my cock enveloped in the wet heat of his mouth. He sucked me relentlessly and when his fingers curled inside me, hitting upon that perfect spot, I felt myself catapulting over the side of the cliff and soaring through the sky.

I must have blacked out for a moment because when I came to, I was lying up further on the bed with my head resting on a pillow as Micah licked the sweat from my spine. His skin rubbed against mine as he moved up the bed then his head was near mine. His tongue traced the shell of my ear and he nibbled at my lobe.

"Glad to have you back," he teased.

"How long was I out?" I mumbled dreamily, keeping my eyes closed.

"Not long, just enough to make me feel like a king." I peeked one eye open and caught his wide smile and we both started laughing.

"You are definitely *my* king," I replied.

He flipped me over with a strength that still took me by surprise at times and I stared at him wide-eyed. "Hmmm. If I'm a king, does that make you my queen?" He wiggled his brows at me playfully.

"Don't push it." I swatted at his chest, but he caught my wrist and raised it above my head, quickly grabbing the other and locking them together. His body lowered over mine and I could feel his breaths on my lips as he stared into my eyes.

"I came too close to losing all of this. I can't ever lose you, Landon; I couldn't bear it." The back of my eyes stung when I heard the pain in his voice.

Pulling my wrists from his grasp, I cradled the sides of his face in my hands. "You won't lose me. Not until we're very, very old and then I'll just be waiting for you on the other side."

"I love you so much," he whispered.

"I love you too. You are all I've ever dreamed of." I offered my lips to him and he met me in a tender kiss.

Micah's tongue swept into my mouth and soon the fire between us was reignited. I lifted my hips and we each gasped as our cocks rubbed together. Our movements were slow, purposeful, having already worked through the frantic need to come. He lifted so that he could gather supplies from the drawer by the bed and I busied myself, licking the sweat from his chest and letting my teeth graze over his taut nipples. He hissed when I bit down and he held my head in place as I soothed him with gentle licks and quick flicks of my tongue.

He settled back on his heels as he opened the bottle of lube, spreading it around on his fingers. I held my legs open and he circled his fingers around my opening. My muscles were still relaxed from his fingering before so it didn't take him long to work three fingers inside of me.

"Please, Micah. I need to feel you," I pleaded desperately. He carefully removed his fingers and reached for the condom, but I stopped him when I laid my hand on his arm. He eyed me curiously and I swallowed thickly.

"They ran a full work-up on my blood in the hospital. I'm clean." I held my breath as I waited for his response. My heart sank when his chin dropped to his chest. *Had I pushed too hard, too quickly?* Then he lifted his head and the love I saw shining in his eyes took my breath away.

"I was tested when I left the SEALs; it's a required part of the discharge process," he explained. "I'm clean too." A smile spread across his face and I felt a matching one pull at my own. I reached for my dick and stroked it gently while he slicked his cock with lube.

"Are you sure?" he asked, looking at me for any sign that I'd changed my mind. That wasn't going to happen.

"I'm sure. Fill me up, Micah." Needing no more prodding, he slid inside of me with one long movement, making me gasp at the welcome intrusion. His long, thick cock filled me so completely that it felt as if our bodies had merged into one.

"Hold still," he said. His body was rigid and he squeezed his eyes shut as he struggled to calm himself. After a few moments, he began to move and I moaned at the feeling of his bare flesh moving inside of me. "You're so warm and your hole is hugging my cock so tight. It feels incredible, baby." His words lit me up and I locked my ankles together around his back, digging my heels into him so that he drove into me even deeper.

"Hang on," he instructed and I scrambled to grab onto the headboard as he raised up onto his knees, lifting me along with him until I was resting on my shoulder blades. He pulled almost all of the way out and then slid back inside of me quickly.

"Yes, Micah!" I shouted. "I need you to fuck me hard."

His body rocked into mine with such force that the headboard began banging against the wall loudly. Sweat rolled down the sides of his face and dripped from his chin. It was an erotic sight to see his powerful body working so furiously to bring us both to the height of pleasure. A tingling sensation began at the base of my spine as I neared the end. Micah shifted his angle and soon each stroke of his cock landed against my prostate until stars began to flash behind my closed lids.

My second orgasm of the night was even stronger than the first and I lost my ability to breathe as I rode out the wave. In the distance, I heard Micah scream and then I felt a liquid heat filling me. He covered me with his weight and I wrapped my arms around him, clinging to him as if I were afraid he would disappear. Micah recovered faster and began laying gentle kisses along the side of my face and over my eyelids before landing on my mouth.

After a few minutes, he pulled back and we each sighed as his cock slid out of me. I felt his seed begin to spill from me and he reached a hand between my legs and used a finger to spread it around my hole. He glanced up at me and I blinked back tears at the awe on his face.

He shrugged one shoulder. "Now you're really mine," he murmured.

"I've been yours from the first time I saw you," I answered back.

With a smile, he climbed from the bed and went into the adjoining bathroom. I heard the sound of water running and then he was back with a warm washrag that he used to clean me up. When he was finished, he tossed it aside and climbed into bed, settling us both beneath the covers. He pulled me towards him and I curled an arm around him, resting my head on his chest.

My head moved up and down with his breathing and it began to lull me to sleep. I forced my eyes opened when I remembered there was something I wanted to ask him. I lifted my head to see him. Moonlight streamed through the windows and spread over his face.

"What is it, baby?" he whispered. His hands feathered through my hair, lovingly.

"I want you to move in with me. That is, if you want to. Or we can look for something else if you don't like…"

Micah pressed a finger to my lips to stop my nervous chatter and smiled at me. "I'd love to live here with you. Wherever you are, that's where I want to be."

I stretched up to give him a kiss and I could feel him smiling against my lips. With a happy sigh, I lay back down, putting my head back on his chest. His fingers played through my hair and within minutes I was asleep.

CHAPTER
Twenty

Micah

I LEANED BACK AND DRAPED MY ARM OVER THE BACK OF Landon's chair. My fingers rubbed absentmindedly up and down his shoulder as I laughed at the antics of the Greene family. Landon and I had been back in Chicago for two months, but Carter and Ryan had been finishing up the tour. They were finally back home and everyone had gathered together at Rick and Kathy's house to have dinner and catch up. *Scratch that, make it Mom and Dad's house.* Kathy kept insisting I call them Mom and Dad since, as she explained it, I was just another one of their kids now. I was trying, but it would take some getting used to. Although I had to admit that I liked the feeling of being a part of a family again. I hadn't ever had that in my life except for the brief amount of time when I lived with the Romeros.

A lot had happened since we'd come home. We'd both agreed that we were tired of travelling so much, so I'd made the decision to hire a few extra guys that could be sent out on long-distance assignments, allowing me to work only in the Chicago area. Landon was back to work at his agency and he told me that he'd had a long talk with Carter and they'd agreed that the band was doing well and that it was time for Landon to stay home and focus on the other bands he managed.

I'd also let go of my lease and moved in with Landon the day after he'd invited me to. I'd been a little afraid that it would be hard for me to adjust to living with someone and we'd end up getting on each other's nerves. Instead, I found myself looking forward to having dinner with him each night after work. We'd tell each other about our day while we cooked and then afterward, we usually ended up on the couch together, my head in his lap or my body stretched out behind his as we caught up on the shows we liked.

At the end of the day we would either make love or lie wrapped in each other's arms, whispering quietly in the dark about whatever was on our minds. I loved finding out everything I could about Landon and because he was working through his problems with Dr. Alberto, he was more relaxed and freer, as if a heavy weight had been lifted from his shoulders.

Landon's sisters had gone into labor just one day apart. Emma had gone first and we'd all rushed to the hospital to help welcome the newest member of the Greene family. Kathrine Elizabeth was named after her two grandmothers and was the prettiest little baby I'd ever seen. We'd all been thrilled for the proud parents, but after being at the hospital for over sixteen hours waiting on her arrival, we'd all stumbled home and fallen into our beds, exhausted. No sooner had our heads hit the pillow than the phone started ringing and bleary eyed, we'd made our way back to the same hospital, that time to wait for the birth of Michelle's son, Richard Kobe, who was named after his grandpa Rick and his daddy's favorite basketball player. Michelle had rolled her eyes at that, but then gave in when Jason offered to do all of the cooking and cleaning over the following three months.

"Don't get me wrong, I love my son, but would it kill him to let me sleep for more than just a few hours?" Michelle said tiredly.

"I know what you mean," Emma chimed in. "I'm so tired that the other day I put the milk in the cabinet and the cereal in the refrigerator."

"I'm so tired that I went out to my car yesterday to go to work and fell asleep right in the driveway. I probably would've missed the whole day of work, but a coworker called to see where I was at," Mark grumbled.

"I hate to break it to you, but it isn't any easier at four years old. Sarah climbs in our bed in the middle of the night all the time. I usually get woken up with an elbow in my eye," Caleb said.

Rick chuckled at the miserable looks on his children's faces. "It never gets easier," he stated. "Even when your children are old enough to live on their own, you'll worry about them. They may be off travelling the world and trying new adventures and you'll wake in the middle of the night, worried because they're not close enough for you to just run into the next room and check on them. But if you're very lucky, like we have been," he said quietly as he looked around the table. "Then your children will meet people who love them so much that they're willing to watch out for them when you can't be around. As a parent, there's nothing more you can hope for than to have your children grow up to be happy and loved. We're blessed that each one of our children have found that." We all sat quietly as his words soaked in and I saw more than one teary eye in the room.

"I still miss sleep though," Mark joked and everyone laughed, breaking the heaviness in the air.

"I miss sex," Jason teased, earning himself a poke to the ribs from his wife.

"Oh I don't know, some of my fondest memories were when the two of us had to sneak around so we wouldn't get caught by you kids."

Everyone turned to look at Kathy who sat in her chair cradling one of the babies on her shoulder. She kissed the baby on his head and then glanced up at us, her eyes shining with mischief. "What? You learn to get creative," she said, fighting back a smile.

"Did you guys really believe we were going to the post office after dinner every Thursday night?" Rick asked, wiggling his brows.

Landon covered his mouth beside me as if he were going to be sick. "Not the family station wagon!" he wailed, his voice muffled behind his palm.

"Why did you think it was so hard for us to get rid of? It was full of memories," Kathy said. The sounds of chairs scraping against the hardwood floor filled the room as everyone stood at once, grabbing their dishes and leaving the room. I could hear Landon's parents laughing and what sounded suspiciously like a high-five. We began working together to clean the kitchen and I wondered idly if that might have been Kathy's plan all along; I'd have to keep my eye on that woman.

Someone touched my arm and I turned to see Caleb looking at me with a serious expression on his face. "Can I talk to you for a minute, please?"

"Sure," I said. I shrugged my shoulders at the curious looks Landon and Giovanni wore as I followed him out of the kitchen and into the hallway. He turned halfway down the hall and faced me with a stern look. He folded his arms across his chest and stood as tall as possible. I cocked my brow at him in question. As far as I knew, I couldn't think of anything I could have done to make him angry with me.

"I like you, Micah, I really do and from everything Landon has told me, you're a great guy, but my loyalty lies with him." His tone was fierce and I stared at him in disbelief for a few seconds, but then something in his words sounded familiar and things started to make sense.

When I first met Caleb, I was worried that he would hurt my

best friend. Giovanni had been hurt before by someone who claimed to love him and so I'd decided to have a little chat with Caleb and make sure he understood that if he hurt my friend he was going to have to deal with me. I'd used every bit of intimidation I had learned from my SEAL training, but he had hugged me instead and thanked me for loving Giovanni as much as he did.

I'd known then that Caleb was the perfect man for my friend to trust his heart with and he and I had been close ever since. Although, it seemed as if Landon's little brother was ready to turn the tables on me. The only problem was that there was absolutely nothing intimidating about Caleb. He was a big softy with a heart of gold and so without meaning to, I started laughing.

He glared at me. "Dude, I've practiced this speech. The least you could do is be respectful enough to listen to it."

"I'm sorry, you're right. Please continue," I said, trying to straighten my face.

"Thank you," he said with a huff, eyeing me closely for more laughter. "As I was saying, Landon is the kindest, sweetest, most loving man I've ever known and there isn't one damn thing he could ask for, that I wouldn't do. I know he got his heart torn to shreds by that asshole, Kyle, and he chose to hide his hurt from us, so I couldn't be there for him like I would have liked. He went through so much pain on his own, but he finally found the strength to tell us the truth and that is in large part, because of you. So, I thank you for that, but I also have to warn you. If you hurt him in any way, if you run off and break his heart, I will be there to hunt you down and you will pray that I never find you."

My humor faded away as I listened to Caleb's speech and I stared down at him silently as he finished. I realized that just like when I'd given him the same speech regarding Giovanni, he had said all of those things because he loved Landon almost as much as I did. Landon had been born into a family that showed their love and devotion to each other and I would be eternally grateful to them for making him into the man he was.

Caleb looked stunned as I threw my arms around him and hugged him tightly. "Thank you for being an amazing brother to Landon. He deserves only the best and I can tell you are," I said, repeating his own words from long ago. "I give you my word that I will never, ever, hurt him, but if I ever do, I want you to hold up your end of the deal. Because I would want to be punished for ever causing him pain."

"Welcome to the family then." He patted my back and then pulled away with a sheepish smile. "Sorry to have to be so rough with you, big guy." He growled at me as I began to laugh again. "What? I can be scary when I want to be."

"I'm sure you can," I said, hooking my arm around his neck and leading him back down the hallway.

Landon smiled at us as we walked back into the kitchen. "Everything alright with you two?"

I glanced down at Caleb who raised his brows at me. "Yes, we understand each other perfectly." I smiled at Caleb and he smiled back before moving over into his husband's arms.

"You ready to go home?" Landon asked. My eyes swept over the room and I saw that Landon's parents had joined the others in the kitchen.

"Not yet. I have something I need to do first." My heart was thumping wildly in my chest and my mouth was as dry as the desert, but I pushed on. "Excuse me, may I have everyone's attention for a moment please?" All eyes turned to me and I suddenly wondered if I should have done things more privately, but then I saw Rick smiling and he gave me a single nod and that was all the encouragement I needed. I was still shocked that the man had trusted me enough to give me his blessing when I'd come to him the week before, but I was grateful because there was nothing I wanted more in the world than to be Landon's husband. I just hoped he felt the same way.

I turned to him and he looked curious about what I had to say, but his face was full of so much love and trust that it stole my breath away. His eyes widened as I dropped down on one knee and I heard several gasps from the others in the room. I pulled the small box out that had been burning a hole in my pocket all night.

"Landon, I thought I was destined to spend my life alone. I thought I was a failure and I was too damaged for anyone to be able to love me. Then, I met you and you showed me that everything that I had thought about myself was wrong. You believed in me, you trusted me and miraculously, you fell in love with me. You are my best friend, the love of my life, and my soulmate. I know, beyond a shadow of a doubt, that I want to spend the rest of my life with you. Will you marry me?"

The tears that had pooled in Landon's eyes, spilled over and ran down his cheeks as I removed the ring from the box and held it up. "Yes, I want to be your husband more than anything," he said through his tears.

I slid the ring onto his finger and then he pulled me to my feet. I cradled his face in my hands and took a few seconds to stare at him because I wanted to remember how he looked in that moment for the rest of my life. His lips met mine in a kiss that spoke promises to each other about our future and then we both began laughing as his family let out a loud cheer behind us. They surrounded us and took turns hugging and congratulating us.

I looked at the faces of each person around the room and a warm feeling filled my chest. When I'd left the SEALs, and moved back to Chicago, I'd just been hoping to be nearer to Giovanni and continue being a part of his life. I'd never imagined that I would fall head over heels in love with his brother-in-law and end up with an entire family to call my own. Giovanni caught my gaze from across the room and gave me a wink. I'm sure he could tell what I'd been thinking and he knew how much all of that meant to me.

I turned to Landon who was staring back at me with a mixture of love and awe and I leaned in for another kiss. "Thank you," I whispered to him.

"What for?" he asked.

"For loving me, for saying yes, for being mine." A smile spread across his face.

"I've been yours since the first time I saw you and I can't wait to be your husband," he whispered back.

I smiled back at him. "Husband. It does have a nice ring to it, doesn't it?"

—· ⟹•(⟸ ·—

The sound of a phone ringing startled me out of a sound sleep. I'd been sleeping with my body pressed up against Landon's back and my arm thrown around his waist protectively, but he wriggled out from under me as he grabbed his phone from the nightstand. He sat up and leaned his back against the headboard and ran his hand over his jaw as he blinked against the brightness of his phone screen.

"Who is it?" I mumbled, scooting closer to him and laying my head in his warm lap. He rubbed his hand over my short hair and I kissed his leg in return.

"It's my brother," he said in surprise as he answered the call. "Carter? What's wrong?" I sat up next to him when I heard the worry in his voice and slid my hand over his. It was hardly ever a good thing to get a call in the middle of the night. I could hear Carter's voice through the phone, but he was talking too quickly for me to make any sense of it.

Landon climbed out of bed and held his phone between his shoulder and his ear as he grabbed a pair of jeans off the back of the chair and pulled them on. I followed suit, figuring he'd want me with him if something had happened.

"Okay, we'll meet you there," he said and then he hung up and went to the closet, pulling out the first shirt he found. His voice was muffled as he yanked the shirt over his head. "Rocko's in the hospital,"

232

he explained. "Carter said Steve was really upset when he called him so he wasn't sure what exactly had happened, but from what he could tell, it was really bad." We quickly darted out the front door and into the Jeep.

"Rocko's been in bad shape for a while now. We've all tried to help him, but there's only so much we could do until he either decided he was ready to make a change or until he hit rock bottom," Landon said. I reached across the seat and rubbed the back of Landon's neck as I drove towards the hospital. "I hope it's not too late for him."

"Try not to worry until we know more, okay?" I said gently.

He smiled at me and nodded his head. "Thanks for coming with me."

"Always," I promised.

I parked quickly and held Landon's hand as we walked through the automatic doors of the emergency room. Landon gave Rocko's name to the nurse at the front desk who ran her eyes over us as if she were trying to determine if we really knew the famous drummer or if we were members of the paparazzi. She was only around five feet tall, but the look on her face very clearly said she wasn't someone to be messed with.

Luckily, Ryan walked through a pair of swinging doors just then. "It's okay, Racheal. They can come in."

The young nurse's demeanor changed when she saw Ryan and I watched in amusement as her face turned pink and she smiled at him shyly. "Hey, Ryan! I just wanted to make sure no one went back there that shouldn't be."

"You're doing a great job and we really appreciate it." Ryan gave her a friendly wink and I had to hold back a laugh when she bit her lip and giggled like a teenage girl crushing on the prom king.

"No problem. You let me know if you need anything else," she gushed. Ryan thanked her and then led us back through the double doors and down a long hallway.

"Looks like you have a fan base of your own, Cryan," I teased.

Ryan rolled his eyes. "Don't start. We've already been called that three times since we got here."

"How's Rocko?" Landon asked.

Ryan's expression was grim. "We haven't seen him yet, but Steve said he was worse than he's ever seen him."

"What happened?" I asked.

"We're not sure, yet. Steve's the one that found him and he's been really upset so we told him to wait until everyone got here so he'd only have to go through the story once. They're letting us wait in his room to give the band more privacy."

Ryan led us into a private room where Carter and the other members of the band were gathered. They all wore the same mixed expressions of worry and sadness and Landon immediately went to his brother and the two of them shared a tight hug. Tyler stood at the window with his arms crossed over his chest, but he turned when he heard us come in and slumped down wearily on the deep window sill. Steve was sitting slumped over with his elbows on his knees and his face in his hands. Kalia was kneeling at his side, speaking quietly to him and rubbing his back soothingly. They both looked up when Carter cleared his throat.

"Everyone's here now. Can you tell us what happened, Steve?" His tone was gentle and Ryan stood behind him, his arms encircling his fiancé. Landon walked back over to me and gave me a grateful look as I offered him my hand.

Steve nodded his head and took a deep breath. "I hadn't heard from Rocko in a few days which was odd. He hates to be alone, so he's always showing up at my place to play video games or watch movies. He's over so much, I ended up giving him his own key." The thought brought a small smile to his face.

"When I realized it had actually been three days since I heard from him, I tried calling. It went straight to voicemail every time. I left a ton of messages and texted him several times, but by dinner I still hadn't heard from him so I went over to his place. The doorman said he'd seen him leaving a few days ago, and hadn't seen him come back." Steve stood and began pacing as he continued.

"I figured he must have gone on a bender so I went around to all the bars and clubs he likes to hang out at. One of the bartenders said he'd seen him a couple of nights before. He told me that Rocko had spent most of the evening dancing and getting drunk and it was nearly closing time when he saw him leaving with a small group of people. I asked him if he knew any of the people Rocko left with or where I could find them. Luckily, he knew one of the girls whose name was Stacy and that she worked at a clothing store not far from there.

"I tracked down Stacy who seemed surprised when I told her that I was looking for Rocko. She admitted that she'd been with him and some other people she'd just met. She told me that they left the club and went to a nearby motel. The next morning, she left because she had to work, but Rocko and the others weren't done partying so they stayed behind. I thanked her for her help and then went to the hotel, hoping someone would have seen him." Steve stopped pacing and shoved his fisted hands into the pockets of his jeans. He stared down at the floor and his voice got scratchy with emotion. Kalia reached for him, but he shook his head at her, needing to get the words out.

"It was a rundown, sleazy kind of place and the manager was all too happy to give me a key for a little cash. The room was trashed; empty bottles of booze were laying all over the floor, along with used condoms and a spilled container of pills. I didn't see anyone and fig-ured they'd all split, but then I heard water running in the bathroom." Steve's bottom lip quivered and he wrapped his arms around himself.

"Rocko was lying completely naked and unresponsive in the tub. Even the ice-cold water of the shower pouring over him wouldn't wake him up. His skin was cold and gray and he was barely breath-ing. I called 911 and he started convulsing when they moved him onto the stretcher. They wouldn't let me ride in the ambulance with him so I followed him here. They took him back right away, but I heard one of the emergency workers tell the nurse that they lost him twice on the ride in; I haven't heard anything since." Steve bent down and put his hands on his knees as he tried to catch his breath. Tyler and Kalia put their arms around him and helped him back over to the chair. Carter turned and buried his face in Ryan's chest and Ryan hugged him tightly, whispering in his ear.

Landon turned to me. "Come on, let's go see if we can find something out. They're all scared and they need to know what's happening with their friend." I nodded my agreement, but just as we reached the door, it opened and a man in blue scrubs walked in. Everyone looked at him expectantly as he pulled the cap off his head and gave us a weary smile.

"I'm Dr. Weber and I've been assigned to Rocko's case. Does he have any family that needs to be contacted?" I remembered Landon telling me once before that despite how close the members of the band were, Rocko had shared very little about his life before he'd met them. Even Steve, who was his best friend, knew better than to ask questions about the man's past.

Carter answered the doctor's question. "We are his family."

The doctor studied him for a moment and then continued. "I don't think I need to explain to any of you how serious his situation was. He coded twice on the way here, but they were able to bring him back. We pumped his stomach and started giving him fluids because he's severely dehydrated. I ran a tox-screen to see what all he'd used and after seeing the results…well, let's just say he's lucky to be alive. I'm going to keep him here for a few days, but then I'm going to recommend that he get checked into a treatment facility."

"We'll make sure he goes," Tyler said.

"I hope so because next time he may not be so lucky. The nurses are cleaning him up a bit and then we'll move him in here so you can be with him." The doctor stood and shook everyone's hand before walking back out. No one said anything for a few minutes as everyone processed what the doctor had told us.

"What do we do now?" Kalia asked, breaking the silence.

"We've tried talking to him, reasoning with him, and even begging; none of that's worked. I think it's time we show him some tough love," Carter responded.

"I'll start looking into rehab centers. We'll get him into the best one in the world," Landon assured them as he pulled his phone out of his pocket. I followed him into the hallway and wrapped my arms around him, kissing his temple.

"What was that for?" He smiled as he slid his arms around my waist.

"Because you're a wonderful man and because I'm so glad you're mine. I love you, Landon."

"I love you too, Micah." The look he gave me was so tender and full of love that I thought my heart would burst. I couldn't believe the path my life had taken from growing up with an abusive father who told me that I was nothing, to finding a man who looked at me like I was his entire world. I knew exactly how lucky I was to have found my soulmate and I was never going to let him go.

EPILOGUE

Rocko

I FINISHED SHOVING MY CLOTHES IN MY SUITCASE AND ZIPPED IT shut, then pulled my long hair back into a loose ponytail. I'd listened quietly as my best friends told me that they refused to stand by and watch me kill myself and that if I didn't go through rehab then I was out of the band. At first I was pissed that they were threatening my place as their drummer, but after giving it some thought, I realized that they'd only said those things because I'd scared them and because they cared about me. As soon as I was released from the hospital, I checked myself into a rehabilitation program.

The first several days had been pure hell as my body ridded itself of all the drugs and alcohol I'd poured into it. Detox was not for the faint of heart and I made a promise to myself that I would stay clean and sober from then on.

Since then I had spent countless hours attending daily group and private counseling sessions, as well as art therapy. I didn't have a clue how making a lopsided vase out of clay was supposed to help me, but

I went along with it. The group counseling sessions were boring as fuck, but I was usually able to get through them without having to share too much.

The private sessions on the other hand were nothing less than an exercise in torture. Dr. Turner and I usually spent the hour staring at each other as he waited patiently for me to answer even the most basic questions. The truth was, I thought Dr. Turner was an alright guy and I wasn't trying to be a dick, but there were just some things from a person's past that were better left alone.

Finally, after two months, I'd completed the program and I couldn't wait to get home. I'd texted Landon and he said he'd arrange for a car to pick me up. I glanced around the room, lifting the blankets on the bed and checking the closet one last time to make sure I hadn't forgotten anything. Satisfied that I wasn't leaving anything behind, I picked up my suitcase and walked out of my room.

Dr. Turner was waiting in the hallway. "I just wanted to congratulate you before you left. You should be proud of how far you've come and I wish you all the best."

"Thank you," I murmured, not quite sure what to say.

He held his hand out and I shook it. "Good luck, Rocko. Try to let more people in; you might be surprised to find that not everyone will let you down."

I watched him as he turned and made his way back down the hallway, his words running on a loop through my mind. A black Escalade was sitting at the curb with its engine running so I opened the door and headed down the sidewalk. It was dark out and I was relieved when nobody jumped out of the bushes to snap a picture of me as I left rehab.

The driver got out and I handed him my suitcase then climbed in the back seat. I was grateful that the privacy screen was up between myself and the driver because I didn't feel like talking to anyone. I scooted down in my seat and closed my eyes, taking a deep breath as the car began moving. While I was relieved to have my freedom back, a part of me was nervous about leaving rehab.

It had been easy to follow the program while I was there because there were no temptations. No one offered me drugs, alcohol, or sex. Out in the real world was another story though and my hands began to shake as I wondered whether I would be strong enough to refuse my old vices when I was faced with them. I knew what was at stake though so I would fight hard to maintain my sobriety.

I drifted off to thoughts of seeing my friends and playing the drums again. I jerked awake when I felt the car slow to a stop. I peered out the window, confused about where I was.

I pushed the intercom button. "Excuse me, I thought you were taking me home. This isn't where I live."

Before he could respond, my door swung open. I climbed out of the car to apologize to whoever lived there and explain that some mistake had been made, but I stopped short when I saw the person standing there.

"Hello, Rocko. I'm glad you're here," Lachlan Edwards said stiffly.

"Where are we?" I asked in confusion.

"This is my home. Please, come inside. We have a lot to talk about."

The End

ACKNOWLEDGEMENTS

First and foremost, I want to thank my family for your patience and understanding as I drive myself crazy with deadlines and for being my biggest fans. I love each of you more than life itself.

To B, you never cease to amaze me. When others would have given up, you've pushed yourself, refusing to let anything take away the kind of life you want. I have no doubt that you can handle anything life throws your way, but please know that you will never be alone because I am always here for you. I love you, baby.

To Aimee, for being an unwavering friend in an ever changing world.

To Deena, for supporting me and encouraging me no matter what.

To Kerry, for being my first and forever friend. I love you.

To my amazing team: Pam Ebeler, thank you for always understanding the vision I have for my guys and for being patient with my never-ending questions. I'm so glad I got to meet you. You are a true inspiration. Jay Aheer, thank you for continually surprising me with the beautiful images you create. You never cease to amaze me. Judy Zweifel, thank you for your kindness and attention to detail. Stacey Blake, thank you for the personal touches you add which bring it all together in the end. To my betas, Lee Rey, Nicci Sleeter, Wendy Maples, Jodi Temple, Melissa Mcentyre and Lori Greis thank you all for your honesty, enthusiasm and encouragement. Without each and every one of you, I would not be able to do this job. I appreciate all of your hard work, input and the friendships we have formed along the way.

ABOUT THE AUTHOR

I am married to my high school sweetheart who let's face it, is a saint for putting up with me all of these years. Together we have been blessed with the chance to raise two amazing human beings and so far we haven't screwed it up; I'll let you know for sure later. I am a business owner and spend more time laughing than actually working most days. I love watching movies, cooking, going to the beach and spending time with my family and best friends. I am an obsessive reader who is a complete sucker for a good love story, but loves to feel a broad range of emotions throughout a book. I think real life is hard enough and so my books offer twists and turns, but always with a happy ending.

I love to hear from my readers. You can reach me at:

Twitter – www.twitter.com/annabellamicha1

Facebook – www.facebook.com/profile.php?id=100011438515157

Blog – annabellamichaels.blogspot.com